Travel Page

Every publication from Rippple Books has this special page to document where the book travels, who has it and when.

The Book of Names

Stories
By
Royce Leville

Rippple
Books

First published in 2015 by

Rippple Books

Editor: Jeff Kavanagh

Cover design: Claudia Bode

Layout: Susanne Hock

Rippple Books

Postfach 304263

20325 Hamburg

Germany

www.rippplebooks.com

A CIP catalogue record for this book is available from the British Library.

ISBN: 978-3-9816249-2-2

Willard

"Basements are useful," he says. "You can escape from the world."

It was supposed to sound romantic and deep, as if down in his basement is some kind of lavish studio, where he paints massive murals and carves driftwood into sculptures. A place where he records albums on which he plays all the instruments. Scatter cushions, home-made candles and racks of wine. The bench seat from an old car, turned into a sofa. A pottery wheel and kiln. A kind of temple to bohemian endeavour that would make any girl swoon, even this restrained software sales rep.

True. It's a studio of sorts, but probably not the kind that would satisfy this girl. Because that basement comment, in response to her hobbies and interests line of questioning, has her looking at him like he's a total weirdo. She's seeing a very different kind of basement; some dank cave where a girl gets locked away.

"Are you into model trains or something?" she asks.

She sips her red wine, using both hands to hold the glass, as if she's taking communion. She's got small, slender fingers, the nails trimmed to the tips, and very thin arms. Desk hands, he decides. They never felt the sting of a hot spark flying off a grinder; never got dry enough for oil to seep into the cracks and stay there.

He'd like to be honest, to tell her about the precision cutter and high-speed grinder. His art and its use. He'd like to go into detail, to prove his ability and knowledge; how it requires the steady hands of a surgeon, and how any small mistake is costly. The walls deserve description, the catalogues and cards. The sublime orderliness of it all. The usefulness. His basement. There's nothing degenerate about it. Nothing untoward. Sure, it has a lock, but he firmly believes every door should.

He folds his arms, hiding his hands. "No. No trains."

"Do you sleep down there?"

"No."

"Because you look pretty tired."

She sips her wine again, her eyes moving, briefly, to the organiser. He follows her glance and sees the speed dating sergeant with the stop-clock in her right hand and her left hand poised above that annoying little concierge bell.

More precious seconds tick by.

"I work with metal," he says. "In my basement. It's art."

"Really."

"Yes."

"Is it worth anything?"

"Depends on how you value it."

She seems to find this interesting. "Have you ever had, you know, an exhibition? Of your art."

He nods. "But most people are too caught up in their own worlds to recognise what they're seeing."

She gives him a steady look. That last comment was clearly unexpected.

"I think I might want to see some of your stuff."

"My basement?"

The bell rings.

All dates end and everyone stands up. That's the last session and the organiser is keen to send everyone home, as it's already late. She collects the forms and goes through the routine. She blows out the candles and takes down the love-heart balloons. People put on their coats. The more gentlemanly men help the ladies; some respond positively, relishing the attention and enveloping themselves like they're getting wrapped up in a rug-hug. The desperate men follow through with shoulder squeezes that linger just a tad too long, causing the ladies to squirm out, politely, from their grasp.

Those who came with friends leave together. Most of the men check their phones, to signal a level of importance and disguise any apparent aloneness. As regular attendees, some of the men nod at each other before leaving.

"See you next week, Willard," the organiser says, herding him towards the door.

He watches the software sales rep shoulder her handbag. She doesn't dig in it for car keys. She suddenly looks rather young to him, a little lost.

He waits, letting her leave, then follows.

Outside, he sees her walk to the next bus stop. She has a strange, slow, duck-footed way of walking, as if one leg is weaker than the other. She walks on her heels, leaning slightly backwards.

The stop is for the Q6, which goes out to the small community college on the outskirts of town.

His vintage motorbike-sidecar is parked around the back of the church's multi-purpose hall. He removes the wheel lock and places it in the sidecar's trunk. With his helmet on, he sits on the bike and waits.

If she's a student, he thinks, it means she lied, and that means she lied about everything. If she plays a role at speed dating, it means she's only herself at home. Research? An identity thief? Sex without attachments? All possible. Her guard dropped when I talked about art. She was the most interesting. She was new. She was the only woman who didn't spend seven minutes trying to recall where we'd met before.

The bus arrives at the stop, then pulls away.

He follows at a distance, knowing the route.

The night is clear and crisp, the traffic light. As he rides, he peeks in the windows of the cars that pass. He recognises some of the drivers and passengers. With those he doesn't recognise, he wonders about their lives. Their secrets. The roles they play; becoming a different person in every different room they enter. Where they live and what kind of locks they have. How do they look when they sleep, when the barriers they put up during the day fall away?

He's jealous of all these people who have places to go and are impatient to get there. But he's glad for them, because he knows that distraction and purpose keep the demons at bay.

Her stop is the last one before the college.

He parks the motorbike in the almost darkness, equidistant from two streetlights. Helmet off and wheel-lock in place, he grabs his pick set from the sidecar's trunk and slinks among the shadows.

Further down the street, she duck-walks towards the gated apartment complex. She takes her keys from her coat pocket and opens the gate.

He's got the key to this gate, but it's at home. In the basement.

When the gate clangs shut, he walks up to it. Through the bars, he watches her enter house B of the complex. He's got the key to that too, to all the houses in the complex.

He picks the lock and eases the gate shut so it doesn't clang. From the path, he sees the lights on the third floor come on. Front apartment, left side.

He's soon through the ground-floor door. The house has a locked basement. He picks that door as well. Once inside, he sits on an old wooden crate and removes his shoes.

An hour passes.

During that time, he doesn't hear anyone enter or leave the building. During that time, he could have gone home, but he likes it down here in the basement. It's quiet, surprisingly clean and dry. There are no rats. No water dripping.

He closes his eyes.

House B, third floor, front left side. Madeline Swaine. He pictures the name written on the circular label at the base of the key. Yellow label, green pen. Everything was fine with her. Just lonely. She slept without an expression, a large boxer at the foot of her bed. One shot of a tranquillizer kept the dog out for about three hours. When she slept on her right side, she snored ever so softly. She didn't appear to dream. She wore pyjamas and woollen socks. The silk sheets were a bit extravagant. She worked in marketing, at the tourist office. Rode a bicycle to work. Her alarm was set for 7:10am. She liked to knit and do tapestry, which bracketed her in an age group much older than she was. The apartment was littered with projects, both finished and un-finished. When her keys first went missing, she called him for help; said she'd found his business card pinned to the notice board next to the mailboxes downstairs. She wasn't distraught or panicking. More annoyed than anything else. He made the required copies, from the keys she gave him, and reproduced the less complex keys for which he had the originals. He showed her the special pen-sized camera he had, which could photograph the inside of locks, allowing him to make the suitable keys. She joked that with such a camera, a thief could break into any home, building or car. He assured her it only worked for very simple locks, like the cheap lock on her bicycle, and the right tools and software were needed to reproduce the keys. With all her keys replaced, she offered to make him a scarf. He refused. At one point she called him a hero. She flirted too, but he guessed that was mostly out of gratitude. He suggested she get a dog, some energetic, lively breed that would require exercise and attention. Hence the boxer. When he chanced upon her at speed dating, she didn't recognise him, and spent their allocated seven minutes trying to place him.

That was months ago.

4

He opens his eyes. Madeline Swaine was gone. The lock for house B, third floor, front left side has probably been changed.

There's work to do.

He picks up his shoes and climbs the three flights of stairs. The single lock is a cinch to pick, the chain easy to slide off with the door just slightly ajar. His hands are steady. The dangling chain makes no noise.

Inside, there's a light on, in the living room. A soft light, perhaps a lamp, orange-shaded.

He edges inside and sniffs the air; it's musty from sleep. No pets. Rice for dinner, possibly take-out.

He finds her on the sofa, a red rug up to her chin, reading glasses slightly askew. Out of its ponytail, her hair is rather stringy. An open book is upside down on the floor, inches from where it fell from her left hand. Anthropology in the title, borrowed from the community college's library.

There's no sign of male life, no evidence of a boyfriend. He creeps into the bathroom and sees only one toothbrush, the bristles splayed and well-worn. She uses anti-dandruff shampoo and coconut-scented face moisturiser.

For half an hour, he stands over the sofa and watches her. She sleeps with something close to a grimace, appearing to grind her teeth. The temptation to pick her up and carry her to bed is strong. Turn off the lamp, close the blinds, pick up the book and flatten the creased pages. He wants to right all the wrongs in this flat. He senses she needs help. Not lonely, necessarily, but struggling.

Money, he concludes.

She seems very small bundled up on the sofa. Helpless. Innocent. Unattractive in her sleep.

He takes her keys from the hook near the door and leaves.

***

On the phone, she's panicking. "They're all gone. I don't understand it. I left the apartment in such a rush this morning."

"Late for something?" he asks. He moves to the corner of the basement, to prevent the echo.

"For work. I just pulled the door shut, like I always do."

"Happens a lot."

"Then I got home and I realised I didn't have my keys."

5

"So, are you locked out, or did you lose your keys?"

"Lost them. My landlord let me in to check. They're gone. All of them."

He takes the keys from his pocket and inspects them. On the key ring is a purple frog, rubbery and soft.

"Your business card says you're available twenty-four hours," she says.

"You can bring the keys to my shop tomorrow and I'll make the copies."

"Tomorrow?"

"Or I can come over now and get them. Do the work tonight."

"What will that cost?"

"House calls are extra. I'm guessing your landlord needs his extra key back pretty soon."

"All three of them. There's the gate and the door downstairs."

Again, he inspects the keys in his hand, wondering what locks they open. She doesn't have very many keys, just half a dozen. There's one very small bronze key, rounded with two teeth. He's curious about that one.

"And then there are the others. They were one-offs. Oh, I'm so screwed."

"Relax. I deal with this every day. You'll be fine."

"I think you better come over now. Right now."

"Okay."

As she gives him the address, he gathers up his gear. After a few more reassurances, she starts to calm down.

"Are you really the only locksmith in town?"

He stands in the basement, looking at the perfect model of their town.

"It's not really big enough. There were others, but there wasn't enough work."

She laughs a little and says, "We're living in a one-locksmith town."

"And there's barely enough work for me. A lot of the new buildings have gone electric. Using cards, not keys."

"My place is a bit more old-fashioned. I'll be waiting at the gate to let you in."

She hangs up, saving him from saying there's no need to wait outside.

The ride over is uneventful. He's sure to stare straight ahead, to avoid any potential diversions. He passes houses and apartments, places he was recently. There are people he'd like to check up on, just to see how they're sleeping; if their expressions have changed. He wonders if Mrs Elena Markins of 127 Rockliff Road is happier now that she's buried her husband. Did she use the key he made for her, to the garage where the bastard kept his navy-blue 1972 Citroen DS21 locked away so she couldn't drive it? Has she removed the car cover and taken the Citroen for a joyride?

He hopes so. He imagines her speeding, the windows down, a big smile on her face, a whole new kind of freedom in front of her. And that lousy fucker six feet under.

He hopes many things as he rides in the direction of the small community college. He can't help but wonder what is going on behind the closed doors. All the houses and apartments. The offices where lights still burn. He needs to know. So many of the cards require updating.

He parks his motorbike and secures the wheel-lock.

She's waiting at the gate, but comes towards him, with that unmistakable waddling almost-limp, when she sees the sidecar.

"That is fabulous," she says. "I didn't think people had these anymore."

He takes off his helmet. She watches him retrieve his gear from the sidecar's trunk.

"It's not for a passenger?" she asks, seeing how it's only for tools and storage.

"It's my mobile workshop. If I take some stuff out, a person can sit in there."

"Need some help carrying anything?"

"I got it," he says, briefly facing her and smiling.

"Hey, it's you. From speed dating last night. The guy who loves basements."

He gestures towards the gate with his pick set. "Shall we?"

As they walk, she says, "I'm so glad you're here. I've just been freaking out. I've never lost my keys before. Never." The gate clangs shut. "They must've fallen out of my pocket at some point today. I even retraced my steps. And I went to the police station."

She holds the ground floor door open for him.

"Thank you."

"The police were completely useless. And they had nothing to do.

They were just sitting around. Looks like there's no crime in this town."

"Not much."

"Makes you wonder why anybody would need to lock their doors," she says, leading the way up the stairs. "I just moved here. From a big city. It's been a shock."

"Do you like it here?"

"It's all right. I grew up in a small town, but I was always trying to escape from that place. It's the circumstances that brought me here that were crap."

"Oh."

"Yeah," she says, her voice trailing off.

Inside the apartment, she closes the door.

"Would you like something to drink?"

As he knows she can only offer water, he says, "I think it's best I do my work quickly and let you go to sleep."

"Your basement calling?" She smiles, rather grimly. "So that's your art. Making keys."

"Part of it, yes."

"What's the other part?"

On the kitchen counter, he sees a key ring with three keys. "Are these for the apartment?"

"Yes."

"If you let me take them, I'll bring them back first thing in the morning."

"Okay. I leave the house at around eight. Can you make that?"

"What other keys do you need?"

She lets out a frustrated sigh. "It's like I said on the phone. They were singles. I can't replace them."

"Can you show me the locks?"

"How will that help?"

He takes the pen-sized camera from his shirt pocket. "I can make a photo of the inside of the lock with this. At my workshop, I've got special software which can create a digital reproduction of the key, based on the lock. Then it's just a matter of making the key."

"You can do that?" she asks. "There's software for that?"

"There's software for pretty much everything these days."

"Yes. Right. There is." She moves closer to inspect the camera. "Looks like a little flashlight."

"It's a camera."

She stares at it. "Think about what you can do with it."

"It only works for very simple locks," he says.

She leads him through the small, sparsely-furnished apartment. He goes through the motions of photographing the lock of her desk drawer, the security box hidden behind her shoes in the closet, and the diary by her bed.

"Can you show me the photos?" she asks, following him to the door. "I want to see how this works."

"It's not that fancy." He gathers up his gear. "I'll be here tomorrow at eight sharp. Sleep well."

The door closes behind him. He hears the chain slide into place.

Back in his basement, the work is done quickly. He copies her keys the old-fashioned way. Like for like. It's easy to do with the originals. He opens the top of house B and lifts out the small rack of keys. He removes Madeline Swaine's keys and puts the new set in its place, with a red label on the key to the apartment door. Swaine's card is also removed from the catalogue. He writes the date on the card's bottom right-hand corner, and puts the card and keys into a sealable plastic bag. He leaves the bag on the work bench, to be filed later, and slides a blank card into his shirt pocket.

It takes a good ten minutes of rifling through his boxes of key-rings to find something he deems appropriate. It's a small black die, with a metal loop on the one side. He manoeuvres the keys onto this ring, hoping she'll like it.

At 1:47am, he's back in her apartment. She's in bed this time, with the red rug thrown over the top. She's sleeping on her stomach, rather twisted. Her left leg is pulled up, the knee bent at ninety degrees, and she has her left cheek on the pillow. Her hair is tucked under a kind of woven hat. He assumes this, along with the shampoo in the bathroom, is for the dandruff.

He watches her sleep for a while. She changes position often, is restless and twitchy. At one point, she takes the hat off and throws it aside. It lands at his feet.

He wonders if the dandruff is the result of stress.

The new keys work. He opens her diary and reads it, using the light from his pen-sized camera. The security box has a few trinkets from her childhood, as well as a hand gun, some photographs, a few police reports, and a bundle of letters that are of little interest; a boyfriend, who appears to have broken her heart during their screwed-up junkie romance. The desk drawer is filled with business stuff, confirming the contents of the diary.

He takes the card from his shirt pocket and writes:

"House B, third floor, front left side. Sofia Wilks. Single. Broke. BA in Social Anthropology, but thrown out of university for falsifying her thesis. Estranged from parents (academics) as a result. Reformed drug addict three months clean. Possibly a compulsive liar. Says she sells software but is actually a cashier/receptionist at the Cyberia Internet Cafe. Confesses everything in her diary but lies in real life. Now in small town trying to start again. Another candidate for reinvention, or a new identity. Deserves sympathy, to a certain point. Sleeps awkwardly, as if subconscious is trying to solve problems. Perhaps reliving mistakes, or wanting to go back in time to do things differently. Scratches at arms and neck during sleep. Has bad dandruff."

He pockets the card, wondering how he can help her.

She's now sleeping on her back, knees bent, the red rug a perfect pyramid.

He edges out of the room and leaves the apartment.

***

She can't pay, but offers to make him dinner instead. He refuses at first, but accepts after her playful pressing becomes aggressive, because he would also like to learn more about her.

Which is why he is now sitting in her apartment. The fold-out table has two chairs, mismatched.

He has decided the dinner, and any possible dessert, is a financial agreement for her; a bill that she can cover without money.

She makes rice, with vegetables and tofu. It's rather plain, and mostly rice. She offers him salt and pepper, and the shakers look like they were lifted from a restaurant. The salt shaker has small grains of rice inside.

He doesn't really know what to say. He eats. She talks. She asks questions about the town and the residents. She remarks that the town is rather affluent, with low crime and little poverty. She tells the story again of going to the police station to report her lost keys.

"They were adamant that if someone finds the keys, that person will hand them in. Come on, Will. Do people really do that here?"

"Sure. Why not?"

She shakes her head a little in disbelief. "Totally unexpected. In the world these days, people are always trying to take advantage of you. They look at you thinking only about what they can get from you."

"Maybe they're thinking more about what they can offer," he says. "Like this very nice dinner."

"Sorry it's a bit dull. I'm still stocking up my kitchen with goodies."

"Why did you move here? You don't seem to like it."

"I just need to get settled. To find my rhythm."

"Maybe first you should find your keys."

She laughs at this, and it comes across as forced. "That's funny. I didn't expect you to be funny, Will. At speed dating, you struck me as a bit strange, like you were hiding something. But you're totally normal. You work, you do your art in your basement. I still want to see some of that."

"You already did. Your new keys."

Her look is quizzical. "You think that's art?"

"Yes."

"A kind of sculpting? Still life with key and lock?"

He puts down his fork. "The art is in the precision. Making a key that perfectly fits the lock. And you don't have to jiggle it or have a special feel. The key goes in and it works, every time." He sits back, folds his arms and adds, "People think all keys look the same, or are similar. But even keys that look identical have minuscule differences, and it's these differences that mean a key will work or not."

"Fascinating. Can you pick locks as well?"

"A lot of my work is helping people get into places they're locked out of."

"Show me."

"I don't have my pick set. You need the right tools:"

"Can't you do it with a credit card?" she asks. "Slide it between the door and the frame."

"That's what you see in movies. It doesn't work in real life. You always end up snapping the card in half."

She points at him with her fork. "I won't believe you until you show me. The same goes with that basement of yours."

"I don't know."

"Get some stuff from your sidecar. Have you got a pick set in there?"

He nods.

11

"Go get it."

"I'm not sure that this ..."

"Go get it," she shouts. Then, more calmly, "My neighbour from across the hall is on holiday. We can pick her lock." She stands up to open the door for him. "I want you to show me how it's done. Right now. Think of it as a little pre-dessert entertainment."

He decides to do what she says. Down at his motorbike, he briefly considers riding home. But something impels him back upstairs, pick set in hand. He doesn't want any of her desserts, but he does want her to accept that what he does is art.

He's getting the feeling she's not right for his town.

She's waiting at the top of her stairs.

When he sees her closed door, she holds up her keys, the ring with the small black die, and says, "I'm prepared. Don't worry."

He takes his time picking the lock, to show it's more complicated than it looks. He thinks about Valerie Charlesworth, divorcee, resident of house B, third floor, front right side. She works in admin at the community college. Her husband was having an affair with Cornelia (Conny) Bracken of house D, second floor, back left side, until a situation was contrived for Valerie to find out about it and kick her deadbeat, unemployed husband out. The cards on Cornelia Bracken and Bernie Charlesworth received final dating and filing a few months back.

As the door clicks open, he wonders if Valerie has taken that holiday to Scandinavia she always dreamed of taking. He'd left some brochures in her mailbox when he'd last visited. He'd found her sleeping well, spread-eagled in the big bed, glad to be rid of her baggage.

"You did it," she says, pushing past him. "We're in."

"Come back," he whispers. "You can't go in there."

"Relax, Will. No one's home."

She grabs his arm and pulls him inside.

"Don't touch anything," he says closing the door.

In the open-plan kitchen and living room, she goes to the kitchen first, opening the cupboards and taking things out.

"We should've had dinner here," she says. "Look at all this good stuff."

"Put that back."

She's holding a bottle of wine in her hands, looking around for a corkscrew. "She won't notice."

"Please. Put it back."

She does so, saying, "You're really not much fun."

She moves through the apartment some more, opening drawers and looking at the books on the shelf. Now that she's out of the kitchen, he's stopped worrying that she might find the coffee container in the fridge; the one Valerie fills with money because she doesn't trust banks.

"Come here."

She's standing on the rug in the living room. He once sat on that rug, cross-legged, while Bernie and Valerie were asleep, and looked through their photo albums. He skimmed through the rejection letters Bernie had received. He read the first few chapters of the novel Bernie was writing, scrawled by hand and about a professional killer named Oscar who gets hired by powerful Hollywood types to kill celebrities and famous people in order to raise the awareness of that person's brand. Death resulted in increased fame and attention, and allowed for back catalogues of work to be rereleased, making the star more profitable and famous in death than they were in life. The novel was interesting enough that he delayed outing the affair of Bernie and Cornelia so he could keep reading the chapters and find out what happened to Oscar.

But Bernie stopped writing, and Oscar's unfinished story tormented him. He desperately needed an ending, and Bernie couldn't give him one. Not even under torture.

"Come here," she orders.

"I think we should leave."

"I think you should come over here." She points at the rug. "Right now."

He does so, dragging his feet like a child in trouble.

She pushes him down onto the rug and sits on top of him.

"What are you doing?"

She's got his belt open and his fly down, and is aggressive in getting a hold of him. She kisses him a few times, but not on the lips.

He struggles, but not very hard, and she's surprisingly strong in the hips. Despite himself, his body responds, and she gets the position she wants. Soon, he can feel the rug moving just slightly underneath him, powered by her gyrations. She seems to really enjoy it, the way an addict might be desperate for a fix and then gets it, and it's more about scratching the itch than the pleasure it brings.

Her hair comes loose from her ponytail and a few flakes of dandruff waft down.

He lets himself get used, hoping it will all be over soon.

He doesn't know what to do with his hands. She solves this issue by grabbing his wrists and pinning his hands behind his head. This gives her more purchase and she really rides him, her hands pressing his wrists so hard he can feel the blood being cut off.

She grunts a little.

"Not so loud," he says.

"Shut up. I'm almost there."

The rug is edging towards the sofa. For distraction, he tracks its progress. He's starting to get sore and is now praying for it to be over.

Millimetre by millimetre, shout after shout.

He braces himself for the final stretch.

Then she collapses on him. He blows a few strands of hair out of his mouth. Her grip lessens and he moves his fingers a little, to get the blood going again.

"Oh, I needed that," she says, standing up quickly and leaving him on the rug.

She duck-walks to the kitchen and takes a carton of milk from the fridge. She drinks straight from the carton, finishing it, tipping it vertically and shaking it so the last drops hit her tongue.

He looks down and sees himself pink and raw. He wants to go home, to take a long shower and change his clothes.

On his feet, with his pants up and belt secured, he sees his body has left a slight indentation in the rug, as a man might if he fell on it from ten storeys.

He watches her poke in the fridge. She opens a box of chocolates and eats a few. She spits out one she doesn't like.

"Ugh. Cherry."

When he gets to the kitchen, she's got the coffee container in her hands. She pops the lid off and looks inside.

"Oh, jackpot."

She takes out the cylinders of notes, tightly bound by elastic bands.

"Put that back," he says.

"Look at all this money, Will. You have no idea how much I could use this."

He reaches to grab the container, but she pulls it back.

"What do you think you're doing? Get away from me."

"Just put the container back in the fridge and let's go."

She viciously shakes her head, causing a flurry of dandruff.

"This is mine now," she shouts. "I found it. It's mine."

She backs out of the kitchen and he chases after her. She's rather nimble and manages to elude his grasp. As they do a few laps of the living room and kitchen, she uses the furniture to keep him at a distance, feinting this way, then that, dodging like an expert. She throws stuff at him – books, magazines, a candlestick – all the while clutching the coffee container to her chest.

When she tries for the door, he's right behind her, and pushes her head against the door with enough force to render her unconscious. She collapses to the floor.

***

Out of the shower and in fresh clothes, he goes downstairs to the basement. She's still out, which is good, but also a worry. He has little experience with tranquillizers when it comes to humans.

He checks again that she's securely in the chair, her arms strapped down, her ankles duct-taped together.

She has a pulse.

He lifts her chin to look at her. There's no grimace, no grinding of teeth. She looks rather content. Her face isn't showing any signs of struggle or fear. She has no expression at all. She's peaceful.

He puts on some latex gloves and goes to the large medicine cabinet. The heroin is located on the shelf labelled F-J. He takes a few needles as well, an unused teaspoon and a short length of thin rubber hose.

All the marks are on the inside of her left elbow, so he ties a tourniquet around her left arm and taps at the skin with two fingers. The veins are thin. He heats up what he deems to be the right amount of heroin and fills the needle with the bubbly, almost caramelised liquid. The smell seems to rouse her, and she comes to just as he injects the drug into her vein. Her eyes glazed and drooping, she looks down at the needle in her left arm, and smiles.

"Hey? Oh, thank you," she says.

"You're welcome."

A bit more awake now, she fights against the strapping around her wrists and her eyes dart around the basement. But then the drug kicks in and she goes limp in the chair.

"Where am I?"

"You're in my basement."

He places the needle, spoon and tourniquet on the bench, to be used again later.

She stares at the model of the town, at all the perfectly arranged cardboard houses and symmetrical streets. She leans to the right side of the chair and turns her head to get a better look.

"What's that?" she asks.

"It's the town."

"You ... made this?"

"Yes."

"That's wild." She laughs. "Oh, I've missed this."

He goes to the northern end of the model and opens the top of a cardboard building. He lifts out a rack of keys.

"I've got every building, house, apartment, garage, you name it," he says. "These are the current keys. I've also got all the keys of every resident dating back twenty-three years. To when I started. I've kept a record of everyone."

She finds this hysterical. Her laughter echoes in the basement.

"Stop laughing. This is very serious."

"A lifetime project, but why?"

"I wanted to know about the people. I wanted to help them. I grew up in this town, and it wasn't always as nice as it is now."

"You think you're responsible for that?"

"Yes."

"You and your magic keys." She starts crying a little. "How are you gonna help me?"

"You're beyond helping," he says flatly.

"Hmm. Get me high and dump me in the river." She looks at the model again, with its blue section snaking through the town, signifying the river, and the small trees lining its banks. "This is beautiful," she says.

"I know."

"This is the art you were talking about."

He nods.

"You stole my keys."

"I did."

"You broke into my apartment."

"Yes. I watched you sleeping."

"What?" she asks.

"I watched you sleeping. You were so unhappy. So many problems. But you don't have to worry about anything. It's over."

She laughs a little. "I think that just might be a voice in my head," she says. "I'm not gonna die. None of this is real. Your model is too beautiful to be real."

"That's very nice of you to say, but ..."

"I don't wanna die."

"Yes, you do. You already tried. You wrote about it in your diary."

Suddenly angry, she fights against the strapping. "You bastard," she shouts. She struggles some more, then stops. "Can I have another shot?"

"You can have all that you want."

"Maybe a bit more. It's good."

"Soon," he says. "You will get all of it."

"A key to every door," she says dreamily. "The things you could steal. Clean the place out and drive away."

"I don't steal. Why does everyone only think of the negative uses for keys?"

"Unlock the secrets." She giggles. "Let the skeletons out of the closet." Then, through gritted teeth, "Everybody's hiding something. Where's the money, Will? I want my money."

"I don't have any money. And neither do you."

Her breathing is shallow. "Always the same," she shouts. "Always the goddamn same."

He ties the tourniquet around her arm again. She doesn't resist. The look in her eyes is one of encouragement, impatience almost. He does the work, filling her with a large amount of the drug.

"That'll do it, Will," she says smiling. "What now?"

She passes out.

He releases the tourniquet and puts it in a sealable plastic bag, together with the needle, spoon and a couple of small packages of heroin. The bag goes in the inside pocket of his coat, together with the pick set. He cuts the duct tape and removes it from her ankles, and gets the strapping loose.

Carrying her upstairs, he thinks she's lighter than before.

There's almost no traffic as he rides to her apartment.

Halfway there, she sits up, finding herself in the sidecar and speeding along the empty streets. The wind blows her hair back and she opens her mouth widely to let out a long, joyous whoop. Then she passes out again.

He stops to buy a carton of milk and a box of chocolates.

At her apartment complex, he parks on the street and carries her upstairs. He decides to put her in the bathroom, with her back against the lobster-coloured bathtub. Her body keeps sliding forward, and she laughs softly, smiling all the while.

He gives her a final, large shot of heroin, and places the needle in her right hand. He leaves the tourniquet tied around her arm and places the blackened spoon on the floor.

A string of white foam dribbles out of the corner of her mouth.

He uses her keys to open the desk drawer and the security box, and scatters the papers on her bed. The gun goes on the bathroom floor, within arm's reach.

It's a grisly scene, and he's not terribly proud of his handiwork, but it had to be done.

He leaves the lights on.

He washes the plate and glass he used, the cutlery as well, and puts it all away.

With the door just slightly ajar, he deftly slides the chain into place with a specially fashioned screwdriver, and pulls the door shut.

In Valerie's apartment, the carton of milk and box of chocolates go into the fridge. He positions the coffee container on the lower shelf, at the very back, where it always sits.

He cleans up, replacing the books and magazines she threw at him, the candlestick as well. He straightens the rug, smoothing it with his hands to remove the indentation his body had made.

Ronald

He makes a pot of coffee, feeds Maxi and readies himself for the evening session. But before he can get started, there's the usual procrastinating and digressing; the cleaning up of his desk and the monitoring of his online auctions. He does some more sorting of his piles. With a little bit of shuffling, the to-do pile, which is nearly all books, becomes a second to-sell pile, which means more work setting the auctions up and getting them started. And then there's the stuff that has to be packed and shipped. He starts in on this, because he's not really interested in reviewing two books, a new Smartphone, yet another car-sharing app and a five-star hotel in Brunei, doing all that work by midnight, allowing for seven hours of sleep before getting into the hamster wheel again tomorrow for the morning session.

For Ronald, a deadline is not the strong motivation it once was. It used to be, back in his days working in busy newsrooms, but not now, in the current 24-hour mess of permanent deadlines. Factor in all the vested interests, the clients wanting returns on their often meagre incentives, the constant reminder emails from brand managers and communications assistants, and it all makes Ronald a busy freelance reviewer, stuck in an endless cycle.

Ronald is motivated by money. He slaves away to pay the bills that never stop coming. He writes under thirteen different pseudonyms, broken down into industry, media and target audience. The twelve hours he spends working each day are broken up into three four-hour shifts. He's old school and doesn't work on weekends, but that's also because there are no post or package deliveries. He spends much of the weekend sleeping, or walking Maxi in the park and trying to meet guys. He visits his mother once a month at the Sunrise Assisted Care Facility. She has Alzheimer's, and the visits are awful.

Filling his weekends has become something of a problem in recent years, as the junket trips offered went from fully comped orgies of consumption and decadence, tailored to the whims of the reviewers on board, to pay-your-own-way marches through the consumer goods desert. Thanks to the internet and the rise of free content, decent incentives went the way of the last century, leaving freelancers like Ronald to cobble together a living by selling the free products and incentives sent to him, and writing as many reviews as possible. But the weekend junkets were over. He dabbled with golf for a while, playing with a half-set which had been gifted to him together with a client's request for an umbrella review, but didn't enjoy the sport. He sold the clubs and bought a dog. His choice of breed was influenced by the numerous reviews rating golden retrievers as the top dogs for male hook-ups.

Ronald wastes an hour packing and addressing envelopes and boxes. From her basket in the corner of his office, Maxi watches him the whole time. But the cleared space renews Ronald's motivation somewhat, the coffee injects him with some vigour, and he sits down to tackle the reviews, deciding to do the books last.

He knocks off the car-sharing app in fifteen minutes, copying and pasting another review he'd written last year for a similar product, but making it negative because all the company had sent was a lousy coffee mug.

The review request from the hotel in Brunei came with a bare bones one-night stay, which Ronald has already auctioned off, but as it didn't include a business class ticket, the five-star hotel gets a three-star review.

Nice try, Ronald thinks, and not for the first time today, he takes a moment to sit back, stare at Maxi and complain.

"A couple of decades ago," he says, the retriever's ears going up, "it would've been a chartered plane, a deluxe hotel suite and a man servant or two. Lobster, caviar, champagne, private massages, anything you wanted."

Sensing her master's tone, the dog whines a little.

"I know, Maxi. I know. Those were the days."

The Smartphone review is another quick copy-and-paste job, with a few crafty, critical asides to demonstrate his technical expertise. The book reviews are more complex, mainly because they're more time-consuming and his heart really isn't in it. He's rather bitter towards books, and he has to be careful not to turn his reviews into lamentations about the woeful state of contemporary literature and the arts.

But Ronald is a seasoned pro and book reviews are his bread and butter. He uses the same formula each time: talking about another book first, then comparing this new book favourably or unfavourably to it, and opening some pages at random to pull out some quotable passages. The publisher usually sends a detailed synopsis and this is enough to get the gist of the story and condense it into one paragraph for the review. Something about love and loss, something general about never being able to outrun your past, something about the impact of history, some quotes for filler, a few ostentatious adjective-noun combos, and voila, the review is done.

He picks up the first book, a huge paperback which, in keeping with the current trend, has a ludicrously long and convoluted title that is supposed to be witty and eye-catching, but which is actually really annoying when viewed a second time, and becomes increasingly annoying the more he has to refer to it in his review. Working in the book's favour is the African coffee angle, plus the several packages of fair trade Tanzanian coffee the publisher has sent with the book. Ronald is drinking precisely this brew as he punches out the review. The coffee is good and there's a month's supply of it, so he's positive towards the book, calling it "breathtakingly, courageously honest" and "an extraordinary achievement of veracious matter-of-factness."

Reading through, he envisions one of his more bloated sentences being placed on the book's cover, or inside the cover.

Ronald tosses the book on the to-sell pile and forces himself to get started on the second. The sooner he's done, the sooner he can go to bed.

It's another fiction paperback, this one sporting a one-word title in type so massive it takes up the whole cover. In the package, there's a big photo of the author, striking a very scornful and serious-looking pose, as if ready to wield his poison pen and rail against the ills of the world. There are also printouts of interviews with the author, in which, from the very first lines, he comes across as a pretentious twat who deserves to be repeatedly stabbed with his own poison pen, who considers himself a genius and a gift to the world of letters but, as Ronald knows, writes solely about misery and misfortune and repeatedly plays the cancer, alcohol and rape cards.

Ronald leans back in his chair and stares at the ceiling. For reasons beyond Ronald, the author is popular and revered, meaning the review will get picked up and published, and republished, whether it's good or bad. Plus, he knows the system; for such an author, the sparkling reviews have already been paid for, in cash and not in incentives. So it won't hurt if he offers a little critical balance.

This is why Ronald is grinning as he starts his scathing review. And there is that matter of the publisher only sending a pathetic gift voucher, to purchase more of their books. That voucher will be auctioned online soon.

He sticks to the tried and true formula, this time pulling out awful passages for quoting, and making reference to excellent books that this novel doesn't even get close to emulating. His referencing is designed to demonstrate just how bad this book is and how far short it falls of reaching its desired goals. He also references the author's previous shit work.

Ronald giggles a few times as he writes, getting a joyful reminder of why reviewing can be rewarding. Destruction is fun.

He's almost finished when the sound of the doorbell interrupts him.

"Must be a neighbour who signed for a package," he says to Maxi.

Ronald opens the door on someone he doesn't recognise.

"Yes?"

The man reads from a crumpled piece of paper in his right hand. "Are you C. Robert Lowenstein?"

Ronald leans on the door, closing it slightly and blocking the entry. There's something about the man that he finds rather off-putting. He's a perfectly normal looking person, quite attractive, but made abnormal by a set of tormented, almost crazy eyes.

"Who wants to know?"

"I'm here about the review," the man says, shoving the paper into the back pocket of his jeans.

"What review?

"For my book. *The Energetic Soul Protector Who Started the Revolution in Peru*. Didn't you get it?"

"I doubt it. That's not a title I'd forget in a hurry."

The man snaps his fingers and nods several times. "That's the idea. It stays with you."

"Double the money," Ronald says. "Much more annoying than clever."

"What was that?"

"Look, I don't think I've received it yet. Ask your publisher to send it to me."

"You are C. Robert Lowenstein."

"Goodnight."

Ronald closes the door, but the man jams his foot in the doorway. Then he pushes the door open, causing Ronald to stumble backwards, and charges into the apartment. He looks around, seeing the spotless living room and kitchen, the spare but tasteful furnishings.

"Hey," Ronald says, following, "you can't just barge in here."

"Where are all the books? I thought this place would be full of books. Or do you do all your reading on an e-reader?"

Ronald is tempted to confess that he hasn't actually read a book, from cover to cover, in over two decades. But the man scares him, a little. He doesn't want to push the wrong button less the man, who fits just about every possible stereotype of a struggling author, right down to his rumpled clothing, pasty skin and very bad haircut, goes nuclear on his orderly apartment. The man is pathetic, and so is his slightly deranged behaviour. As the man pokes around his apartment, Ronald decides it's all a caricature; a regular guy playing at being a writer, wanting to live that idealised life and be that lauded artist. Ronald thinks the man should just get a job like everyone else and let go of the writer dream.

"I'm still on paper," Ronald says.

"Where are the books then? Where's my book?"

The man goes into Ronald's office. Maxi barks loudly.

"Nice doggy."

When Maxi continues to bark, the man suddenly starts barking back, causing Maxi to retreat to her basket in the corner.

"Hey, don't get angry with Maxi," Ronald says from the office doorway. "She doesn't write the reviews."

The man looks around, his face moving robotically, accumulating stimuli and information and processing it all. His eyes stop on the piles of books, placed just to the side of the desk.

"Hah. Books. I knew it."

He bends down and starts rummaging through them, scouring the to-do pile first, casting books aside as he goes.

"It's not here." He looks at Ronald and shouts, "You threw my book away."

Despite the shouting, Ronald is not really scared of the man. He finds this disruption rather annoying. The floor is now scattered with books, the piles mixed.

"Try the ... that's the wrong pile." Ronald points at the to-sell pile and adds, "Try that one."

The Energetic Soul Protector Who Started the Revolution in Peru is at the bottom of the pile. The man plucks his book and holds it aloft.

"There. You got it. My publisher assured me that they'd sent it to you."

"But they didn't send anything else," Ronald says under his breath.

"What was that?"

"Oh, I was, ah, well, your publisher ... " Ronald cranes his head slightly to view the book's spine and sees that it was published by a small publisher, probably of the vanity variety. "They didn't send all the required information. I was waiting for more. Photos and interviews and such. When I get that, I can write the review."

"I haven't done any interviews yet," the man says. "My publisher said the five-star review of C. Robert Lowenstein would trigger all that. Sales and awards and magazine profiles, and more sales."

Ronald laughs, then stops when the man's eyes widen. "Is your book that good?"

"It's brilliant." The book gets slammed onto Ronald's desk. "When you read it, you'll know."

"Okay. I'll look at it tomorrow."

The man pulls out the chair and points at Ronald, gesturing for him to sit. Ronald does so. The man hands him the book, opening it to page one.

"You want me to read it now?"

"Reviewers are speed readers, aren't they? So, get started."

Ronald closes the book. "That's not how it works. What you're doing is not how it works. Your behaviour is wrong. You're actually damaging your chances of getting reviewed. Now, I think you should leave."

The man sits down on the floor, cross-legged. "I'm not leaving until the review is done. You can interview me while you're writing it."

"You must be joking. I can't work under this sort of pressure."

"You have to."

Ronald attempts to be reasonable. "Listen, I've got your book and I'll read it. If I like it, I'll review it. But you can't come in here and demand a review like this."

"I'm being creative," the man replies. "My publisher said I had to be creative with my marketing efforts."

"Creative is good. Bullying and violence are not." Ronald reaches for his phone. "Now, you either leave or I'll call the police."

"Read!" the man shouts. From his position on the floor, he leans across and yanks the telephone line out of the wall. "Read."

"And if I don't?"

This catches the man off guard, as if he hadn't thought that far ahead. Ronald concludes the man is here spontaneously, on perhaps a drug or alcohol-induced whim, and that planning and plotting may not be his strongest points as a writer.

The man looks around the office, his eyes falling on the large pair of scissors Ronald uses for packing books and products.

Grabbing the scissors, the man says, "Start reading or I'll cut your doggy into furry little pieces."

"Leave Maxi out of this."

"Just read my book. It's easy."

Ronald looks at it. His hands shaking, he flips the pages to the end. *The Energetic Soul Protector Who Started the Revolution in Peru* comes in at just under 600 pages.

"We'll be here all year," he says. "I don't have time for this. I've already reviewed three books today, among other things."

"Three? You must be the world's fastest reader."

"I don't ... " Ronald trails off, unsure if he should confess.

"What was that?" The man looks at Ronald searchingly, until it clicks, and Ronald is impressed that the man is much smarter than he looks.

"You don't read the books?" the man asks, and he sounds heartbroken. "But how can you write an objective review if you haven't read the book?"

Ronald laughs at this. "An objective review. That's an oxymoron."

"No, it isn't."

"There's no such thing. Never was. Not for books, not for anything. At least, for the most part. The reviewers write what they're told to write and there's very little that's objective about it. And the authors who write reviews to make a buck just write about themselves and their own books. It's all rather pathetic really."

The man looks like he might cry. Maxi, with her admirable sense of empathy, walks over and sits down next to him, resting her muzzle on his thigh.

"But that would mean it's all a lie," he says, patting the dog. "It's all meaningless."

Ronald agrees, but says nothing.

25

Maxi whines some more.

"It's business," Ronald says at last, echoing the words of his first editor-in-chief, who years ago had outlined the concepts of "paid content" and "incentive advantage" to Ronald when he was a cadet reporter, just before Ronald was sent off on his first sponsored assignment.

The man processes Ronald's brief statement. "I guess that explains why bad books get good reviews."

"And films," Ronald adds. "And products, hotels, services, pretty much everything. A lot of it depends on how much of the marketing budget goes to the reviewer."

"I can't believe it." The man slaps his ears with his palms a few times. "It's not true."

"Believe what you want. At any rate, you now understand why I can't read your book tonight, and why I won't read it all, no matter how much you threaten me or my innocent golden retriever. There's no point."

"But what about the internet? All the reviews people write."

Sensing he's getting the upper hand, Ronald crosses his right leg over his left. "Yes, the internet," he says, gesturing with the writer's doorstop novel. "Where everyone's got something to say. The internet has made things much worse."

"How?"

"Well, it's like this. The internet caters to popular opinion, with aggregate reviews and popularity scores, and that means you simply have to sway that opinion your way. Which is why the top-shelf pros get paid off. Down on the lower rungs, it's a bit different. Because if you think your neighbour's a moron with absolutely no taste, why would you read a book he recommends? And anyway, more than a few online reviews are fake. They're written by people somehow connected to the product, whether they're friends and family or employed by the companies themselves. There you go. If you want some reviews, ask your friends, not me. Ask your publisher. Or pay me. Offer me something."

The man shouts, "That's not the way it should be."

"That's the way it is. It's the business. I'm in it to make money. To do that, I need to write as many reviews as I can."

"What about merit? What about the cream rising to the top?"

"I think that still sort of happens, despite the business," Ronald says, and he's starting to enjoy the conversation, glad to see the man is seemingly resigned to the situation. He briefly watches the man patting Maxi, reminded that his dog has proven herself an excellent judge of character. "The crap usually gets left behind," Ronald continues, "because even the Emperor eventually realises that his new clothes leave him naked. If a film tops the box office, there must be something about it that's good, because a lot of people enjoy it, even if you and I might find it rubbish. Same with books and music. Same with art, but that's a bit more complicated."

The man leans back against the wall, but his head is still lowered and his hand is still gently stroking Maxi's head. For her part, Maxi is just loving the attention, and this makes Ronald feel guilty, because he sits at his desk all day when he should be lavishing more attention on his dog. No, he thinks, when he should be out enjoying life and lavishing more attention on himself; not writing about apps he'll never use and hotels he'll never visit, and paying all his mother's ever-increasing medical bills.

While waiting for the man to reply, Ronald flips open *The Energetic Soul Protector Who Started the Revolution in Peru*. Chapter one begins:

"Draped in an embroidered silk robe of red, green and white, with silk boxer shorts in matching colours pulled up to the widest, roundest point of his impressive belly, the diminutive President of Peru entered his ballroom-sized boudoir to a regal fanfare of trumpets with the intention of consummating his marriage to wife number eleven and to get a good night's sleep. Waiting on the bed was the luscious Maritza, all sixteen years of her, naked and raw, yet clever enough to have used the pre-wedding governmental briefing - 'This one shall not be ruined by pregnancy,' the President had charged - to her advantage by lacing the insides of a condom with poison. Thus, deep in the act, the President would meet with an untimely, yet ecstatic end and the revolution would begin."

Ronald smiles and closes the book. "A decent start."

"Not that it makes any difference."

"No. Not really. There are thousands of books out there with openings as good as that."

The man looks up at Ronald, as does Maxi. They have similar expressions: pining, desperate and mournful. "I thought this book would change my life," he says. "I'd win all sorts of big awards and make lots of money."

"You don't want to win a big award. Believe me."

"What?"

"It's the worst thing for a writer. Because of the weight of expectation that follows." Ronald gestures to the books on the floor. "You win a big award, and you're most likely to disappear as a writer, because everyone expects something brilliant, and you can't produce brilliance under that sort of pressure. Besides, awards these days have got their own funding and marketing to think about. You know, big sponsors to win. They want superlatives, the youngest this and the longest that, anything to get in the headlines. They gave up on artistic merit and good storytelling decades ago."

"Stop it. You're killing me, Robert."

"I know. Reality is awful. You're probably best off quitting writing. Play the lottery instead. You've got about the same chance of success."

"I think that's just about the most depressing thing I've ever heard," the man says.

"Now don't jump out of a window or anything like that. It helped a few writers in the past, but suicide no longer makes good marketing."

The man stands up, and Maxi gets to her feet as well. "I guess it's back to law," he says.

Ronald can't believe it, can't possibly picture the man clean-cut and presentable in a suit. "You're a lawyer?"

The man nods. "Trusts and estates. Boring stuff. I was hoping writing would get me out of it."

Holding up the man's book, Ronald asks, "Is this a legal thriller?"

"I don't write genre fiction. I hate those pop-law thrillers."

"A shame," Ronald says. "There's good money in it, when it's done right and when the publisher invests heavily in marketing."

"You mean when they pay off the reviewers."

"And the book shops, and some celebrities. That's the way it works."

"Right. It's business." The man starts to leave. "I'm sorry I bothered you, Robert. I didn't mean to charge in like that. I thought I could talk you around. I thought I had to get proactive."

"Sorry," Ronald says.

As the man walks for the door, mopes really, Maxi is at his side, Ronald gets up and follows. He knows he should feel the empathy that Maxi is clearly feeling, but it's just not there. He's not even at the sympathy stage. Instead, he's thinking of himself and his own writerly quest for meaning that's getting him nowhere, and quietly wishing that his mother would just go ahead and die already.

"I'll review your book," Ronald says. "And I'll do it tonight."

The man turns and smiles, but it's a resentful smile. Ronald is relieved to see the man's eyes are now simply tormented and sad, the crazy gone.

"Thanks. I appreciate it."

Ronald closes the door on the man, double-locks it and slides the chain in place. Back in his office, and with Maxi in her basket, he sits down to write his review of *The Energetic Soul Protector Who Started the Revolution in Peru*.

He uses the same old formula, cleverly bringing in Kafka as the example this author doesn't get close to. The vitriol and spite pour out of him.

Halfway through, he becomes aware that this will be his last review. Relieved, and with plenty of bridges to burn, he doesn't hold anything back.

As Ronald gets more riled up, his dog senses the change in atmosphere and starts whining.

"Don't take that tone with me, Maxi," Ronald says, typing furiously. "I'm doing this guy a favour."

Mikelis

He lies down on the bed and begins to die. He gets comfortable, moving his head slightly on the hotel pillow, creating a shallow bowl. It's just a matter of closing his eyes, nodding off to sleep. He knows that, understands the process, the hows and whys.

The room smells wonderful.

Staring at the ceiling, he sees a long tunnel lined with doorways, but there are no doors. The doorways lead into doctor's waiting rooms, hospital wards, pharmacies, supermarkets stocking discount man nappies, a single room in a retirement home. There are so many doorways and entrances, none of them appealing. Rooms stocked with all the food he will eat, all the nurses who will tend to him, all the funeral invitations, all the complicated paperwork he'll have to deal with, all the clothes that will have to be washed, all the pills he'll have to take, piles and piles of soiled man nappies. He sees there's about a two-metre gap between each doorway. And if this tunnel – no, this corridor – if this corridor is a hundred metres long for every year he will live from now until he's ninety, that makes twenty-five years, with a corridor that's 2.5 kilometres long, if he lives that long, with doorways on either side two metres apart, meaning a hundred doorways for every hundred metres, and 2,500 doorways altogether. But then he decides to widen the gaps between the doorways a metre per year, so that by his ninetieth birthday, there's twenty-seven metres between the doorways, and that would mean a total of ... of ...

X number of doorways. An unknown, but limited number.

He blinks.

He doesn't want to die. The sight of that long corridor, all those doorways, it scares him. It's another journey, one that would lead to deteriorating health and senility, and all that that includes, but it's still a journey he'd like to take. Another escape, into a realm with new factors of probability and chance; things he can control and things he can't.

Control. Chance. They have dictated his life.

Calculations. Luck. Statistics and forecasts. People dealing with numbers, but not with people. No. People dealing with numbers that are people. Were.

He blinks again. Now, the ceiling is showing faces.

His quota started at five people per week, sixteen years ago, not including the standard thirty days holiday and public holidays. So, five people per week over forty-something weeks. Forty-four. Two hundred and twenty people per year, until the quota was upped to ten per week. Then fifteen.

The faces stare down at him. No expressions; just staring, maybe blaming, a little.

Two-twenty a year for five years, then four-forty for the next five, then six-sixty, making ... people ...

"Nē."

X number of people. An unknown, but limited number. Not enough to make a real difference, but when taken together with all the others out there like him, then the statistics change for the better.

So he was told.

So Raif said when he was here.

"The program's expanding, Mike. Your calculations were right. We needed more people, on the road and in research. We're so close to balancing out, thanks to you. The ministers are very happy."

Raif unwrapped the flowers and arranged them in the vase, taking his time with it, moving the stems around with his gloved hands.

"Good."

"Look, sorry, Mike. You were right about Hayate. Bringing him on board was a mistake. All that talk of suicides and natural disasters, what was he thinking?"

"Big wins all at once. Going for broke."

"Like dropping a bomb, but that's not what we're about."

"He took the dignity out of it."

"He did. And we have to be selective. People notice that kind of stuff."

"Hayate tried to put the odds in his favour. That never works."

"He ruined what we were trying to do."

"Yes. Did he go back to Japan?"

Raif looked at him. "You don't know? He was going to be put into another department, another special team, but he killed himself. Jumped from the top of the parliament building and landed on the Esplanade. Just missed an MP from Italy."

"What?"

"Awful."

"I didn't see that coming."

"None of us did."

"The Japanese have the highest rate of suicides."

"This is Belgium, Mike, not Japan."

"It's Europe."

"Remember Hayate trying to take credit for those suicide figures during his first presentation?"

"Yes, but why didn't anyone point out to him that the wrong people were dying? Young people."

Raif shrugged and checked his watch, a gloved hand covering his mouth. "Best be off. Take care now. You look tired. Have a nap."

Then Raif was gone, the door closing behind him with a kind of suction that drew the air out of the room and sealed the door tight once more. The smell of the flowers filled the room, a warm, muggy scent that dragged Mikelis to the bed, where he lay down to die.

He turns away from the faces on the ceiling. A deep inhalation through his nose makes his eyes sticky, but he forces them open.

He's in a small room in the Hotel du Parlament, on Rue du Parnasse, across the tracks from the main buildings. A standard double, painted a non-standard colour: peach. His colleagues, those who don't live in Brussels, stay at the Radisson Blu around the corner, but he prefers the boxy, sparse rooms and the garish colours of the Parlament. It makes the place seem exotic, and not just another generic room you wake up in and wonder where the hell you are.

He finds it fitting that he will die here, in this peach-walled cube, far from his homeland, where he'd spent so many years in cubes: his bedroom in the house in Jurmala, the university dorm in Riga, the Soviet cell, the endless succession of two- and three-star hotel rooms spread out across Europe. Always three dimensional cubes. A man forever locked inside dice. Shake and throw. Cast the die and see what comes up. One in six, each time, no matter what numbers came before. One in six.

Unless the die is loaded.

He regrets nothing. Maybe not marrying and having children, sharing a life, but then he wouldn't have ended up here, wouldn't have killed X number of people, but he would've had the chance to journey down the 2.5 kilometre corridor with X number of doorways.

It's fine. He knew it would end up like this, knew it was coming. He doesn't want to be a burden on the state. Because the numbers don't lie. The numbers never lie. Hayate didn't understand that. Maybe it was a language problem. Hayate wanted big change, to take people out in chunks, in target groups. That was what he was brought in to do, head-hunted from Tokyo where he'd done some admirable work with demographics, albeit with a large amount of tragic luck. He never took credit for the earthquake, the tsunami and Fukushima, but he wasn't sad about it either. He'd even gone as far to say that there was a future in natural disasters. "Potential." Man-made earthquakes targeting coastal villages populated by retirees. He was still on about it as Mikelis marched him up the stairs to the roof.

"You never went for it, Mike," Hayate said, in his stop-start English that made everyone think of the old guy in the *Karate Kid* films, that made them all crack stereotypical jokes. "Never understood it."

Hayate took the stairs reluctantly, the gun in his back not hurrying his progress; if anything, it was slowing him down.

"You don't mess with nature. You don't swing the odds."

"But, Mike, that is exactly what you do. Kill people for better odds."

"No. We work with numbers. And we remove specific people. They won't be missed."

"Ah, then your number also up. You are at retirement age."

"I am."

They reached the top of the stairs and stepped out onto the roof.

"Why you do this, Mike?"

Mikelis motioned with the gun for Hayate to step to the edge of the roof.

"For the team. For Europe. You are bad for us, and I believe in Europe."

"Yes, yes. The new empire." Hayate turned and looked down at the Esplanade, at the MPs, aides and lackeys running around. "The bureaucratic continent. These people get nothing done. They move papers, argue, talk. They cannot agree on anything. Everything in triplicate. Everything translated."

"They are focused on the good of all citizens. You were always focused on the good of the one. You."

Mikelis pushed Hayate from the roof. Surprisingly, he didn't scream or flail his legs and arms. He just fell backwards, arms at his sides, body stiff, like it was a trust-building exercise and ten of his friends would catch him.

He hit the ground hard.

X number of people plus one, making his final total an odd number. He would like to sit at the desk and figure out the total, do with paper and pen what he used to do so easily in his head, but the bed is comfortable, and it's difficult to move.

He doesn't like that it's an odd number. There's no symmetry. It's a loose end. A die still rolling, or spinning on one of its corners. Spinning and spinning.

He feels extremely tired. The fight has gone out of him. Even all those years in the Soviet cell, he had fight in him, because the numbers don't lie. The USSR wouldn't last. He knew that, had calculated it. Communism was a corridor with a limited number of doorways and rooms. Latvia would be free. He would be free. Eventually. He knew it, and was right.

There's a knock on the door.

"Housekeeping."

The voice sounds like it's coming from far away. It echoes. Before he can answer, the door is opened and a woman enters, pushing a trolley laden with a tower of towels, a pyramid of toilet rolls, and little soaps and shampoos in plastic baskets. She sees him lying on the bed.

"Oh. I thought the room was empty."

"It's fine."

"Are you all right?"

"Yes. Tired."

She stands next to the trolley, deciding what to do. She's small, her roots unclear. He thinks she could be Spanish as much as Serbian; Algerian as much as Iranian. But she's not wearing a headscarf. Her English is accented. She pronounced it "Ousekeepen." She's not pretty and she's not young. He gets the feeling that this is a second job for her, and the probabilities extend before him, one leading to another. He quickly theorises that she's saving for something. Escape has the highest probability. To get away, or even get back to wherever she came from. Or to send it all back. No. She wants to escape home.

She goes to the desk and smells the flowers.

"Very nice," she says. "Strong."

She pulls out the chair and sits down. She seems to deflate slightly.

"Long day?"

She nods. "Day. Week. Month. All long."

"Where are you from?"

"Bulgaria. You?"

"Latvia."

She sits more languidly in the chair. "And here we are in Brussels."

"Both of us Europeans."

"Twenty-five years ago we were both Russian."

He laughs. "Well, this is our capital now. This is who we are."

"I don't feel home here. I don't feel part of it."

"Do you feel welcome?"

"I think is my fault. I feel … temporary. Just visiting."

"I know the feeling. This is supposed to be your home, but it isn't and it never will be."

"Hmm."

She stands up and shuffles to the trolley.

"You don't have to go."

"I should not have sat down. You look like you need sleep. I leave you."

"No. Please. Sit. Tell me your story. I'd like to hear your story."

"Why?"

"People, they are fascinating. We try to put them in boxes and give them numbers and say they are like this, but … but people are full of surprises."

"Not me."

"A Bulgarian in Brussels is a surprise, for me."

"There are thousands of us here."

"You came when Bulgaria joined the EU?"

She nods, then sits down in the chair. She slowly crosses her legs. The dress lifts a little, revealing her knees. He'd like to sit up and get a good look at her, but can't seem to lift his head from the pillow. His whole body seems frozen, numb.

She rubs her thumb and index finger together. "Better money."

"What is your profession?"

"I'm a teacher."

"That's why your English is good. You're educated. But working here in a hotel."

"I earn more cleaning rooms in Brussels than teaching children in Sofia."

He smiles. "Yes. The numbers don't lie."

She unbuttons the top of her blouse and rubs the leathery bare skin with her hand. "It's warm in here."

"I don't like the cold."

35

"But you're from Latvia."

"I think cold is more a state of mind. Not so much a temperature. I'm cold from the inside out."

"Like a snake."

"Yes." He closes his eyes and opens them again, glad to see the ceiling is just the ceiling. No corridor, no faces. "A snake. Poisonous."

"Do you work for the EU? Everyone who stays here has something to do with it."

"I do."

"You don't look like a politician."

"You don't look like a housekeeper."

She laughs slowly, sinking further into the chair. The dress lifts some more, bringing a dimpled square of thigh into view.

"We're both in the wrong film," she says. "What do you do for the EU?"

"I'm in demographics. Population control."

"Is that something you can control?"

"Of course."

"With pills and condoms?"

"We operate at the other end of the scale."

She yawns. "Old people?"

"Yes."

"Tell me about it."

"I'm not sure you want to know."

"How bad can it be?"

He blinks with effort, struggling to stay awake. "Europe is ageing."

"I know. I read the paper."

"People don't really understand it. The numbers, I mean. What the numbers mean. We're losing balance. And control."

"What can you do?"

"Try to restore the balance."

Yawning again, she asks, "With more children or less old people?"

"Ideally, both."

"All the locals do is complain that only the immigrants have children."

"Again, they don't understand what the numbers mean. Immigrants are a minority. There will be no out-populating. We live in an era of selfishness, but it's just a trend. It will change. People will have children again."

"Do you have children?"

"No. Do you?"

She nods. "They are back home."

"You send your money to them."

"They ... it was the best chance. I want them to have good lives."

She grips the arms of the chair and pushes herself up. She looks groggy, drunk. She manages to get herself onto the corner of the bed, where she falls sideways at his feet, her back to him, in the foetal position. He could touch the bottom of her spine with his toes, if he could move.

"What's happening?" she asks.

"You see those flowers?"

"Hmm."

"For the last sixteen years, I delivered flowers like those to old people. I entered people's homes saying I was doing a census for the EU. And I always brought flowers, which made the people very happy. They always let me in because they had no one. No family. No wives or children or grandchildren. They were alone, alive, taking money from the state. No one would miss them."

"I see."

"You must understand. This has saved Europe. I have saved Europe. Me and my team. We travelled Europe, deleting people. For balance. You can't imagine the burdens these people put on Europe's social systems. They bleed us dry, make it bad for everyone."

"But I have children. I am not alone."

He sees that she's very still, can feel that she is resigned. "I'm sorry. We were never meant to live this long anyway."

He closes his eyes and drifts off into something deeper than sleep. X number of people plus two. An even number.

Sandra

They stand on the boat, waiting for the last of the guests.

"I think that's everyone," Pete says.

"Wait. Vicki's not here yet," Sandra says.

Pete shakes his head. "She's not coming. You haven't seen her, what, since high school? I don't even know why you invited her."

"We were best friends. I thought we might become close again if I invited her. You know, if I made an effort."

"What happened between you two anyway?" Pete grabs the hand rail to steady himself as the boat thumps against the dock. He's keen to get this party underway.

Sandra turns slightly to him and says, "Our parents gave us money and we went to Europe for the summer after graduation."

"You never said you'd been to Europe." Pete tries to smile, but he's really forcing it, because he thinks there's probably a lot he doesn't know about Sandra, as there's plenty she doesn't know about him. He's glad that with each new girl he can improve on all his old lies.

Sandra watches with expectation as a taxi pulls up to the dock. She extends her neck a little, bird-like, to get a better look. "No, I didn't," she says, "but there's not much to tell. We were having a great time right up until we met this Australian guy in Verona and Vicki went off with him. Literally, ran off. With him."

"Those Aussies pop up everywhere," Pete says, though he wasn't that well-travelled and had only heard from others that Australians often show up in every country. He wonders if Sandra had also been interested in the Australian and this had caused the rift between the girls. She's the jealous type, he thinks. A bit of a drama queen. And a screamer in bed, as if she knows people are listening. "And that was it?" he asks. "You never spoke to each other again?"

"Vicki followed Skye to Australia," Sandra says, still staring at the taxi, still craning her neck.

"Skye? What kind of name is that?"

"It suits him. He's a free spirit." And the look she gives Pete makes him feel this is a prime quality he's lacking.

"I bet he doesn't make a hundred grand a year." Pete follows

Sandra's gaze to the taxi. A girl gets out. "And I bet he doesn't have friends who let you use their boats for parties either."

"That's her," Sandra says, watching Vicki walk along the dock.

"How did you know she was in town anyway?" Pete asks, watching Vicki as well, liking the short skirt, the knee-high boots, and the way her upper body shakes ever so slightly when each heel hits the dock.

"Our mothers are friends." Sandra waves rather girlishly to Vicki, like she's clapping with one hand. "I guess we both know everything that's happened to each other."

"Sandy," Vicki says joyously as the two embrace on the gangway. "It's so good to see you."

"You, too. But it's Sandra now."

"Oh. Okay."

"This is my boyfriend."

"Very pleased to meet you," Pete says smoothly, liking Vicki straight away. Her face has the kind of openness he missed in Sandra, an eager parting of the lips that hints she's more willing to react with feeling than with guarded emotion. She has long, wavy hazelnut hair, streaked blond by the sun, and it lends her, along with the cheeky glint in her eyes, a certain rawness that Pete is attracted to and intrigued by. He holds her hand a little too long – thinks about raising it to his lips – and tries to make eye contact. But Sandra steals Vicki's attention.

"He's a lawyer," Sandra says.

"Whose boss owns this boat," Pete adds. "And now that everyone's on board, we can get started."

"We have to wait for Skye," Vicki says.

"Skye?" Sandra exclaims. "He's coming?"

Vicki nods, her mouth slightly open. "By train." She turns to Pete. "He doesn't believe in cars."

Pete laughs, rather maliciously, as is his habit when encountering people who believe in certain things he thinks ridiculous. "But he flew over here from Australia, right?"

"Of course."

"So, he has no problem with burning fuel then. These eco idiots are full of contradictions."

"How do you survive in Sydney without a car?" Sandra asks, embarrassed by Pete and silently wishing he would talk to some other guests and not be at the gangway when Skye arrives. She hopes Vicki won't be there either.

"There's plenty of buses and trains," Vicki explains. "I drive to work, but Skye never goes anywhere with me in the car. He bikes everywhere." Again, Vicki turns to Pete. "He's a lifeguard at Bronte Beach."

"He's an amazing swimmer," Sandra says, recalling that time in Italy when Skye, his tanned chest taut and glistening, had plunged into Lake Garda and swum out so far that she and Vicki couldn't see him anymore; they got so scared that they ran to the police station to send out a search for him. But when they got back to the beach, he was sunning himself on the sand. He had looked up so casually and asked, almost bored, as if he didn't care if he ever saw them again, "Where youse been?"

"Well," Pete says, "I was second base for my high school baseball team. And, I rowed at Oxford."

Sandra, wanting to show him off, needing Pete to be more than he was, eagerly grabs his arm and says, "You never said you went to Oxford. You're full of fabulous surprises."

Pete's all modesty: "Oh, I just did a semester there on exchange."

"Aren't you a bit short to be a rower?" Vicki asks, looking him up and down again.

"Well, I wasn't in the eight." Having been to Oxford as a child, Pete now racks his brain trying to remember it, just in case they ask any specific questions. "I rowed for fun and to keep fit. I'd like to row here, but there's not enough time in the day."

"Hey, Pete," a man calls out from the level above, from where all the guests are drinking and trying to talk over the music. He already has his tie around his head and is wearing a ridiculous eye patch; but wearing it self-consciously, making it seem as if he had brought it with him. "Is this barge actually gonna move or are we staying at the dock all night?"

"We're waiting for one more," Pete shouts back.

"Come on, Petey. The high seas are calling us." He leans over the rail, nearly falling, and then stumbles backwards laughing.

"Your boss?" Vicki asks.

Pete smiles his disarming, suave courtroom smile. "An intern. I invited everyone from work so I had to invite him, too. Unfortunately, he was the only one who could come. Our practice has a mentor system and ..."

"And you're his," Vicki says. She looks up at the intern dancing precariously close to the railing. "You taught him well."

Sandra looks down at the dock. "There's Skye," she says, watching him walk slowly and deliberately towards the boat, taking his time, never rushing, just like she remembers. He always walks at his own pace; if you want to walk with him, you have to adapt your pace to his. She wants to say something, to show how easy she is with this situation, but she can't speak. To improve her position, she grabs Pete's arm and draws him close.

"G'day," Skye says, walking up the gangway. "Hey, Sandy. I'm glad I lived long enough to see you again."

Sandra blushes slightly, but in the growing darkness, gets away with it. "It's ... it's Sandra now. I'm happy you're here." She looks at him and their eyes meet briefly. It's been almost five years. He looks heavier; still loose-limbed and strong, but with a fullness of body that speaks of middle age. How old was he when they met? She can't remember, but surely he wasn't much over thirty.

"Better late than never." Skye drapes an arm languidly over Vicki's shoulders. He nods to Pete but doesn't reach out his hand. He looks around, bored and unimpressed. The wind blows back his blond hair, revealing a high forehead with the hair receding at the sides. He subconsciously flattens his hair, then asks Pete, "This your monstrosity?"

Pete smiles thinly, preying on what he perceives to be an easy, inferior target. "No, but now that you're finally here, we can get going. We were all waiting just for you." He removes the gangway and signals to the boat's hired captain. The engines power up and the boat edges away from the dock.

"Where can we get a drink?" Vicki asks.

"The bar's upstairs," Pete says, leading them in that direction. "Everyone else's up there."

Skye puts his hands in his pockets. "What're we celebrating anyway?"

"I was made a partner," Pete says. "I'm the youngest ever."

"Good for you." On the deck, Skye looks around at the guests, frowning and looking like he would rather be any place else. "I guess that means something to someone somewhere."

Pete bristles. "Well, not even David Hasselhoff can be a lifeguard forever."

"Who's he?"

"We don't have a television," Vicki explains. "Skye doesn't believe in that either."

Pete picks up two glasses of champagne and hands one each to Vicki and Skye. All around them, the party grows louder and more boisterous as the boat picks up speed. A few people stumble and lose their footing, and every spilled drink is cause for more laughter. "What do you believe in?" he asks.

Skye sips his champagne, barely taking any. "Living life on your own terms," he says slowly, his accent thick.

"You haven't changed at all," Sandra says. She turns to Vicki in order to cover any outward show of feeling. "Neither have you, Vic. I'm really sorry we lost contact."

Vicki expresses her sadness aptly, though both are making a show of it. "I can't believe it's been five years. It seems like it was only yesterday we were in Europe."

"I know." Sandra thinks that trip felt like a lifetime ago. It was at least ten boyfriends ago, and that counted almost for a lifetime. "I want to take Pete there, especially to Verona and Venice."

"Sounds great," Pete says, wondering where this talk was coming from. Sandra had told him she hated to travel.

"It's so romantic." Vicki looks at Skye and they share a pathetically contrived moment, but they are interrupted by the music stopping. Like all the other guests, they look towards the intern who is holding a microphone. He has lost the eye patch, but still has his tie around his head.

"All right," he slurs into the microphone, "who wants to hear a song?" All the guests cheer, urging him to make a fool of himself, in the same way many will once they're drunk enough. With the help of the karaoke machine, the intern launches into a lyrically liberal version of *My Way*. He even tries to sing a verse in Spanish, much to everyone's delight.

"Did he learn that from you as well?" Vicki asks, sidling up next to Pete.

"Only the lines he's getting right," Pete replies. "I sang in the choir at high school."

Vicki smiles, her lips wet and her mouth tantalisingly open. "Why don't you get up there then? Show him how it's done."

"Maybe later. Let the others have some fun first. I don't want to show everyone up."

"You ever sing with Sandy? She's got a great voice."

Sandra laughs nervously, sneaking a look at Skye, who seems not to be listening, but she knows he doesn't miss anything. "She's lying. I never sang in a choir or anything like that. And it's Sandra now."

"Come on," Vicki pushes. She turns to Pete. "We made a record once. One of those record-yourself-on-a-CD-for-a-dollar things. We sang *Dancing Queen*."

Pete laughs loudly. "I'd never have picked you for a Beatles fan, Sandra."

"It's an ABBA song, partner," Skye says. "I guess your musical history begins and ends with Poison. You look like the hair-band type."

Pete wants to let rip at Skye, pull his pathetic, lackadaisical act to pieces, but decides this wouldn't impress Vicki. So, he turns to the girls, smiles and says, "You two made a record? That's amazing. You better get up there and sing that song."

"No," Sandra says. "That was a one-off."

"Thank you, thank you," the intern shouts into the microphone. "Who's next?"

Vicki pulls Sandra towards the makeshift stage. "Come on, before I lose the courage."

"This is too embarrassing." Sandra resists at first, but then decides to totally out-sing Vicki, just as she did on the record.

"I've never heard Sandra sing," Pete says, standing awkwardly with Skye and glad to have something to look at, to divert his attention away from the Australian. He's even happier when the intern comes up to them and introduces himself.

"Australia, eh," the intern says, struggling to keep his footing. Having slowed down, the boat is now cruising at a distance from the city, close enough for them all to see the small lights in the windows of the skyscrapers. "Always wanted to go down under. You look like one of them crocodile wrestling types."

"Yeah, mate, all we do is wrestle crocodiles, drink beer and pull out big knives."

"That's exactly what I hear," the intern says as Sandra and Vicki begin to sing. They giggle through the first few lines, but Sandra is clearly trying to better her friend, making Vicki rise to the occasion, her voice becoming louder; they struggle a little sharing the one microphone.

"They sound good," Pete says, vaguely impressed, his eyes on Vicki.

"Vic sings in my band back in Sydney."

"I thought being a lifeguard was your thing."

Skye sips his champagne, again barely taking any from the glass. "I do a lot of things, partner."

"Encore," shouts someone in the crowd when the song is finished.

"Your turn, Pete," Sandra says into the microphone.

Pete holds up his hands. "Later, later. I can't follow that."

"You got that right." Vicki hands the microphone to another man taking the stage. He swings the microphone around his head and the crowd cheers him on.

"That was brilliant," Pete says to Sandra and Vicki.

"Where's Skye?" Vicki asks. "Didn't he watch us?"

Pete looks around. "He was here a minute ago."

"Excuse me," Sandra says. "I have to visit the bathroom. I'm all flushed."

Glad to be alone with Vicki, Pete gets closer to her and says, "I hear you sing in a band."

"It's just for fun. We played a few gigs. Skye's brother Steele has big plans for us. He plays the drums and writes the songs. I don't have the heart to tell him the songs aren't that good."

"But you're good. Maybe you should go solo."

"I'm happy doing what I do."

"Which is?" Pete asks, liking the sound of her voice and the way her mouth moves. He wants her, but is, for the moment, at a loss as to how to go about getting her. He has already achieved some Olympic-standard pick-ups and often just picks up girls for the challenge of it. The way he got Sandra was especially rewarding and was why he stayed with her despite his interest diluting with every passing day. Because for Pete, holding the catch is never quite as rewarding as landing the catch.

"I work at a kindergarten and study in the evenings. Only one year left."

"And then you'll be what?"

Vicki smiles, showing her teeth. "A legal assistant."

Pete pounces on the opening. "Is that right? Well, I happen to know a freshly-minted partner who could use a new assistant, qualified or not."

"The youngest ever?" Vicki asks. "I don't know. I like Australia. Down there, the sky's the limit, know what I mean?"

Pete laughs, pretending to be relaxed and undeterred, yet

wondering how often she's tried to impress people with that line, or variations of it. "Living life on your own terms is a recipe for selfishness if you want my opinion. It also sounds like an excuse for non-achievement."

"Oh, really? Well, Sandra's only been gone ten minutes and already you're hitting on me. Are you like this with all her friends?"

"I thought it was a set up. She ran to the bathroom the minute Skye went."

Vicki's face falls slightly. "I knew she'd try something." She heads down the stairs and only just manages to keep herself from falling when the ship suddenly starts to tilt. The music stops and people start to panic as the boat begins tipping slightly backwards.

"Oh my God, we're sinking," someone shouts. Everyone screams at once and many hands jostle for the limited hand rail space.

From below, the captain shouts, "Everyone stay calm and stay on the top deck. I need some of you guys to come down here and give me a hand with these life rafts."

Pete helps Vicki back up the stairs. "Stay here," he orders, thinking it's his role to take command of the situation. He beckons a few of the men to follow him down the stairs and the intern leads the pack.

"The boss is not gonna like this," he says, remarkably sober, making Pete wonder if he had been faking his drunkenness all along. "Hey, Pete, where are you going?"

"Help the captain," Pete says, moving away from the life rafts and towards the stairs that lead down to the engine room and bathrooms. "I wanna know what happened. Maybe I can stop it from sinking."

"This is no time to be a hero, Pete." The intern is holding one corner of an inflatable life raft and helping to flatten it out. The captain flicks a switch and the raft begins to inflate. A few people hanging onto the hand rail above see the raft and start pushing each other to be the first downstairs and the first into the raft. All the others follow.

"We're not all gonna fit," one man shouts, looking around him to see who should be left out, his eyes stopping on the larger people.

"Well, I'm already in," a woman says, pushing a few people aside to get into the raft. But her short skirt is too tight and she can't lift her leg high enough to step into the raft. She tries to jump but lands on the edge of the raft with the heel of her stiletto. It punctures the raft, the air hissing out as it deflates. She falls over.

"You stupid girl," the captain says.

"What a flimsy raft," she shouts in reply, getting pulled back to her feet by a couple of people.

"There's another one and we all would've fit in two," the captain replies. "But now there is only one. Stay the hell back while we inflate it, all of you."

Downstairs in the engine room, Pete hears the shouts. "Only one raft," he mumbles to himself. The water is already two feet high. It's bubbling from a closed door on the far side of the room.

"Help! Help!"

Pete runs to the door. "Sandra?" He tries to pull the door open, but it's stuck. "Hang on." He bends down and feels a large gas tank, which must have tipped over when the ship started tilting. He gets the tank out of the way and door opens, a surge of water coming with it. Drenched, Skye is first through the door, almost shoving Pete aside and then running through the water like he's running in the surf, lifting his knees high. He stumbles and gets to his feet. He doesn't even stop to look at Pete and is up the stairs before Sandra comes out. The water has made her make-up run from around her eyes and down the sides of her face.

"Pete," she shouts, hugging him tightly.

"Sandra, what happened?"

Sandra squints at Pete. "I don't know. It just ... happened."

Pete points to the exit. "Go upstairs." Sandra nods and starts wading slowly through the now waist-high water. With the door open, the engine room is filling quicker than before. Pete looks into the room and sees the hole in the side of the boat. A generator had been shunted against the side, causing the hole. He smiles grimly, thinking that this incredibly cheap boat must be made of plywood, and thinking that Skye must really have been giving it to Sandra, physically and aggressively, in a way she had always pretended not to like, despite her theatrical vocalisations, to move a generator of this size with force enough to put a hole in the boat. Water continues to gush in and a pair of black panties floats gently past him. He scoops them from the water and turns towards the stairs. Sandra is standing there, watching him.

"You forget something?" Pete asks, holding up the panties.

She looks at him sadly, but then scowls, an expression he's never seen from her before. Her menace scares him a little and he's glad happy when she goes up the stairs.

On the deck, the captain is trying to maintain order. "Everyone stay calm." The second life raft has been inflated and all the women are crammed into it, shivering and crying. When the water is high enough, they will float away. All the men have been given life vests.

"Vicki, get out of the raft and let the captain get in," Skye orders. His blonde hair is wet and pulled back, revealing his widow's peak.

Vicki reluctantly climbs out of the raft. "What happened?"

"This is the cheapest, crappiest shit-box I've ever been on." The boat tilts further and the life raft, with the captain now inside, starts to float and drift away from the boat.

"The Coast Guard's on the way," the captain shouts. "Don't try to swim for it." All the men jump into the water. A few of them shriek at the coldness of the water. They float close together as the captain had ordered earlier.

"Skye, there are no more life vests," Vicki says. Skye looks around and sees a life buoy hanging from the side of the rail on the top deck.

"Come on," he says, heading for the stairs.

But Pete and Sandra are already up there. Pete's holding the round buoy in his hands. "Don't worry. I've got it," he says. The boat is almost entirely underwater and he tosses the buoy over the rail.

Sandra steps forward and punches Skye in the face. "You're an asshole."

"What are you doing?" Vicki steps between them and pushes Sandra overboard. She lands ungracefully in the water and swims over to the life buoy.

Slightly stunned, Pete decides it's time to take his chance. He asks, "Would you like to have dinner sometime?"

"What?" Vicki exclaims. "Are you insane?"

"You know what they were up to down there," Pete says. "They cheated on both of us." He reaches into his pocket, pulls out the black panties and spins them around his index finger. "They were so into it, they moved the generator so it made a hole in the boat."

"You're crazy, Pete." Vicki turns to Skye, who's holding the side of his face and, despite everything, still looking lackadaisical and unimpressed.

"Well?" Pete pushes. "How about it?"

"I never should've come to this party," Vicki says. "Everything I do with Sandy always turns to crap somehow." She jumps over the rail and swims to the life buoy. Sandra pushes the buoy towards her and they both hook one arm over it.

Pete says to Skye, "You are a completely useless human being. Almost as useless as Sandra. You two deserve each other."

"Nothing happened down there, partner."

"Well, I'll still be telling the police about how you sank this boat."

"It was an accident."

"Right." Pete scrunches up the panties and throws them at Skye. "I guess you'll be needing these more than me." To Pete's surprise, Skye folds the panties carefully and puts them in his pocket. Then, he jumps over the other side of the railing and begins swimming towards the life raft. "Loser," Pete says. "They're probably his panties." The boat has sunk and he's in the water now. He swims towards the two girls, who are shouting abuse at each other.

"Bitch."

"Slut."

Pete hooks his arm over the buoy. "Best party ever."

"We were gonna get married," Vicki says, calming down a little, and more sad than angry.

"Yeah? Well, Skye practically raped me down there."

"You went after him. That's why you invited me to this party. You knew I'd bring him."

"That's not true. Why would I do that? I already had him once and it wasn't that good."

"What? Skye said he never slept with you."

"Well, he did," Sandra says, crying now and shaking from the cold. "Right before you stole him away from me."

"You can have him back. I don't care."

"I don't want him. I've got Pete."

Pete laughs. "Not anymore. Nobody cheats on Pete."

"Like you're so pure," Sandra says. "Mr I-rowed-at-Oxford and I-played-second-base. Every second thing you say is a lie."

"I didn't believe a word of it," Vicki says. "He even tried to pick me up, right when the boat was sinking, and right in front of Skye."

"I never want to see you again, Pete."

"That'll make us both happy," Pete looks around, hoping there might be something else he can cling to, to get away from these two bitches, but there's nothing.

"You know," Sandra says to Vicki, moving around the buoy and huddling close to her, "he told my mother he played the guitar in high school and then two weeks later told one of my friends he played piano."

Vicki sneers at Pete. "You must be the most insecure man in the history of humanity." The girls laugh together. "Are you even a lawyer?"

"That much is true," Pete says. Against the shadowed outline of the city, he sees a light coming straight towards them. It's the Coast Guard, and he wonders how much abuse he will have to endure before being rescued.

"I missed you, Vicki," Sandra says. They hug with their free arms.

Esmeralda

He wants to leave, but his wife insists on staying, and he can't be bothered arguing. So after the intermission, he buys a bag of peanuts and two cups of wine, and they return to their seats in the fourth row. He takes the aisle seat this time, so he can stretch out his legs and maybe dash off to the bathroom for an extended toilet break if things get too crazy. The bag of peanuts is warm in his hands, the nuts still in their shells. He starts breaking them open, dropping the remains on the already shell-covered floor. He offers the bag to his wife; her hand stirs around inside, seeking out the biggest of the nuts.

The audience gets settled and the lights are dimmed. As with the start of the show, there is a palpable air of expectation. The audience members remain strangers to each other, but are connected by their collective desire to see more feats of the amazing and witness the grotesque. The show's first half had bordered on violent, the performers pushing the limits of taste and physicality in order to extract the necessary gasps and screams from the audience. There was a rather bizarre tooth removal, which he thought was staged. There was quite a lot of blood when a knife trick went wrong. An ambulance was called, and the paramedics exhibited a fumbling intensity that led him to believe it wasn't part of the act. The knife-catcher's screams were very real. This was followed, rather cunningly, he thought, by chainsaw juggling that had everyone on the edge of their seats, expecting a limb or two to be lopped off. The paramedics hung around, loitering to the side of the centre ring, just in case. Their crackling walkie-talkies ruined the atmosphere somewhat. But the trick went right, the juggler stayed whole and the medics left. The rest of the performances were just outright strange; they only seemed interesting for their strangeness. He didn't think there was a terrible amount of talent or skill involved. It was all just weird.

This circus was definitely not for children. He likened it more to performance art. The artistry of torture, almost. He was glad the show hadn't drifted into the realm of the pornographic. At least, not yet.

The murmurs of the audience die down as the ringmaster walks towards the circle of light projected from the lone spotlight, positioned just slightly to the left in the centre ring. He's skinny, quite tall, and wearing a dark purple suit that appears to be made of velvet. The suit jacket has tails, and there's a monocle attached to the lapel. He puts the monocle in place, in his left eye. It lends him an old-world sense of entitlement and grandeur, like a faded aristocrat fallen on hard times.

The ringmaster proved in the first half that he was a man of few words, that these incredible acts required little introduction. But he actually appears rather bored with the whole thing; that he had, perhaps, once failed at a more regular and respected profession, and somehow through the course of happenstance and wrong turns had ended up here, in a purple velvet suit introducing amateur weirdness passed off as entertainment.

He raises the microphone.

"Ladies and gentlemen," he says in a monotone. "I give you the astonishing, the mesmerising, Esmeralda."

The lights go out. There's a soft humming as several ultra-violet lamps are switched on, bathing the centre ring in a soft, neon-purple glow. Small specks are visible on the carpet, and could be bits of confetti or drops of the knife-catcher's blood.

For a while, nothing happens. Then, something starts moving behind the curtains, an animal on all fours, black and white, with the white glowing through the thin curtains.

An animal on the prowl, moving slowly.

Everyone watches for movement, for this animal to appear. He thinks it's some kind of big cat, maybe a tiger. He hopes so.

Esmeralda the white tiger.

His wife's hand digs noisily into the bag of peanuts and stirs around. The sound makes the animal stop. Even from behind the curtain, it's clear that the tiger's head moves and looks directly at him and his bag of nuts.

His heart starts to beat very fast, imagining Esmeralda coming straight for him, devouring him and the nuts.

But the animal doesn't move.

His wife's hand slowly withdraws a nut from the bag, careful not to make a sound.

Others in the audience have responded to Esmeralda's reaction. No longer are they shelling nuts or chewing. They are held spellbound by this animal prowling behind the curtain.

She starts to move again, gracefully, slowly. The curtains shimmer as she passes.

Esmeralda walks the length of the curtain and back again, stopping in the middle. Then, a section of the curtain is parted. At the same time, the ultra-violet lamps are switched off and the main lights raised, albeit at a dim level.

When Esmeralda's head appears in the parted gap, there's a collective gasp from the audience; the fear of this dangerous animal wandering around just metres from them, unattended. But there's excitement too. A white tiger, up close and in the flesh.

Unfortunately, Esmeralda is not real, he knows it. It's an authentic mask, perhaps the remains of a real white tiger, a rug turned into a costume. Yet the eyes are lifeless and the mouth doesn't move. There is no sense of danger. And when he looks closely, leaning forward in his seat and almost dropping his bag of nuts, he can just make out the profile of a person's face, nose and lips painted in white and black, tucked underneath the tiger's head. In full light, the profile would be even more visible.

He's still astounded though, because as Esmeralda enters the ring and starts walking around, she delivers a very convincing impression of a big cat. He sees that she's walking on her knees, with her ankles somehow fixed to the top of her thighs, giving her the right proportions for a tiger's hind legs. There are fake paws attached to her knees.

She gets very close to the front rows, making those audience members lean back and away as she approaches.

He wonders if he is the only one in the audience aware that it's a person in costume. A woman, lithe and supple as a feline and an expert in mimicry.

A quick glance around assures him he's not alone, as they are shelling nuts again and drinking from their plastic cups of wine, enjoying the show. Esmeralda seems to sense this too, that the facade has dropped. She deftly executes a few tiger-like gestures, keeping her head low so the tiger's head is always in full view. It all looks rather routine, and somewhat rushed. Finally, she unclips the binds holding her ankles to her thighs and stands up straight. When she removes the tiger's head and shakes her hair loose, he actually thinks it's something of a relief.

The audience claps. A few people shout, "Bravo."

Esmeralda smiles and bows. She's so flexible, that when she bows, her hair sweeps across the carpeted floor.

An assistant comes into the centre ring carrying a steel tub sloshing with water. He has a black and white striped towel draped over his left shoulder. The tub is placed on the floor. At first, Esmeralda bends down and delicately washes the black and white paint off her face. Then, as if acting on impulse, she proceeds to get into the tub, folding her body and manipulating her limbs until she is fully inside and can't be seen anymore. Audience members stand up to see if she is still there, until everyone is standing, trying to get a look. Peanut shells crack under their feet.

He stands as well. Being tall, he's able to see over the heads in front. Esmeralda is impossibly curled up inside the tub, fully submerged and her body slightly magnified by the water; an embryo in a halved egg. Her mouth and nose are just above the surface so she can breathe.

Everyone claps.

As she slowly starts to emerge from the tub, theatrically stretching and struggling as if exiting the womb, the people in the audience go back to sitting. Out of the tub, Esmeralda is now all in white, some kind of body suit. The black tiger stripes were only painted on.

He's somewhat disappointed that she's not naked, as he'd thought the whole costume may have been body paint, apart from the tiger's head and fake paws. Because she has a tremendous figure, all soft muscle and supple tendons, curved and taut. She's as good as naked in that tight body suit, but he'd much prefer to see her in the flesh.

Still employing graceful, rather feline movements, she towels herself down. The assistant holds up a mirror so she can check if all the paint is gone from her face. She pulls her wet hair back and secures it in a short ponytail. She even playfully licks the back of her hand and uses the hand to smooth her eyebrows. The gesture draws soft murmurs of laughter and she smiles in response. She wraps the towel around the assistant's neck like a scarf. He lifts the tub and carries it out of the centre ring.

The lights are raised further, making Esmeralda's body suit shine and glow, almost gold. She moves into the very centre of the centre ring.

He can't stop staring at her. The way she moves, her very presence. There's something other-worldly about her, something fresh and pure. Untainted, virginal, sexual. A woman transformed into a white tiger, then into a foetus and a newborn, and now into this glowing, mesmerising embodiment of feminine perfection. Every single part of her is perfectly formed and in exactly the right place.

He's feeling something deep inside he's never felt before. Something primal. He's struck by the intense desire to pick up a club, pound her on the head with it and drag her away by her ponytail. And he'd kill anyone who tried to stop him.

He's suddenly aware that he has never been in love. Until now.

As the stunning Esmeralda stands in the centre ring, readying herself for whatever her next performance will be, he sneaks a look at his wife. They've been married for nearly five years, and only her commitment and proximity turn him on. It's his second marriage. Between the marriages, there were a few girlfriends, plus the handful before his first marriage. But none of those girls and women made him feel like this, and it all seems like so much wasted time and effort.

Because this is what animal attraction feels like. This is pure carnality.

He fixes his eyes on Esmeralda as she balances on one leg and raises her other leg behind her. Raises it and raises it until it's perfectly straight above her, and she arches her back slightly and grabs that leg's shin with her up-stretched hands. It seems impossible, and audience members gasp and cough in amazement, but she appears to do it with ease.

He thinks it would be just incredible to have sex with Esmeralda, with someone who could manipulate her body like that. Imagine the tricks she could do in the bedroom, the positions she could achieve.

As she stands there, legs so unbelievably extended, his sexual imagination takes him far beyond the dull scenarios and standards he knows. The possibilities seem endless. He envisions small elevators, telephone booths, economy-sized cars, closets, airplane bathrooms. He could fit Esmeralda in anywhere.

She lowers the raised leg until it's at ninety degrees to her other leg, and bends over so her hands touch the floor.

She'd be good in the kitchen too, he thinks. She could stir a pot with her foot while chopping vegetables or doing the dishes with her hands. Perhaps all three at once. Fold the laundry and paint a picture. Now that would be performance art, and practical too.

He feels suddenly foolish for taking his carnal feelings towards Esmeralda and making them domestic.

Her hands on the floor, she raises her body into a handstand, perfectly straight, but then goes further, her spine arching backwards, folding almost, as her legs go over and past her head, almost to the floor. She holds the sickening position.

"Oh my God," he hears his wife say.

Esmeralda doesn't smile. She doesn't appear to be in any discomfort or pain, but she also seems to gain no pleasure from her movements.

He thinks this is sad, that she's just performing. Perhaps that's how it would be at home with her as well; getting close would require her to perform, to put on a show of sorts, that he'd never really get to know the real Esmeralda.

He wonders if that's her name.

She lowers herself out of the handstand. An assistant brings out two chairs and Esmeralda executes the splits with a foot on each chair. The weight of her torso causes her legs to bend in a very slight U-shape.

The audience claps. Several members are simply staring and clapping dumbly. Others look away.

He imagines her giving birth to her own baby, able to bend so far forward that she could see the baby's head. They wouldn't need a doctor or a hospital. They could live in a cave, or roam the world like gypsies, with Esmeralda performing her contortions for fast money. He could be her lone ringmaster, in a natty suit with a top hat that people could put their cash inside. Esmeralda would be more than enough talent for a carnival of one.

But no. He doesn't want to share her. He doesn't want her to perform for people like this. A cave would be better, living wild. Or he could pack her way in a box every day. Fold her into a trunk and lock her inside, like a precious jewel. Or a prized toy. Bring her back out after he comes home from work. Then, she would perform just for him.

Out of the splits, and with one of the chairs removed from the centre ring, Esmeralda turns her focus to the remaining chair, impossibly winding her body and limbs on, around and through it. In doing so, she morphs from feline to serpentine, almost strangling the chair, consuming it. And sure enough, in one particularly complex position, Esmeralda grimaces hard, her whole body flexing, the muscles, tendons and ligaments going piano-wire tight. The chair breaks into pieces. The loud and unexpected crack makes some members of the audience jump in their seats. Esmeralda falls to the carpeted floor and untangles herself from the mess, to the wild applause of the audience.

He claps as well, stunned, but also now fearing Esmeralda somewhat. Would a girl that strong and powerful let herself get boxed away each day? He thinks she would fight back, talk back, and probably have positions contrary to his. Flexible in body, but not necessarily in mind. He wouldn't be able to tame her. No one would, and he thinks himself an idiot for having entertained such thoughts. Because if he could tie her down and own her, she would lose all of her appeal.

This makes him want her more. He wants her to crush him like she crushed that chair. Envelop him and squeeze with all her strength.

But he's married, holding a bag of peanuts, merely a witness to this show. How could he ever get her to notice him? What could he offer? And maybe all the other men present are harbouring the exact same thoughts and desires. From these contortions and tricks, they see only their own pleasure. They are also being awoken to the sexual possibilities of tight spaces.

The assistant removes the remains of the chair and places a champagne bottle on the carpeted floor, next to Esmeralda. She lies flat on her stomach, the bottle inches away from her face. From behind her, she brings both legs up and over her head. With her toes, she manages to loosen and remove the wire frame holding the cork secure. A second assistant enters the centre ring. From her toes, he plucks the wire frame, shows it to the audience, then pockets it.

Things start to slow down a little.

Esmeralda takes a long time to bring her legs back to the floor, and an even longer time to raise her hips high, balancing on her hands and feet, in the very likeness of a stretching cat. She even lets out kittenish yelp of pleasure once her hips reach their zenith.

The champagne bottle and the tension being created by the slow movements make him think they're reaching the climax of her performance. He wonders what her sexual climax would sound like. If she's a kitten when stretching, does she roar like a tiger when she orgasms?

He grunts with amusement, getting a sharp elbow in the ribs from his wife.

Standing straight, Esmeralda raises her right leg. One assistant holds it while the other reaches down and lifts her left leg. Now in the splits position, with an assistant holding each foot, Esmeralda is carried over to the champagne bottle and slowly lowered on top of it. She gets herself comfortable, manipulating her hips to achieve the desired position. Because of his angle of viewing, it's not quite clear with what she's actually gripping the cork, but she's definitely got hold of it. A third assistant comes out and lies on the floor behind her. He grabs the bottom of the bottle with his hands.

The four performers stay in this position for a minute or so, during which time all the members of the audience stand in order to get a better look.

Then, the two assistants holding Esmeralda slowly begin to walk in a circle, turning her around. Held in place, the bottle remains unmoved, but the cork goes with Esmeralda.

In the stunned silence, he swears he can hear the squeak of cork against glass.

Around and around they go, stepping over the assistant lying on the floor.

Some members of the audience move out of their rows to get closer to the action, to find out just how she's gripping that cork so tightly, and with what.

A circle. Another circle.

What if the cork explodes from the bottle? he wonders. How is she applying downward pressure to keep that from happening?

His wife pushes him out of the row and jostles with the others to get closer.

He finds this painfully slow uncorking very arousing. And from the looks on the faces of the men around him, some with their hands deep in their trouser pockets, he sees he's not alone in wanting to be the bottle.

But Esmeralda's face is expressionless. She simply lets herself be turned.

Finally, there's a soft, gaseous hiss as the pressure is released from the champagne. The audience lets out a collective breath, a sigh that sounds vaguely sexual, and as Esmeralda is lifted away from the bottle, they join together in giving her an incredible amount of applause.

Her arms raised in theatrical triumph, the assistants carry Esmeralda backwards, out of the centre ring and behind the curtain. The remaining assistant picks up the bottle of champagne and pours it into the cups extended by audience members.

The cork is nowhere to be seen.

He falls back into his seat, exhausted, and just a little bit disgusted. With his wife clamouring for a cup of champagne, he leaves the bag of nuts on her seat and dashes outside.

It's dark. The peanut and wine stall, which glowed during intermission, has been closed and shuttered.

He follows the edge of the enormous tent, where a slither of light is shining from the gap between the canvas and the ground. It's a marked trail that leads him to the caravans behind. He finds the makeshift stage door, which is a black curtain, and peers inside. Other performers are getting ready. Some are gathered together, drinking. He sees the man who was wounded in the knife act, his right arm heavily bandaged, playing an accordion. One of the assistants is milking a goat. There's a donkey dressed up like a piñata, with a handler nearby holding a baseball bat and wearing a sombrero.

He decides that's one act he can miss.

There's no sign of Esmeralda.

He looks towards the caravans. Only one has light in the window, and it flickers like candlelight. He heads for it. From another caravan, a chained up dog barks and tries to run towards him, coming up short because of its metal leash. Scared, he edges around the still barking dog and gets to the caravan's door.

He knocks.

The dog suddenly stops barking and sits down. He turns to look. The ringmaster is standing in front of him.

"Help you?" the ringmaster asks.

Up close, he thinks the ringmaster is taller and more filled out than when seen from the seating area, more threatening and vicious. Hardened by experience.

"You want to talk to Esmeralda, yeah? Tell her how great she was? Well, she doesn't associate with audience members."

They stand for a few moments in silence. He thinks the ringmaster is possessive of Esmeralda, is possibly her guardian of sorts; had once fought for possession of her from a previous master and has since fought off others. He wants to challenge the ringmaster, to win Esmeralda for himself, but is too intimidated.

The purple-suited man just stares at him, his expression rather bleak.

"Why don't you go back to your seat and enjoy the rest of the show," the ringmaster says.

He nods.

The ringmaster reaches out a hand to open the caravan door, then stops. From his pocket, he plucks the champagne cork.

"Here," he says, giving him the cork. "A souvenir."

He takes it, letting the cork sit in the palm of his hand.

58

The ringmaster offers a very faint smile and opens the door to the caravan. Once inside, the door is closed and locked.

He tosses the cork to the ground and walks back to the tent to find his wife.

Pavel

It's just before 1am when Dave gets home. He's in a bad mood, made worse by the fact he sees no lights on in his apartment windows. The darkness means Natalia hasn't made a surprise appearance, as she sometimes does on Friday evenings.

He locks his bike and heads inside.

Guess she doesn't want to hear any more of my horror stories, he thinks.

His hand jitters a little as he slides the key into the post box. A lot of the evening's imagery is still vivid. It's the kind of stuff that's hard to shake, even when he's seen it before, or seen worse. Unlike the other paramedics, he doesn't get high in order to make it through the dreaded 4pm-midnight shift; those eight hours getting progressively hairier as the night marches on. And tonight, there were all those May Day idiots. But many of his workmates just float through it all, smiling and dazed, but still doing their jobs well. Driving the ambulance in between toking on joints.

Not Dave. He's clean. He's in training. That means no drugs, not even any sleeping pills.

He wonders how he'll get to sleep tonight, without Natalia to pour all his garbage on and without the calming relief and temporary distraction of sex.

He takes out his post, considers calling her. But he doesn't want to be needy. He has the feeling she's lost interest anyway.

It's mostly junk mail, put in nice white envelopes and disguised as real mail, with his name and address on it. The Hausmeister put a special paper-recycling bin near the post boxes, and these envelopes go straight into it.

The latest issue of *Modern Triathlete* has arrived. That lifts his spirits.

There's also a formal-looking letter addressed to Pavel Brazda. It looks like it's from one of the local Behördes. Einwohnermeldeamt, he assumes. Or some kind of registry office. He checks the other post boxes, but doesn't see Brazda's name written on any. So he places the envelope on top of one post box, thinking that someone in the house has done Brazda a favour by letting him register at their address.

He's done the same for a few Americans in the past; gave them an address to help them get settled, organise bank accounts, health insurance and such. He knows the authorities seldom check to see if the person is actually living there.

He carries his backpack and triathlon magazine slowly up the stairs.

***

The route is free of traffic, as it often is on a Wednesday evening. Keeping a 30km/h average, he does five loops of the Grünewald: heading down Kronprinzessinnenweg to Havelchaussee, then up and down the hills before making a right onto Am Postfenn, and detouring to Teufelsberg to climb the man-made hill, built up from World War Two rubble. With each loop, that short, steep climb gets harder, but he likes the challenge. He can feel the morning's pool session, when he really pushed it doing sprints. It's a good kind of tired.

Dave loves Wednesdays, that ray of sunlight that shines in the middle of his dour working week. It's when he's riding in the twilight on a Wednesday evening that he thinks his life is not all that bad: two days work, one day off, two days work, the weekend off.

If only the work wasn't so traumatising, he thinks.

On the final loop, he sees a family of wild pigs.

He cycles over a hundred kilometres and is fortunately spared the hassle of a flat tire.

It's dark when he gets home, as are the windows of his apartment. Natalia had earlier sent a text that she might come over. He decides to call her later.

He puts the bike on his right shoulder and clears his post box, grabbing all the mail with his free hand. He'll sort it out upstairs.

He showers.

Wrapped in a towel, he sits at the table as he eats. He finishes the salad left over from lunch and follows this with a vanilla protein shake with fresh strawberries and ice cream.

He's nibbling on some mixed nuts when he calls Natalia.

"Hi, Dave."

"Hey, babe. Where are you?"

"Work."

"Still?"

"Oxana, she ask me to cover her shift. We made switch."

61

"You're not coming over?"

"I can later. Midnight."

"Come on, babe. I've been training all day. I'll be asleep by then."

Natalia doesn't reply. Dave can hear the sounds of the Babuschka Café, in full swing with all the Russians having come in after work. Someone is playing the accordion.

"David, I say you training is more important than me."

She hangs up.

Dave doesn't call her back. He tosses the phone on the table and starts going through his mail. He's pragmatic about these things. With it being late May and with the first race just a few weeks away, he'd have to say that yes, his training is more important than her. This year, he's determined to qualify for Team USA to race in the triathlon at the World Age Group Championships in September. He needs to set fast times, to race better than he ever has. And that means training. The last few years, he always came up short. Three years ago, he made the reserve list for his age group, but didn't get to race. He went all that way with all his gear and all he got was a Team USA shirt. But he's worn it proudly since.

He has a letter from his mobile phone provider, saying his invoices will now be generated electronically, and that if he wants a printed copy, he'll have to do it himself.

More junk mail.

A postcard from his father. He's in Prešov, looking into the family's roots. He devotes several sentences to explaining how a scoop of ice cream costs thirty cents there. He's found an uncle, he writes, but he wasn't too welcoming. He hopes to be in Berlin by the following weekend, but he's not doing too well with the rail pass he's on, getting on the wrong trains and ending up way off course.

Dave smiles at this, sure that his father is enjoying himself. As they're both ex-army men, they like getting off the beaten track.

There are two letters for Pavel Brazda, both from the Berliner Bank. He feels one, getting the outline of the bankcard inside. He assumes the other envelope has Brazda's pin.

You fool, he thinks, tossing the envelopes on the table.

He decides to take them downstairs in the morning, when he goes for his dawn run, and put them in Herr Michalik's post box. He's the most likely to know someone with a name like Pavel Brazda.

***

He goes through the automated telephone response system, putting in his subscription number and finally getting a person, but one who speaks heavily accented English.

"Hi. My name's Dave Cibulka. I didn't get my June issue of *Modern Triathlete*."

There's some tapping at a keyboard.

"Our records show that it was delivered last Monday."

"Well, I don't have it."

"Is it possible someone else in your household has it?"

"No. I live alone."

"Is your post box secure?"

"It is."

"Okay, Mr. Cibiluka ..."

"That's Cibulka."

"Sorry. My apologies. Mr. Cibulka, I'll organise a new delivery of that issue."

"Thank you."

He hangs up, and wonders again why there was no post. He really could use his triathlon magazine to get his mind off the night's events. Especially that last call out to the apartment in Hohenschönhausen, with the drunk woman locked in the bathroom; they had to kick the door down and then unwrap her from the mouldy shower curtain. The bruised, unwashed quartet of kids cowering in the bedroom they shared. All the empty liquor bottles. The stink. He'd wanted the father, if there was one, to come home just so he could kick the shit out of him. And even Thomas, his colleague for the night, totally high, but left speechless and sombre by this scene.

Those kids, Dave thinks. Those poor little kids.

He sits down on the sofa, now folded back into position after his father slept on it the previous night. Just one night, and they'd spent most of it arguing.

It started with his father complaining about how Berlin wasn't the same as when he was posted here. Not nearly the same. And out came the old stories. His father making horrible comments about Commies, about how Berlin was being overrun by Polaks and Reds. Dave coming to the rescue of his adopted home, even after having seen the city's darker side regularly, four nights a week, for nearly ten years. Still, he stood up for Berlin, his Berlin, and if his father didn't like it, he could go back to Philly and stay there.

Dave picks up the remote, but doesn't turn the television on. Seldom is there anything good on German TV at 1am; just soft porn, reality rubbish and advertorials.

He misses Natalia, resolves tomorrow to buy her flowers and surprise her at the Babuschka. After his morning pool session.

He goes to bed.

***

His cold is getting better, and it's been good having a few days off. He misses the training, the structure it gives to the day. The purpose.

He knows it was after that first race in Berlin that he picked up the cold. With the water sixteen degrees, the air eleven, and with the pouring rain, there was little chance he would come out of that race unscathed. Guys were crashing all over the place during the bike leg. He recognised some of the paramedics who were scraping riders off the street. They cheered for him as he went past, riding conservatively.

Dave thinks he's lucky to have just a cold.

Natalia has taken care of him the last few days, but with the detached attentiveness of a nurse rather than the care of a girlfriend. Still, he wasn't complaining.

She's working today.

He lies on the sofa, watching DVDs of American shows.

He spends an hour doing stretches on the carpeted floor.

Just after noon, he goes out for more anti-cold supplies. When he comes back, the post has arrived. He takes it upstairs, smiling, because he's got the June issue of *Modern Triathlete*.

Standing in the kitchen, he makes some tea and goes through the post. There are three letters for Pavel Brazda. One is from the insurance company DKV, and has a card inside. The second is from Berlin's medical university, the Charité. The third has been addressed by hand and is rather bulky. He spends a bit of time feeling this envelope, turning it over and around, pressing at the corners. He thinks there's money inside. A rather large amount of money.

The kettle comes to a boil. He holds the letter from the Charité over the steam and slowly pulls the flap open.

He reads the letter.

Among the other formalities of starting his PhD studies, Pavel

Brazda needs to be at the medicine faculty on August 7 for the welcoming event.

So, you're on the way to becoming a doctor, Dave thinks. More specifically, a sports doctor.

He's impressed, almost glad for Pavel.

Dave had wanted to become a doctor, but his parents couldn't afford to send him to med school after his older sister ate up the family's college fund. The best he could do was follow his father into the army and become a paramedic. Once discharged, he followed a girl to Berlin and, having been trained at only one thing, became a paramedic there. Before starting the job, he took a crash course in German and made his then girlfriend, and all subsequent girlfriends, speak German with him. But Natalia the Russian wanted to improve her "Angilish."

He puts the letter back in the envelope and holds the other, bulkier envelope over the kettle.

The cheap envelope opens easily.

There's a handwritten letter inside, on pale blue paper with black lines. The language looks like Slovak, and the shapes of the letters and words bring back memories of his grandfather reading to him, those strangely illustrated children's books, with the elongated faces and sad endings.

The stack of notes adds up to €500. It's in tens and twenties, wrapped in aluminium foil. The notes look used, and not like the fresh notes that come out of an ATM. Someone worked and saved, or perhaps stole, in order to send this well-worn money to Pavel.

Dave's in a bind. He can't put the envelope in Michalik's post box, because when he did that with the bank card and pin, he'd seen the letters placed on top of the post boxes the next day. Meaning Pavel is not getting his address from Michalik.

He wonders if the contents of the letter will help.

At his desk, he labours over typing in what he thinks is written. It takes the better part of an hour, but that's fine. He's got nothing else to do. He puts the text into an online translator and gets a garbled English version.

He's surprised how much Slovak he remembers.

The things you learn as a kid, he thinks.

It's enough to piece together a story.

The letter is from Pavel's sister, and she's even signed it, "Your sister,

Danica." This makes Dave think their relationship is not that close. Danica lives in Košice. She often refers to someone called Jarek, and Dave assumes this is her husband. The first few paragraphs consist mostly of news, referring to people and places Dave doesn't know. It's rather dull, with Košice sounding like a very small village; a quick online search reveals it to be a city of a quarter of a million people, and about an hour south of Prešov. On the second page, Danica starts admonishing Pavel for wasting money. Danica is a coming across as the bossy older sibling, and as a nasty piece of work.

Dave grimaces as he reads.

The family – especially Danica – has sacrificed a lot to send Pavel to Berlin to do his PhD. The Dunkin' Donuts that Jarek bought a quarter-percentage in is now starting to make some money, but she can't keep sending it to Pavel. She orders him to get a part-time job. On an upbeat note, she says Jarek plans to open his own Dunkin' Donuts shop out at the Košice Airport, which is now getting more flights from cheap airlines, but none of those future profits will be sent to Pavel.

The letter ends with several more orders. Pavel shall stay out of trouble, put his head down and study hard. Don't waste time chasing girls or playing football, basketball or whatever sport he's into. What their parents really want, and what Danica demands, is that Pavel get his PhD and come back to Košice to work as a doctor. And she's not sending any more money, because it's dangerous to send money in the post.

Dave sits back, feeling sorry for Pavel. Actually, feeling really sorry for Pavel. It reminds him of his own troubles with Rhonda. Like Pavel, Dave has an older sister prone to giving orders and being bossy. He's never actually said so, but he believes it was Rhonda's negative influence that led to their parents getting divorced; that she fought so much with their mother, who then took it out on their father, who then couldn't stand being at home and went off looking for someone else. It was also Rhonda who exposed their father when he was having an affair. And it was certainly Rhonda who blew his chances of going to med school.

Dave last saw his sister when he was home for Thanksgiving last year. Her twin boys are now three and as bratty as can be. They fought for her attention, but Rhonda was too intent on getting stuck into Dave, for living in "Krautland" and for not being married and for not having kids of his own and for not being around to take care of their ageing parents. Repeatedly, she said it was all up to her and she had to organise everything. She called their father senile – he wasn't there – and their mother depressed; she was there, and Dave thought she was looking rather happy. It had been an utter relief to go to the airport and fly back to Berlin.

He doesn't have any flights booked to go back home, but his mother is coming over in late September. He's looking forward to it. The triathlon season will be over. He can show her the city.

He folds the letter, placing the money inside, and glues the envelope's flap back down. He does the same with the Charité letter.

Dave is fully aware that Berlin is a tough city. Pavel's going to need that money, especially as a student. So he can't leave the letters lying around.

He heads out and knocks on the doors of everyone in the building. He starts on the top floor and works his way down.

No one knows Pavel Brazda, and they show no interest in who he might be.

Downstairs, Dave shakes his head a little, wishing his neighbours were a little more neighbourly.

He checks the names on the post boxes again.

Nothing.

But someone is collecting Pavel's mail, perhaps Pavel himself. Back upstairs, taking them two at a time and feeling sprightly, he puts the three envelopes in a small box and seals it up with packing tape. He puts Pavel's name and address on it, and takes it back downstairs to place on top of the post boxes.

He feels more energetic, glad to be recovering and happy to be helping Pavel out. He resolves to take an easy run in the morning.

He wonders where Pavel is living. He's worried about him.

***

Dave's in a rush to get home. He made sure he finished his shift right on midnight and cycled as fast as he could back to his apartment in Charlottenburg. Because he's racing tomorrow, and he needs to sleep well and get up early.

Lucky for him, it was an easy night. No one died. There's no nasty imagery playing back in his head like some macabre highlights special.

It had actually been a rather enjoyable shift. He likes working together with Thomas, despite his colleague's penchant for getting stoned on the job. They're almost on the way to becoming friends.

He grabs his post and runs up the stairs. After a really hot shower, he has a glass of warm milk to calm his nerves. He's drinking this as he goes through his post.

In amongst the junk, there's a postcard from Dresden; from a triathlon buddy who moved down there last year to teach at the new international school. Craig starts off friendly as usual, but then asks why Dave didn't contact him when he was in Dresden, racing in the nearby Schloss Triathlon Moritzburg. But Craig is nice enough to congratulate him on his great result, finishing third in his age group and twelfth overall.

Dave wonders what Craig is on about. He didn't race in Moritzburg, and there's certainly no other Dave Cibulka racing triathlons in Germany.

A quick online check confirms what Craig wrote. There it is: Dave Cibulka of Berlin, twelfth overall, slow in the swim, but with the kind of run split he could never manage. He finds Craig's name way down on the list.

He sips his milk thoughtfully. He thinks he should just forget it and go to bed. Although, checking those splits again, with such a result, he might qualify for Team USA in the 35-39 age group.

Then he remembers: back in June, chasing after his Deutsche Triathlon Union card. It normally comes by late spring, but a few weeks from the first race, it still wasn't there. He couldn't race without it. On the phone, the DTU said they'd sent it, but Dave said he never received it. So they sent a new card, which arrived with typical German efficiency three days later.

Back in the kitchen, he finishes off the milk, wondering what to make of it all. Who raced under his name?

I need to sleep, he thinks.

He goes through the last of his mail. There are two letters for Pavel. He recognises Danica's handwriting and doesn't open that letter. There's no money in it. But the letter from the bank makes him put the kettle on.

It takes forever to boil.

When it does, he holds the envelope over the steam and gets it open. There are bank statements inside. Pavel is in debt, the balance showing -€694.31. Sure enough, there's a record of Pavel taking €60 from an ATM in Dresden.

"What the fuck?"

He runs down the stairs and checks his post box. Everything's fine with it. The lock isn't damaged, and there's no way a hand could reach through the flap and down to pull out the letters. A magazine, maybe, but not envelopes.

You'd have to have a key, Dave thinks, or have the postman hand you the mail.

He's about to head upstairs when he sees a tiny piece of paper glued to the bottom right corner of his post box. It's got "Brazda" written on it in black pen.

He stares at it momentarily, then starts scratching it off; first doing it carefully with his fingernails, then attacking it with his keys.

***

During his regular Wednesday morning swim, he really pushes it. Because the last race was a disaster and he needs to up the ante on his training. Which is why he runs to the pool and back as well; the kind of brick workout he had always hated and shunned.

Running with a backpack is not much fun, but he forces himself to do it.

For the last few kilometres, a light rain falls.

He thinks about Pavel Brazda, that crafty Slovakian soon-to-be doctor who had perhaps gone around the whole of Charlottenburg looking for someone with a Slovak surname. What annoys Dave is that Pavel could have asked; could have rung his bell and told Dave his story and Dave would have listened. But because Pavel did it secretly, putting his name on a tiny piece of paper and sticking it to the post box, and using Dave's name and address for his registration and God knows what else, Dave is really starting to dislike Pavel. He assumes Pavel stole his DTU card, and his June issue of *Modern Triathlete*, and perhaps a host of other things he doesn't know about.

Because Pavel's been getting into his post box.

Dave wishes now that he'd kept the money.

At home, he's too early for the post. He showers quickly, puts a bowl of muesli together – with sliced banana and lactose-free milk – and sets himself up on the balcony. He turns his computer on, switching his gaze from the screen to the street in order to see the coming postman.

He checks his time from Saturday's race. It's awful. Natalia had said she'd come and watch, but she wasn't there. He'd looked for her at the swim start, through transition, on the bike, during the run and at the finish. He'd been more intent on seeing her than racing well. Totally wrong focus, he knows.

Then, packing up his gear and hating himself, he'd seen the text she'd sent. It was over. She'd "meeted" someone else.

Dave is not loving this Wednesday. Today is the last day to lodge his application for Team USA. He doesn't have the results he needs, apart from that guy racing as him in Moritzburg.

Then it clicks.

He puts the bowl of muesli down, half-finished, and starts surfing around the triathlon results from the last few weeks. He starts with races in and around Berlin, then expands his search to include neighbouring states and nearby cities. He finds his name in triathlons in Hamburg, Rostock and Schwerin. With each race, the results get progressively better. This Dave Cibulka finished fourth in Schwerin.

"Fourth?" Dave says.

He makes a list of the results. The finishing times are just what he needs.

"Fuck it," he says, and he lodges his application for Team USA.

He hits send and picks up his bowl of muesli. Chewing, not really sure how he feels about what he's just done, he looks down at the street. The postman, dressed in yellow and labouring with that big heavy bicycle, is coming towards his building.

Dave stands up and drinks down the rest of the milk and muesli. As he lowers the bowl, he sees a man standing across the street. He's in the shadows, leaning against, and slightly behind, the thick trunk of a chestnut tree. As the postman reaches Dave's building, the man readies himself to emerge from the shadows and cross the street.

"Pavel," Dave says.

He dashes down the three flights of stairs. When he gets to the entrance, the postman is calmly slotting the mail into place.

"Wo ist er?" Dave asks.

The postman shrugs. "Wer?"

Outside the building, Dave scans the street. He sees the man duck around the corner and chases after him.

But he only makes it to the corner, because he's finished from the morning's brick workout. Plus, the big bowl of muesli has given him a stitch. And Pavel is fast. There's no sign of him when Dave rounds the corner.

He trudges back to his building and clears his post.

There's no mail for Pavel.

***

The weeks pass. Dave has basically moved onto the balcony. He set up a sun chair with a pillow and blanket. He bought a pair of binoculars. He moved his winter stationary bike onto the balcony to save him from doing long outdoor rides. He switched his shift to start working the even more dreaded midnight-8am. It's changed his whole life rhythm, but he's adapted all right.

Whenever he's not training or working, he's out there on the balcony, scanning the street, waiting.

There's no sign of Pavel, but he hasn't changed his address. His mail is piling up. Dave has opened all of it. Anything written in Slovak has been carefully transcribed and translated. Dave finds himself getting better in the language. He can take that poor internet translation, work with the Slovak text, and the big dictionary he bought, and turn it into understandable English. In fact, he's getting so good, he thinks about quitting his job as a paramedic in order to become a Slovak-to-English translator. He decides to contact some Slovakian companies, publishers and communications agencies, to see if they need translations.

Dave now knows all about Pavel's family. He thinks about writing to Danica, but decides not to.

Because all his Team USA gear has arrived, including a spanking new racing suit in red, white and blue, and he's booked his flight to Madrid and rented a bike case. The World Champs are in late September and his mother will be there to cheer him on. Bursting with pride, his dad has said he'll come too, and Dave's hatched a kind of elaborate plan to get his parents back together. The plan hinges on Dave having a bad result – probably finishing last, because he won't match those qualifying times – and his parents consoling him. The family together again.

Exposing Pavel would mean jeopardising all of that.

71

But Dave does want to meet him. To confront Pavel. Part of him wants to help. He feels he owes Pavel, and that Pavel owes him.

Dave wants Pavel to thank him for taking the mail.

He also wants to ask Pavel about how he does so well in the triathlons.

Sometimes, sitting on the balcony, waiting, enjoying the endorphin-inspired glow of post training, he thinks they could become good friends. Training buddies even.

Other times, usually in the sour mornings after a long and horrific eight hours riding in the ambulance, he hates Pavel. Wants to punch him in the mouth. He's a sports doctor, a better athlete, probably better than Dave in lots of ways.

He hears the familiar crank and grind of the postman's bicycle and heads downstairs. They're on a first name basis, using the informal du to address each other, and Udo doesn't bother putting the post in Dave's box because Dave is usually there to meet him.

There's the usual junk. Even Pavel is getting junk mail addressed to him.

The August issue of *Modern Triathlete*.

A large, bulky A4-sized envelope addressed to Pavel.

Upstairs and back on the balcony, Dave scans the street. No Pavel.

He opens the big envelope and pulls out the stack of printed papers. There's a letter from a publisher in Bratislava, plus what looks like the introduction and first chapter of a book.

His thesis, Dave decides. He hasn't even started at the Charité, yet he's already writing it.

Dave translates the letter first. The publisher has informed Pavel that his thesis is not right for their publication list, but wishes him every luck with placing it elsewhere.

"Sucks to be you," Dave says. He moves on to the introduction of Pavel's thesis, the title of which is translated as "The effect of performance-enhancing drugs on amateur endurance athletes."

"Jesus," Dave says, and he gets to work.

***

It's 7:42am.

Dave yawns. Thomas blows out some acrid smoke, aiming it out through the open driver's side window, and yawns as well.

"Don't fall asleep," Dave says.

"I want my bed," Thomas replies. Part of his decision to switch shifts was to keep practicing his English. "But not you. You go biking or running or whatever. How's the training going anyway?"

"Yeah, good. Bit tired. I'm not sleeping enough."

"Are you excited? For Madrid?"

Dave nods. "I'm nervous, Tommy. All those great athletes. I've got this feeling I'm gonna finish last."

"Come on. You're Deadly Dave. You can do it."

A call comes in. Dave takes it. Through the muffled German, he deciphers that there's a runner unconscious in the Tiergarten and they're the nearest to him.

Thomas hits the siren and floors it. There's a lot of traffic, Berlin being very much a car city with rush hour gridlock, but the well-taught drivers comply to let the ambulance through.

The runner is near the Spanish Embassy, close to the Café am Neuen See and the big Biergarten. There's a crowd of people around him. They part to let Thomas and Dave through. Dave hears some people describing what happened, that the guy was running pretty fast, then collapsed.

They're just in time.

As often, when a life is on the line, things start to blur for Dave. He's spoken with Thomas about this, who replied that the dope makes him think with total clarity, making everything slow down. But for Dave, it goes all fuzzy. He works from muscle memory, from repetition, distancing himself. He knows what to do.

He sets up the defibrillator, puts the handles in the right place, and they bring the guy back. His heart starts beating again, but he's still unconscious.

They get him on the gurney and into the ambulance. Thomas drives. Dave stays in the back. As he works, it's all a little less hazy.

He yawns some more.

When the guy's stable, Dave checks his pockets for some ID. He's picked up runners before, and seldom do they have anything to identify them, which makes it hard to contact the right people. But that's the hospital's problem; he and Thomas just have to get him there and dump him. Then Dave can go home to continue his balcony vigil.

The guy's wearing a plain white singlet, which Dave ripped apart, and red shorts. His legs are shaved. He looks very fit. All muscle, greyhound lean. Dave finds himself staring at the guy's incredible physique.

In the left pocket of the shorts, he feels the outline of a card. He digs in and pulls out a small, sealable plastic bag. Inside is a DKV insurance card, belonging to Pavel Brazda.

***

Dave waits for Udo. He's got everything ready. All the post is sealed up; the envelopes he ripped open have been replaced with new ones. He puts it all in an old shoe box and gets ready to go to the hospital.

He's on the balcony, enjoying the space. He cleared all the stuff away – the sun chair, stationary bike and bedding – and cleaned up. The balcony seems bigger now.

Dave's mind is occupied by two thoughts. First, that Pavel experimented on himself with performance-enhancing drugs, as research for his thesis, and took it too far with the EPO, turning his blood into a sludge that his heart couldn't pump, but even with all that, the best he could manage was fourth in Schwerin. So, Dave wonders, what about the guys who beat Pavel? What are they on? And, what about the guys who do the kind of times required to qualify for Team USA, and all the other national amateur triathlon teams? Because Pavel was doing those kinds of times, and he was more pharmacy than athlete.

The second and more troubling thought is whether Dave should ask Pavel for some PEDs.

Udo's early. Dave hears the clunky bicycle and picks up the shoe box.

Downstairs, he makes small talk with the postman. There's no mail for Pavel, but there's a big envelope for Dave; his first big translation job, from the same publisher who rejected Pavel's thesis.

Holding the envelope, Dave realises he won't have to ride in an ambulance and survive the Berlin nights any more.

Outside, it's a warm day. With the shoe box under one arm, Dave rides to the hospital, still consumed by thoughts of Pavel. He has no motivation to train; he's even cycling slowly. Because he can train all he wants, but will always get beaten by some guy who cheats.

Like Pavel, he thinks. Pavel cheated, but he was doing it for science. For research.

He hopes Pavel is awake. He's got a lot of questions for him.

At the hospital, he locks his bike and heads inside.

Some of the staff recognise him and greet him. When he reaches Pavel's ward, the small gaggle of nurses give him a round of applause. They're all smiles.

He finds the room and enters slowly.

"Hi, Dave," Pavel says.

Barbara

They've made her comfortable, given her a cup of tea, even a thin pillow to sit on. The younger policemen have been especially kind, doting on her, and she's put on some grandmotherly airs to milk that kindness.

"It'll only take a minute," one had said, leading her into the office.

"Just some standard questions," added the policeman who politely pulled the chair out for her.

And she'd smiled, impressed with their good manners, and said, "I want to do the right thing."

The first cop brought her the tea while the second went in search of biscuits.

She wonders if he has gone to the shop across the street to buy some.

She takes a handkerchief from her handbag and dabs at her eyes with it. Even with all that they've told her, it's still hard to believe that Robert is dead.

The house will be so empty without him, she thinks.

"Lifeless," she says out loud, dabbing at her eyes again.

She's tired. The thought of sleeping in the big bed on her own makes her feel even more tired.

The door opens and a man in his late fifties enters. He's wearing a rumpled corduroy suit. His ultra-modern, sharp-cornered glasses clash with his shock of white hair, which is combed up and back from his forehead. He's rather short, and she concludes that the mad-professor hair is meant to lend him a few more inches.

"Good afternoon," he says.

She nods.

He's rather fidgety as he sits down and sets himself up, opening the file and placing a tape recorder on the desk. A slightly trembling right index finger hits the record switch. He's got a blue pen and a red pen, and he positions these either side of a yellow legal pad. The pencil he slides behind his right ear, under the wispy strands of hair. His left shoulder jiggles up and down all the while, like he's trying to shrug something off.

"I'm Doctor Roland Vanderberg," he says.

"I don't need a doctor," she says. "I'm fine."

He laughs a little, that left shoulder bouncing as he laughs.

"No, no. I'm not that kind of doctor. I'm a psychologist."

"Oh?"

"Yes."

"Well, I'm all fine in the head, too."

"That's good to hear. You are," checking the file, "seventy-seven years old. I must say, you're in excellent shape."

"Thank you."

He checks the file again. "I'm serious. You don't look a day over sixty."

"Careful, doctor. I'm wary of flattery."

Roland stares at her for quite a long time, a soft smile on his lips.

Then he catches himself. Taking the yellow legal pad, he leans back in the chair, with the pad on his lap. He writes something in pencil and underlines this with the red pen. The pencil stays in his hand and it's the pen that goes behind his ear. He drums the yellow pad lightly with the eraser end of the pencil.

"Barbara Pickett," he says. "My condolences for your loss."

She nods again, dabbing at her eyes some more.

Another man enters. He's well-dressed in sharp suit, but is exuding a rather grim air. He takes a seat in the corner and folds his arms.

"That's Detective Spinosa. He asked me to interview you."

The detective's hard stare seems to make the doctor even more nervous.

"I didn't," Spinosa says. "None of this was my idea. Now, get on with it, Vanderberg."

The doctor nods. "So, I have some questions regarding the day's events, and the events leading up to today," he begins. "That is, the events that might explain what happened today, and in all the days before today, so we can ascertain that, ah, what happened today might be explained. By you. You will give me an idea why things happened today the way they happened."

"Shouldn't the detective do that?" she asks, tilting her head in Spinosa's direction.

"Yes, yes. Normally, yes. But because of your, well, how shall I say it, your, er, your condition, and bearing, I was asked to conduct the interview."

"'That came from upstairs," Spinosa adds. "Not from me."

"Yes, that's correct. But really, it's all just a formality," Roland says. "Some things to clear up."

"I see." She wraps the handkerchief around her fingers and pulls at it a little. "I once spoke to a psychologist."

"Yes? When was that?"

"Oh, a long time ago. When I was teaching. There was a situation with a problem student and the psychologist interviewed me about him. I remember very clearly that the psychologist didn't talk nearly as much as you do. He would ask very short questions and let me do all the talking. I guess times have changed. Even psychologists have become caught up in themselves."

Detective Spinosa chuckles, and as he does so, the atmosphere in the room changes.

Doctor Vanderberg's head moves backward a little and his shoulder stops jiggling. He's grimacing as he makes some notes on the pad. One sentence in particular gets a work over with the red pen as he repeatedly underlines it, almost boring through the page.

"Methods change," he says. "Listen, I'll be honest with you. I'm actually a bit nervous. I've never questioned a suspect before."

"I'm not a suspect," she replies. "I would never kill Robert. How dare you say that."

"I'm sorry. That's not what I meant. That is, I didn't mean to imply that you, uh, that you may in any way have something to do with today's events."

"I don't even understand why I'm here."

"We just have some questions," Spinosa says. "At least, he has. Answer them honestly and then you can go home."

The doctor adjusts his glasses and asks, "Do you want to go home?"

"Why wouldn't I?"

"Well, it's just that you were married for, let me look at the file, for forty-nine years. It will take some, quite a bit of adjusting. Because Robert was part of your life for such a long time. It will be unusual for him not to be there. For you to have him not there. And the house will be a constant reminder of what you had together and what you've lost."

"Yes." She flattens the handkerchief on her knee. "I know that, and it does scare me a little. I've seen it with some friends of mine. But I would still like to go home. I'm very tired. You made me wait so long."

"My fault," the doctor says, holding up one hand. "I had to cycle over from the community college. There's no psychologist on staff here."

"You're not a criminal psychologist?" she asks.

"No. Ahem. No, I'm not. But there aren't many of us in this town, so here we are. Shall we get into it?"

She takes a sip of what is now tepid tea and nods.

"May I call you Barbara?"

"Yes."

"You can call me Roland. My students call me Doctor Roller." He chuckles as he says this.

"Dear God," Spinosa says, rubbing his forehead slowly with his fingers.

"Let's stick with Roland and Barbara," the doctor continues. "Keep it simple. That is, we'll try not to complicate matters. Right. So. Maybe you can start by telling me what happened today. Describe today's events and how they happened."

She takes a deep breath and says, "Well, I came home from doing the shopping just after lunch. I took a taxi because I don't like driving in the rain. It's too difficult to see and everyone drives in such a mad hurry these days. And the car park at the supermarket is always full. I got home and unpacked the shopping. I called out to Robert, but heard no answer. That happens quite often. He's out in the shed doing something. He gets so into what he's doing, he doesn't hear me calling. When it's dinner time, I have to go out to the shed and get him. Well, I used to do that."

"Hmm." Roland writes in a flurry. "Go on."

"I put the shopping away and made myself a cup of tea. I didn't go out to the shed to tell Robert I was home. I know that he likes to be left alone. He usually asks me to make him a sandwich and a thermos of coffee that he takes into the shed. He spent whole days in there tinkering with something. Some new-fangled device that would make us rich. He was always doing that."

"Inventing things?"

"No. Trying to make us rich. 'The better life, Babs.' That's what he used to say. 'It's what we deserve.' But we never got close to it. He tried hard, but he just wasn't meant to be successful. It was my income that kept us going."

"Your teaching?"

She nods. "Robert never wanted me to work. But he knew that it was my work that allowed him to try all the different careers he tried. Try and fail. He thought all his ideas were gold, but everything he touched turned to stone. I had to comfort him a lot. Make him feel better about himself. But he never lacked motivation. Sometimes, he'd get up in the night. Shout something silly like 'Eureka' and head off for his shed. Those were the nights I slept very well. He was a restless sleeper, you know. And he snored when he was sad."

"Fascinating. But back to today. That is, what happened today. You went to the shed in the early evening."

"Yes. To tell Robert that dinner was ready." She sniffs. "There he was. Lying on the floor. I shook him a little, then went inside to call an ambulance."

Roland stops writing and looks across the table at her. "It's unfortunate it happened like that," he says softly. "I'm sorry, Barbara. It must've been very hard for you. But from what you've said, it doesn't sound like your marriage was very good."

"Why do you say that?" she asks. "We were married for almost fifty years. Are you married? Can you say you've spent that much time committed to one person?"

"No. That's not what I meant. That is, I didn't mean to imply that you were unhappy together. It's just the way you describe ... "

"We were happy," she says emphatically. "We both got what we wanted. And I think we were good together."

"Yes, yes. I believe you. I'm not saying you had a motive to kill him."

"You are saying that. Or at least you're trying to. You should be ashamed of yourself. I'm an old woman." She grunts audibly and adds, "Believe me, Doctor Roller. If I had wanted to kill Robert, I would've done it a long time ago."

"Yes. Of course."

"So that's why I'm here," she says, pointing a finger at him. "You think this is murder. You all should be ashamed of yourselves."

"Please, Barbara. Calm down. We're not accusing you of anything. Robert has died in suspicious circumstances. That is, his manner of death is not easily explained or dismissed. There's a chance a third party is involved."

"Slow down, Vanderberg," Spinosa says. "You don't know what you're talking about."

"Somebody murdered my Robert?"

"It's possible," the doctor says, turning to the detective and shrugging. Spinosa glares at him in return.

"Who would do that?" Barbara asks.

"This is what we're trying to ascertain."

"But the shed was locked. He always locked it, even when he was inside."

"Did you have a key?"

"No."

"Then how did you get inside?"

She starts to speak, then stops.

"Barbara?" Roland asks. "How did you get in?"

"Are you one of these psychologists who can pick when someone's lying?"

"Perhaps. That is, if I had such a skill, I'd be very careful about letting people know I had it."

"That's clever," she says, giving him what she knows is a sweet smile. "But I see no reason to lie to you. I climbed through the window."

"Really? But you're seventy-seven years old. That is, I mean to say, that's very impressive for someone of your, uh, age, that you could get through a window without hurting yourself. Ahem."

"Without breaking a hip?"

He flips a page and continues writing.

"I do water aerobics twice a week," she explains. "I like to think that's one of the things that's kept me vital. And I always walk to the Paulus Home. There and back."

"Where your son lives?"

"That's right. I visit him every day."

"Can you tell me about him? That is, would you like to talk about him?"

"He's a wonderful boy."

"Did Robert visit him as well?"

She shakes her head. "Rarely. Christmas and his birthday. Never more than that, and not every year."

"How does that make you feel?"

She puts her hands together neatly in her lap, the handkerchief nestled between her palms. "We were told from the beginning that it would be difficult with Bobby. They told us that it wasn't necessary to be part of his life. Other parents kept their distance too, letting the Home take care of all the boys and girls. I couldn't do that. He was my son."

"But Robert stayed away."

"Yes. We never talked about it. Robert always had other things on his mind. He was sometimes rather difficult to talk to. Whenever I confronted him with something, he ran off to his shed."

"How old is Bobby now?"

"Forty-six," she says proudly. "They didn't think he would live this long. He's a marvel. A miracle of nature."

"Why didn't you have more children?"

"Well, after Bobby was put in the Home, and the way Robert reacted to Bobby, I decided to go on the pill."

"Oh?"

"It was still quite a new thing back then," she says wistfully. "But I felt it was better than producing another child with Robert's toxic genes."

"Toxic?"

"Anyway, he was far more interested in his projects and getting rich than being a father."

"I see. I, uh, I admire your honesty, Barbara. That is, this is not the kind of thing I expected to hear from you."

"Well, you asked, and you also said you can tell when someone's lying. I want to tell you the truth so you can let me go home and get some rest."

"Yes. Certainly. But I have a feeling I could talk with you all night, Barbara."

"You wouldn't be the first."

"Oh no?"

"Men have always enjoyed talking with me," she says. "They're always more open with the other woman."

Roland uses his pencil to lower his glasses slightly. "I don't follow you. What do you mean by other woman?"

"Robert wasn't terribly interested in sex," she says dismissively. "Like I said, he always had other things on his mind. And I think he also didn't want to make another Bobby. But I'd already taken care of that. So, when Robert went off to his shed, I had some fun."

"You had intrigues?"

She laughs at this. "Intrigues? How old are you?

"Ahem. You had, er, affairs then. Committed adultery."

She nods. "You make it sound horrible, but it was far from that. I didn't just get involved with anyone. I'm no tramp." She gives her hair a fluff and adds, "I was quite a looker when I was younger."

"You still are. That is, I would say that you are still very attractive."

"Agreed," Spinosa says with smile.

"For my age you mean. Well, you're both very kind to say that."

Roland has stopped making notes. He places the legal pad on the table, the pencil on top.

"Are we finished?" Barbara asks.

"Not just yet. I'm still trying to work out two things. Why you married Robert in the first place and why you didn't divorce him. Can you explain that to me?"

"I already did."

"But from what you've just said, it doesn't really sound like love to me. It sounds like you were almost using each other. Or were stuck with each other."

"You don't use someone for forty-nine years," she says. "It seems to me you have absolutely no idea what love is."

"If love is the husband locking himself in his shed and never visiting his son while his wife has one affair after another, then really, I don't know what love is. That is, this version of love has nothing to do with the love I know." He turns to the detective and adds, "I think we're just about done here, don't you? I've heard enough."

"You're the one who's flirting," Barbara says.

"What? I am most certainly not."

"Your denial is more proof. You don't have to be ashamed about it. Flirting is fun. And we all deserve to have a little fun. Sex is fantastic fun."

Spinosa chuckles a little.

"I think you've had too much fun," Roland says. "I'm starting to sympathise with Robert. All the time you were cheating on him. He suffered long enough."

She laughs, and it's a delightful, musical laugh that seems to add colour to the dull office. "Oh, he suffered all right, but it had nothing to do with me. Believe me when I say I had to talk him down from the roof a few times. Ask the neighbours."

"He was suicidal?"

"I wouldn't say that. He was disappointed. A very disappointed and sad man. I felt sorry for him."

"Why?"

"Because his abilities never got close to matching his ambition. He lived with constant failure and rejection. Every business he started went bust. Every gadget he invented was useless. Every pitch he gave died before the end of the presentation. And all the time he kept making these promises. 'The better life, Babs. A big win.' No, Robert. Not even close. But I was always happy. I didn't want to be rich. I liked teaching, and I had a lot of wonderful sex over the years. I still do."

"You still have affairs?"

Barbara dabs at her eyes. "Technically, I'm a widow now. I'm no longer committing adultery, as the stuck-up Doctor Roller would call it."

Spinosa chuckles some more.

"I never thought of it as adultery," Barbara continues. "It was a hobby. A very enjoyable hobby. Some women like to sew. I like to fuck."

Spinosa laughs, but is cut off by Roland coughing uncontrollably, coughing so hard he nearly falls off the chair. His shock of hair shakes with every cough. The red pen falls to the floor. It takes a good minute for him to get the coughing to stop.

"You're the first person I've told all this to," Barbara says, and she sounds rather relieved. "I never could have hurt Robert. I kept everything secret."

"He, uh, ahem, he had no idea?"

Again, she smiles sweetly. "That's very well put. Robert had no idea. That was always his problem."

"Hmm." After a few more coughs, Roland says, "You may go, Barbara."

"Do you have the permission to say that?"

He grins at her cheekiness.

They both look at Detective Spinosa, who nods.

She stands and says, "But you haven't told me how he died."

"Oh, no? Well, he was poisoned," Roland says. "That is, he had injected some kind of poisonous substance and died as a result."

"If the door was locked and he had been dead in there for hours," Spinosa adds, "then the most likely explanation is suicide. But we're still investigating. And you'll never be asked back here, Vanderberg. You're hopeless."

While the air goes out of the doctor slightly, a rather disgruntled sigh passes Barbara's lips.

"Why are you angry?" Roland asks. "I'm sorry that you've lost your husband, but you're free to go. That is, go back out into the world and pursue your, er, your hobby."

She looks at the ceiling, then at Roland. "I had life insurance. For Robert. I thought he might blow himself up in that shed of his and I'd get something for it. With that money, I could've moved Bobby into his own room upstairs at the Home. But that's not to be. Robert's disappointed right to the very end."

"Ah, I see. There'll be no payment. Of course, that also works in your favour. That is, for your innocence. For proving that you didn't kill Robert. That money could have been a motive."

"Give it a rest, Vanderberg," Spinosa says. "You don't work here."

Barbara smiles, nods at the detective and says, "A good evening to you both."

As she walks for the door, slowly and with grace, Roland admires her figure.

Karl

Today is Karl's fiftieth birthday.

The party is being held at the Landgasthof Mörsbergei, a large restaurant in Bubenreuth. The tables are set up in a square, with an open point at one corner to allow waiters and servers access.

Every seat is taken. The attendees sit shoulder-to-shoulder, and are mostly men.

There are landscape portraits on the walls, of northern Bavaria. Meadows and farms and cows. Above the doorway, two old-fashioned duelling swords are hanging crosswise.

Along one table, Karl sits in the middle, his wife to his right and his father-in-law to his left. Never one to enjoy being the centre of attention, Karl isn't comfortable sitting where he is, as the focal point among all these notable friends and extended-family members who have come to celebrate his birthday.

When not eating or drinking, Karl sits, in what he considers to be thoughtful repose, with his right arm folded, his left elbow nestled on his right wrist, his left thumb under his chin and the fingers of his left hand placed just under his left cheek bone; the fingers perfectly positioned to hide the two-inch scar that starts from near his left ear and goes towards the tip of his nose. This gesture is a habit from childhood that Karl has never been able to shake.

Conversation is loud and boisterous. Karl gets involved, making the odd comment and sometimes laughing with the others.

A few times, groups of men break into song, linking arms and swaying side-to-side with the rhythm. Karl moves with them, but doesn't sing.

The food is very good; hearty, local fare. The alcohol flows. Karl is sure to keep pace with his father-in-law in drink. Even though Hans-Peter is nearly eighty, he can still put the beer and schnapps away with ease.

The speeches begin after dinner.

The first to stand, with beer glass in hand, is August Feuerbach. As he stands, he reaches into his jacket to pull out some cards, and this movement reveals that he's wearing a red-black band over his white shirt; it's like a single suspender, running diagonally from his right shoulder to his left side. Quite a few of the men present are wearing such red-black bands, and like August, they arrived wearing floppy red caps with gold trims and short black visors, caps that are now hooked over the backs of their chairs.

A handsome man in his late-thirties with an affable smile, whose good living is starting to get to him as his metabolism slows down with middle age, August Feuerbach works for Karl at Siemens. He considers Karl to be his mentor, even if Karl has been less than reciprocal in the relationship. This is nothing against August; it's part of Karl's strategy, honed over many years, to always let others come to him and to never give too much away.

"Ladies and gentlemen," August begins, flashing that smile of his and checking his cards. "It is an absolutely special occasion that brings us all together today. The birthday of our beloved friend and colleague, Karl Hoffstadt. I'm aware that many of you have known Karl for much longer than I have, but I've worked with Karl for over five years and I can tell you with all honesty that he is simply the worst boss I have ever had."

Loud laughter.

"Now, now, don't misunderstand me. He's not a bad man. Not at all. He's the worst boss because I don't see any chance of overtaking him. He's just so damn good at what he does, better than I could ever hope to be. In fact, the only chance I have for promotion is for Karl to retire." August gestures with his cards in the direction of a few other men, also members of Karl's team. "We're all in that boat, aren't we? Worshipping the ground Karl walks on while also trying to usher him out the door."

More laughter.

"We'll do anything to please him. Work like dogs and do overtime just to get a single compliment. Because Karl's a tough man, probably the toughest man I know. Very demanding, a perfectionist, and a man of few words. But when he speaks, he's very honest and direct, and I have nothing but respect for him. I'm not shy about saying that we are all a little bit in awe of Karl. When I first met him, he just about scared the pants off me. Not an easy thing to do, let me tell you. The Bubenreuther are made of strong stuff."

"Hear, hear," one man shouts out in support.

"With just one look at Karl, I knew he'd been through some tough times, and that he had real courage. He'd taken some blows and stood strong. That's a quality I admire, and I believe many of us here today do as well. Believe me, I was fully aware right then that I'd have to work hard to win Karl's approval. I'd like to think I've done that in the last five years."

"Getting there," Karl says, and appreciative laughter follows his comment.

"See? Hard as steel, and not about to soften in old age. So, I ask you all to raise your glasses and toast the half century of the world's worst boss. Karl, may you continue to be better than us, to teach us and to lead us for another fifty years. To Karl."

"To Karl," the group echoes.

Glasses are raised and everyone drinks. As August sits back down, Karl, still sitting in thoughtful repose, gives his underling a very slight nod.

The next to get to his feet is Hans-Peter. It takes a while, and the old man puts both hands on the table and pushes himself up. He waits for complete silence, getting his red-black cross-band in order, then begins.

"Thank you, August. It does my heart good to hear you speak so warmly about Karl," he says, slurring his words a little. "But you're talking about the man that Karl has become. Twenty-five years ago, when he first came to work for me at Siemens, he wasn't quite the way you describe him. But even then, he most certainly had the qualities we cherish. Things like honour and loyalty. Karl would always stand by your side and support you, when you needed him." Hans-Peter turns to Karl. "And just like your namesake, Karl Ludwig Sand, a man we all admire greatly, you're not scared to take a stand when it's necessary." Turning back to the group, he adds, "That includes standing up to me when I rejected his request to ask for Franzi's hand in marriage."

Hans-Peter pauses so people can laugh; a few of the older men oblige him.

"But I relented in the end. It's not easy saying no to Karl. He's a persistent man, and he's not a man you want to cross. He also doesn't give up on things easily. August, you should hope that Karl leads you for another fifty years, because it's men like Karl who have made Germany such a strong economic power. Hard work and industry, that's what put us back to where we belong."

An uncomfortable silence follows. Hans-Peter takes a sip of beer.

"For me, Karl represents everything good about Germany. He has an excellent education. He takes pride in his work. He's committed to his family. That's why I have never regretted allowing Franzi to marry Karl. Not for a second. I'm very glad Karl joined our family, and over the years, he has become a son to me. As many of you know, both of Karl's parents died when he was studying in Munich. While his mother and father could never be replaced, I feel Karl found a new family with us. A new home."

Hans-Peter puts a hand on Karl's shoulder. Karl feels the weight.

"You got a lot of help along the way, from me and some others, but I'm very proud of you, for all that you've achieved. Happy birthday, Karl."

As Hans-Peter raises his glass, Karl feels even more weight on his shoulder.

Everyone drinks. Hans-Peter sits back down, his face as red as the cap hooked on the back of his chair; the scar on his cheek is a slightly darker red than the rest of his face.

Karl would like to visit the men's room, but he's blocked in where he's sitting, and the timing is all wrong.

No one is brave enough to follow Hans-Peter's speech. A waiter uses the lull to clear away empty glasses and take orders for fresh drinks. A second waiter comes in bearing a tray of schnapps; the tray empties quickly, sending him back to the bar for another.

Finally, Professor Doctor Gottlieb Winter bangs a knife against his glass. He's doesn't stand, and when he speaks, not everyone can hear him.

"Each year," he says sombrely, "out of all my new students, almost none of them were worth a second glance. But every now and then, a student would come along and get my attention. Through the course of my long and distinguished university career, I would say I had three such students. Karl Hoffstadt was one of them."

The professor stops to take a few breaths. He coughs a couple of times. Everyone waits politely, even those at the other end of the room who can't hear him.

"He came from a small village near Würzburg," the professor says.

"Bamberg," Franzi corrects.

"Yes, quite right. Bamberg. He wasn't the smartest kid, or the best looking. And he wasn't one of those boys who tried to make themselves the centre of attention. But Karl really stood out from the crowd. From day one. I knew there was something special about him, and I was right."

Some more breathing and coughing. A few people shift in their chairs.

The professor gestures with his knife towards August, with a rather aggressive stabbing motion. "You, you talked about honesty and courage, but I don't think you know what these words really mean. Especially what they mean to me and to my contemporaries, because we are the ones who brought Germany back from the brink. That took courage, let me tell you."

Hans-Peter and the other older men are frowning and nodding their heads. Nearly all of them have scars on their left cheeks that still show despite their faces drooping with age.

"I'll give you another word," the professor continues. "Sacrifice. Even as a student, while all around him the others were only concerned about themselves, Karl understood the meaning of sacrifice. You can't teach that, in the same way you can't teach courage. I knew Karl had all the qualities to become a great man. It's why I took him under my wing and helped him through university. It's why I wrote him a letter of introduction to my old friend Hans-Peter. It's why I made the trip from Munich to be here today." Looking towards Karl, he adds, "Thirty years ago, I knew that you would become the man you are now. I knew that you would be surrounded by very good people, and they would respect and esteem you. Here's to you, Karl. We did it."

Everyone drinks some more. For those further down the tables, what the professor said is relayed in cursory form.

Karl leans forward, looks down towards the professor and nods a few times. Then, he resumes his thoughtful repose. Again, he'd like to go to the bathroom, but the moment isn't right.

The next to stand and speak is Franzi. "Well, I could talk all afternoon about Karl," she says brightly, "as I know our children could. We love him dearly. But I think it's time we brought in a very special guest. They haven't seen each other for a very long time, but I managed to convince him to come, and I'm very glad he did."

Karl's left hand drops from his cheek. He places both hands on the table, as if readying to stand up.

"Franzi?"

She gives Karl a loving smile and works her way along the table, with those seated having to pull their chairs in to let her past. She knocks a red cap to the floor, which she picks up and hangs on the back of the owner's chair. As she goes out of the room, conversation begins in murmurs as people discuss who the mystery visitor might be.

Karl knows who it is, and he wants to run. His need to relieve himself is suddenly much more acute.

He stands up and starts to move awkwardly along the table, but stops as Franzi comes back into the room, bringing a tall man with her. Everyone turns to look.

"Siggi," Karl says, astonished to see how old his brother is; to see how much he looks like their father did at the same age.

They'd last seen each other at their parents' funeral, and even then, they hadn't said a word. Siggi had tried, but Karl ignored him, and Karl, wanting separation and closure, had let Siggi inherit everything.

"This is Siegfried Hoffstadt," Franzi says. "Karl's older brother."

There's a round of applause that quickly becomes rhythmic; the attendees clapping in time. A waiter brings in a chair and space is made at one corner for Siggi to sit down. But Siggi ignores the seat and walks into the square towards Karl.

"Happy birthday," he says, extending a hand across the table.

With everyone watching, Karl is forced to take his brother's hand. Their handshake is short.

Looking into Siggi's eyes, Karl begins to resent his brother in a whole new way.

"What are you doing here?" he asks, sitting down.

"This was Franzi's idea. So you can blame her. She reached out to me and we both thought this would be the perfect time for us to make peace."

Karl doesn't reply. He stares at Siggi, the brother he once loved and trusted, but who as a teenager just threw that affection and trust back in Karl's face. The dominating older brother, the centre of attention in the Hoffstadt house, taller and smarter and more handsome, and destined to go on to great things.

Karl thought he'd closed that book.

Seething, he takes on his position of thoughtful repose.

"Still trying to hide the scar, aren't you, Karl?"

A waiter brings Siggi a beer and he takes a long drink, smiling as he swallows.

"Sit down, Siggi," Karl says.

But Siggi turns to the group, relishing the attention. "I gave him that scar, you know. How old were you? Ten? Eleven?"

Karl feels many of the men staring at him. From the corners of his eyes, he sees Hans-Peter looking at him curiously.

"No one wants to hear that story," Karl says. "It's good that you're here, and I'm happy to see you, but I think you should sit down."

Watching his brother, Karl sees that Siggi hasn't changed at all; still desperate to be at the centre of things, to have everyone looking at him. Siggi even takes a few steps away from the table, to put himself in the middle of the square.

"You never told them that story?" Siggi asks. "Didn't anyone ever ask about that scar?" He turns to the group and says, "We were kids, playing in the forest near our house."

"You were fifteen," Karl says. Under the table, he presses his thighs together.

"Yes, and I was a good two heads taller than little Karl here. He used to run after me all the time, wanting to be involved and tagging along with my friends. I kept telling him to go away, but he kept on following. To teach him a lesson, I let him run after me into the forest, and then I hid behind a tree."

"Siggi, stop. Please."

Smiling, thinking it all in good fun, and turning in a slow circle to address everyone, Siggi continues: "I held a branch back and waited for Karl to come running by. When he did, I let go of the branch and it whacked him in the face. Ha-ha-ha. You should've seen the way little Karl fell to the dirt. Like he'd been shot. And he held his hand to his face and went crying to mother."

While Siggi continues to chuckle, nearly everyone present starts staring at Karl. They're all looking at him differently now. He thinks he just might lose control.

"A tree branch," Hans-Peter says.

At the end of the table, Professor Doctor Gottlieb Winter manages to get to his feet. His jacket opens, showing the red-black cross-band he's wearing over his shirt. "It's not a duelling scar?" he asks.

Emily

Smiling, Emily goes to bed and has a good, long sleep.

She's up at six, feeling refreshed, but slightly overtired. As it's still dark outside, she has a cup of instant coffee in bed and waits for the first light of the day. She doesn't like running in the dark. Neither does Chantelle.

Emily's feeling ambitious today. There's time enough for a long run before work. Chantelle should join her at some point.

After a big glass of water, Emily leaves her apartment in Kits Point and jogs down Whyte Avenue. It's rather cold for late-October – she's breathing out steam – but blessedly dry. People are out walking their dogs. There are other runners, Nordic walkers too. The Seaside Bicycle Route is busy with cyclists, some with backpacks and the blank-faced determination of people riding to work.

Emily is very relaxed this morning. Running seems easy and natural. It's effortless.

Once she's over Burrard Bridge and heading through Seaside Beach Park, things start to blur. The people on the path appear as coloured blobs, glowing a little at the edges. This luminous surrounding light has a different colour for each person. Emily likes this, being reminded that no two people are alike. But what she likes the most is that people can be reduced to light; that they can be judged by their luminosity and colour, and not by their looks and physique.

Because Emily isn't very pretty. She has a long, mannish face, with thin lips and broad cheek bones. And while she's an excellent athlete, she moves without grace. Her athleticism is more suited to endurance sports with repetitive actions rather than team sports or ball sports requiring highly coordinated movements. Endurance sports also better suit her temperament. She's a strong runner. As a teenager, she was a regional cross-country skiing champion.

Emily sees Chantelle waiting at English Bay Beach, her fetching pink singlet and knee-length tights not nearly warm enough. But she doesn't look cold.

"Aloha," Chantelle says brightly.

"Aren't you freezing?"

"Nuh."

They head in the direction of Stanley Park. Chantelle's fit and she forces Emily to pick up the pace.

"How are ya, Em?"

"Great. I'm great."

"Been on any dates?"

Emily lets out a short laugh. "One. Last night, and it was terrible." After another laugh, she adds, "No, it was actually quite fun. He just didn't like me. He kept looking at his watch."

"Sorry, Em."

"It's all right. Worth a try."

They run in silence, both getting in the rhythm, circling around Lost Lagoon and taking the Bridle Path towards the north end of the park. A Vancouver native, Chantelle knows the park well, and always leads them on a different route. Most of the leaves have turned and fallen. There's a nip of winter in the air.

Emily works hard to keep her breathing steady.

"I've been doing what you told me to do," she says.

"Flirting?"

"Yeah. With limited success. But I'm trying."

"Guys like to flirt," Chantelle says. "Especially married guys, and guys in relationships. It turns them on. They need it."

"Why do you say that?"

"It keeps them going at home."

"Oh, I get it. These guys flirt with me and then go home fired up to sleep with their wives or girlfriends."

"Right. The dads bring their kids to see Vancouver's best paediatrician and flirt with her because she's so good with their kids."

"And this turns them on?"

"It does. So think of all the good deeds you're doing with your flirting, Em. You're keeping so many relationships going. You're keeping families together."

"Well aren't I a saint. A lonely saint."

"You're certainly not a lonely runner."

Emily and Chantelle smile at each other. Seeing Chantelle's beautiful smile, cherubic and cute like that of a small child, Emily thinks her love life would be a lot more successful if she looked like Chantelle. But she doesn't, and never will, so she has to do the best with what she has.

"Keep getting yourself out there," Chantelle says. "Keep smiling. The worst thing you can do is get all misery guts and walk around like some tortured bitch. The right guy will come along. And when he does, you need to be open to it."

"I know, I know. You've said all this before."

"And I know that deep down inside, you're a nasty little flirt."

Emily laughs. "I wasn't always like this. It's your influence."

"My positive influence," Chantelle says with a nod.

The Bridle Path is mostly empty. A few coloured, luminous blobs come from the other direction, but Emily knows most of the runners prefer the water-side path around the park. When she runs with Chantelle, they end up criss-crossing the less-populated trails and paths inside the park. The tall trees and relative quiet keep Emily calm and relaxed. Her breathing is deep and regular.

"What did you do before?" Chantelle asks.

"You mean before you turned me into a nasty flirt?"

"Hey, you were always that. I just encouraged it to come out."

Emily takes a deep breath and says, "I was always too busy. High school, university, summer school to catch up. Then med school. Interning and residencies." She pauses to take a few quick breaths. "The only exercise I got in med school was yoga, if you can call that exercise. There was never any time for dating. My head was crammed full. No one else could get in."

"And now?"

"It's much better working in a practice. It's what I always wanted. A couple more years and I'll open my own. Or I'll stick with Patricia until she retires."

"When will that be?"

"Not sure. She's talking of taking early retirement. To move out to her farm in the Okanagan Valley."

"Sounds boring. Van's the place to be."

"It's actually really nice inland."

"You would say that. You're a yokel from out there, too."

Emily nods. "Further east of the Okanagan. The Kootenays."

"Do you visit?"

"Haven't for ages. Not since my parents retired and hit the road. They sold the house, bought a campervan and just drive all over Canada and the States."

"What about your friends?" Chantelle asks.

"Everyone moved away. After school, we all split up, went off to universities or jobs or whatever. I only had a few close friends. One's in Toronto. Another's in Halifax. They've turned into Christmas card friends."

"No old boyfriends?"

"No. Just Jed."

"Who's Jed?"

Emily doesn't reply.

They loop around Prospect Point Café and get on the North Creek Trail, heading for Beaver Lake.

Emily is starting to get tired. Her breathing is a little more laboured.

Chantelle, running with ease, asks again, "Come on, Em. Who's Jed?"

The memories seem like a long time ago. Skiing along the old railroad tracks out to Cottonwood Lake. Or further, to train on the groomed trails at the Nordic Ski Club. The dogs that came from nowhere and chased her along the tracks. The one time she saw a cougar. The other time she saw a bear. All the animal tracks in the snow. But she was never scared, because Jed often appeared and skied with her.

"Hello? Earth to Emily? Who the hell is Jed?"

"Huh? Oh, just the first guy I fell in love with," Emily says. "The only guy I've ever been in love with."

"First I've heard about it."

"You never asked."

"And you never said anything," Chantelle replies, sounding annoyed.

"What do you want to know?"

"Everything. The first love, Em. It matters. Give me the details."

Emily is thoughtful for a moment, her head cluttered with memories. She hadn't thought about him for a long time, but her date last night had a physical resemblance to Jed, and she'd carried thoughts and memories of him into her sleep. And slept well, dreaming of him. Those memories were so comforting and warm.

Chantelle gives Emily a playful push in the shoulder. "Talk woman."

"I don't know where to start. It's a bit weird."

"Most men are."

"Can we walk a bit?"

"Only if you tell me everything. And I mean everything."

As they walk, Emily says, "He was only around in winter. And he didn't go to school. He was home-schooled. His parents were divorced. In the winter, he stayed with his dad, who was a tree-planter and didn't work during winter. Jed said his dad had a cabin out near Cottonwood Lake, but he never took me there, and I could never find it. I asked around the town, but no one knew of people living out there."

"Okay," Chantelle says. "This is weird. You fell for the love child of Grizzly Adams and a mother bear."

Emily laughs at this. "Not that bad. Jed was normal, considering. I think he was embarrassed. He said his dad would drink and take mushrooms, and they were living a pretty rustic life. Jed used to go hunting, on skis. We often ran into each other out by Cottonwood Lake. And we'd ski together, deep into the woods. It was magical. The winter, the snow. And Jed was this really good-looking guy who liked me. He was smart too. We talked about everything. But sometimes I wouldn't see him for weeks. He said his dad took him on hunting trips. And when the winter was over, he'd be gone."

"Didn't say goodbye?"

"No."

"Didn't write?"

"Nuh."

"Could he write?"

"Of course he could. You've got Jed all wrong, Chantelle."

"Hey, you're the one who painted this picture of the backwards woodsman. The boy raised by wolves. Hunting deer and living in some far-off cabin no one knows about."

"You asked," Emily says.

"When was the last time you saw him?"

Emily is thoughtful for a moment. "My last winter in Nelson. Senior year. In the summer, I moved here to go to UBC."

Chantelle starts running again and Emily follows. They reach the yacht club and head back around Lost Lagoon. Chantelle, still running easily, asks more questions about Jed, turning her head slightly to get the answers because Emily is struggling to keep up. Emily manages to keep pace with Chantelle until they reach English Bay Beach, where Chantelle bids her farewell.

Alone, Emily stops to catch her breath. She walks for a while, her hands on her hips.

She thinks of Jed.

The morning is clear, but the wind is picking up, making soft white caps on the waters of English Bay. People cycle, run and walk past. Emily smiles at them, getting some smiles in return, but is mostly ignored.

She runs slowly back to Burrard Bridge.

***

Emily takes the 99 up to Whistler. It's a rainy Friday afternoon and there's a lot of traffic. Though once past Squamish, the cars start to thin out.

Closer to Whistler, she's surprised to see snow on the ground. It's early this year, and she wonders if there's enough for skiing. Her plan had been to run in the morning, but now she thinks about renting some cross-country skis instead.

The GPS directs her to the Crystal Lodge. She parks her car, checks in and gets her conference accreditation. The lobby is busy with attendees, women mostly, but she doesn't recognise anyone. It's her first time attending the annual conference of the Canadian Paediatrics Society, and she's here in place of Patricia, who decided to spend the weekend with her alpacas in the Okanagan.

It's a busy conference, with meet-and-greets, talks and panel discussions. Emily's presentation is slated for Sunday morning.

In her room, she takes a closer look at the schedule; there's a two-hour window before the opening reception and dinner.

She quickly changes into her running gear and jogs to the Olympic Park. She knows it's too early in the year for it to be officially open, but with this much snow on the ground, there might be some teams training, and if there are, the main shop might be open as well.

After more than ten years in Vancouver, this is Emily's first trip to Whistler. She never liked downhill skiing, and she doesn't know anyone who likes to cross-country. At UBC, her classmates often went to Whistler to do the downhill thing, or drove up to Grouse Mountain to take the short runs there. She was never invited along, but heard all the stories. How they got drunk and went night skiing. The Santa Claus outfits at Christmas. The nude skiing and garbage-bagging on New Year's Day. It was all so childish and attention-seeking, yet it hurt to be left out.

She wonders what's happened to her classmates. She hasn't kept in contact with any of them, but there will be a reunion eventually. Would she go if invited?

The Olympic Park is easy to find. Inside the shop, there's a stoned-looking guy waxing skis. He says they're technically closed and not renting skis, but after a bit of talking, it turns out he's also from the Kootenays. He pockets her money and gives her one of the better rental sets. She leaves her running shoes in the shop.

Getting set up, she tries to remember the last time she did this. That final, stressful Christmas in Nelson? The house already sold and everything packed up into boxes. Helping her father move all the stuff into storage. Arguing with her parents about so many things. What year was that?

There's just enough snow for it to be packed and groomed. As she clicks her boots into the skis, a training group shushes past, all seven of them skate-skiing in unison. The long, gliding movements are beautiful to watch.

She wonders if she can still do that.

Of course she can. This is why she got into paediatrics. Because if kids are taught things the right way as children, if they learn things correctly, they never forget them.

The movements are ingrained in her muscle memory. The correct movements, the perfect technique. She doesn't even need to think about it. Her body knows what to do. And soon she's skate-skiing with ease, feeling graceful, and being reminded that she only ever felt graceful when on cross-country skis.

She goes up and down the straight to warm-up. The stress of the week, and the anxiety she feels about her first conference and presentation, slowly drifts away. She skis and breathes. She can't believe how much she's missed this. Running is no substitute.

The red trail is groomed and she takes this, weaving and shushing her way around what was the Olympic course. The five kilometre loop is easy to follow. She won't get lost, doesn't need to think about the way.

Just ski.

The snow-covered trees look a little blurry. A training group passes her, but she barely gives those coloured blobs a glance.

Darkness starts to fall.

She decides to do another lap of the red trail, upping her tempo. Her breath comes out in large clouds of steam.

There's no one on the trail now. The snow holds the light for a little longer.

Just past kilometre two, she sees a man standing at the top of a short rise. He's leaning on his ski poles, looking at her. He's dressed ruggedly, like he's been out in the woods rather than training on groomed trails. Up close, she sees he has a deer slung over his shoulders, the hooves tied together, and he's leaning forward because of the animal's weight on his back.

She stops, but keeps her distance. She breathes in deeply.

"Emily?"

"Oh, my God. Jed?"

He smiles and nods. He has a full beard, but apart from that, he hasn't really changed. A bit heavier set, a bit more lined. More weary.

"This is amazing," Jed says.

Emily can't believe it's him. She feels a buzzing of synapses she hasn't felt for years. She suddenly feels warm and calm all over.

"How long has it been?" Jed asks.

"Ages. What are you doing out here?"

He shrugs the deer on his shoulders. "Hunting. You?"

"I'm in Whistler for a conference." She wipes her nose on one of her gloves and adds, "Paediatrics conference."

"So, you did become a doctor."

"I did."

"That's what you always wanted."

She nods. "It took a lot of work to get there. What about you?"

"Still doing things the old-fashioned way," he says, giving the deer's hind legs a stroke. "I'm spending the winter in a cabin near Garibaldi Lake."

It's then Emily sees the rifle slung over Jed's right shoulder. She can't think of anything to say. Though she's calm, Jed's presence scares her a little. But it excites her as well. She can smell him, and the scent is exactly the same as it always was.

"It's been a long time, hasn't it, Emily?"

"It has." She breathes in through her nose. "Too long."

"What have you been doing with yourself?"

"Fixing sick kids. You? Apart from shooting animals."

He laughs, and its deep, familiar sound seems to awaken things inside Emily that she had long forgotten.

"It's a living," Jed says. "Gotta survive the winter somehow. I spend the summers tree-planting. On the Queen Charlotte Islands."

"With your dad?"

"He got me into it, yeah." Jed looks down at the snow. "But I lost him a couple of years ago. Avalanche."

"I'm sorry."

"Yeah. But I think he's still out here somewhere. Skiing, hunting and getting high."

Emily feels herself becoming cold. She checks her watch.

"I have to go."

"Okay."

"Look, if you're ever in Vancouver, come and visit."

Jed smiles. "I will."

He gives her a scrap of paper and a broken pencil. She writes down her address and telephone number.

"I could also visit you," Emily says. "At your cabin."

Jed shakes his head. "It's rough country up there. I'll come to the city. You can show me the sights."

"Sure. Good."

They stare at each other for a few moments, before Jed says, "It was wonderful seeing you again, Emily."

"You too."

"I missed you a lot."

"But you never even said goodbye."

"I wanted to. I used to wait for you up on the tracks. But you never came." Jed gets a grip of his poles with his ungloved hands. "The important thing is, we found each other again. I always knew we would."

Emily shivers from the cold. With one last smile, Jed turns and heads into the woods, where he's enveloped by the darkness.

Tired, her breathing shallow and laboured, Emily skis back to the Olympic Park.

***

An outbreak of lice at local kindergartens and elementary schools makes for a busy, stressful week. By Friday, Emily is glad to put the week behind her, and even more glad that she managed to avoid getting lice herself. But when she heads out for a run on Friday afternoon, her body feels like a collection of knots.

It's hard to let all those crying kids go. Hard to push aside the parents, the helicopter dads and tiger mums all over their kids like a rash, needing them to be healthy in order to make piano recitals and soccer games and those after-school classes for supposedly gifted kids. And then there are the parents at the other end of the spectrum, who don't seem to give a damn. The mothers who believe too much in the powers of Ritalin. Who drive big sport utilities and bring their own magazines to read in the waiting room. Who have more than one phone and get their hair done every week. Who seem to be marking time until the kids are old enough to be out of the house and they can have their lives back.

Either way, the kids were the ones suffering.

Emily wants to run away from all that stress. Run fast and far enough to put the week into her past. She's not up for the long haul to Stanley Park, and runs west towards Jericho Beach instead.

There's been no sign of Jed. All week, she's been wondering if she imagined the whole thing.

On the drive back from Whistler, after her rather disastrous presentation, she passed the turn off to Garibaldi Lake and considered searching for Jed's cabin. But fresh snow had fallen and her car still had summer tires, and she just wanted to go home. Because the jitters had invaded her presentation. The uhs and ums and ehs. Just like in med school, when that fucker Derek had made tallies of her grunts and fillers every time she gave a presentation, which only made things worse for her. But he stopped after she took her battered hardcover of *Clinical Anatomy* – on the advice of her yoga buddy Alison – and clocked him so hard in the jaw with it that she fractured the ramus of his mandible, requiring him to have his jaw wired and leaving him with a slight speech impediment. It was also Alison who told her that uhs and ums were good; that they were effective compensation strategies and could be used to one's advantage.

As she runs, Emily thinks of Alison, her one friend during med school. She sure could have used a reminder of Alison's advice before her presentation to the half empty room at the paediatrics conference. It was Alison who once said the uh could be quickly turned into aha, as if you had an idea, while the dopey-sounding um could morph into a thoughtful hmm, with both giving you time to recover without looking completely like a goose.

Good advice, Emily thinks as she runs past the Kitsilano Yacht Club, but remembered too late.

She doesn't miss Alison, or the yoga, because those stretches and movements, and the friendship, are tied in with the unhappy, angry time that was med school. She hasn't done yoga since, and thankfully, Alison was out of her life.

The fact that somewhere in the world, Doctor Derek is speaking in uhs and ums to his patients makes her smile. And the smile makes her relax a little. All that med school stress and frustration that came out as she swung the *Clinical Anatomy* hardcover through the air and made sublime contact with the side of Derek's face. The satisfying sound of bone breaking. His look of stunned fear. Sure, they would never invite her to parties or night skiing or whatever – not that they ever did – but they wouldn't fuck with her either. There would be no teasing and tallying, because she carried that book with her everywhere, holding it in her hand like a loaded gun. If only she'd smacked Derek with it in her first year.

She's still got the book. She decides to take it with her to the ten-year reunion, if she goes.

A sleety rain starts to fall, slanting with the wind and prickling the skin on her face where it makes contact. Her rhythm is terrible today, but she keeps on running, past Margaret Piggot Park and Volunteer Park and Jean Beaty Park and Hastings Mill Park until she's skirting the Jericho Tennis Club, where one poor kid in shorts and a t-shirt is being tortured by a ball machine. His parents are standing on the court under separate umbrellas and taking turns yelling at him as he hits back ball after ball.

The run is hard work, and lonely without Chantelle. But she knows it's her own fault.

In Jericho Park, there are several games of ultimate Frisbee underway, the grass churned into mud and the players caked in it. She stops to watch and catch her breath. Someone asks her if she wants to play. She declines with a smile and a shake of her head.

The run back is slightly easier with the wind behind her. The sleet is now hitting her in the back, slicing through her fleece like acupuncture needles.

Her breathing is forced. She thinks about getting tested for exercise-induced asthma. She had that as a teenager, when she was training so much in the cold winter air. But she knows her breathing trouble is stress.

It's dark when she finally gets home. She has a long shower and washes her hair, first with anti-lice shampoo, finishing the bottle, then with her regular shampoo and conditioner.

As she's staying in tonight, she dresses frumpy and warm, and puts on a thick pair of socks. In the kitchen, she makes a pot of tea.

Through the window, she sees that the sleet has turned into snow. But it's still too warm, so the snow's not sticking.

Emily decides to drive to Nelson in the morning and get her cross-country ski gear out of her parents' storage. Then, she'll be able to go up to Grouse Mountain, or even Cypress Mountain, and go skiing.

Her kitchen is narrow and cramped, barely an arm span wide. As she waits for the water to boil, she places her right hand on the stove and her left hand on the counter opposite. She slides her feet along the floor, doing the movement of cross-country skiing. She closes her eyes and breathes.

It's very relaxing. Backwards, forwards, the graceful sliding. Slow-motion and repetitive.

She hears the kettle click off, but keeps her eyes closed, keeps sliding her feet back and forth.

All those kilometres she did in her youth. Out to Cottonwood Lake and back.

Her breathing becomes very deep.

There's a knock on the door. It sounds like it comes from far away, like someone knocking on her neighbour's door. But the knock comes again and Emily goes to open it.

It's Jed.

***

Emily sleeps late. When she gets up, Jed is gone. As she pads around the apartment naked, she looks for signs of him. There's no note; just a single, very large and very beautiful maple leaf left on the kitchen counter.

And she thinks that is just so Jed.

She wonders if he's gone out to see the sights, walking around Vancouver with a compass in his hand, but hopefully not with his rifle. Or he's gone back to the peaceful solitude of his cabin.

Whatever. The important thing, Emily thinks, the most wonderful thing, is that Jed is back in her life.

She feels fantastic. So loose and relaxed. Good all over.

She puts on her running gear and has a spring in her step as she heads over Burrard Bridge and in the direction of Stanley Park.

104

It's cloudy and damp, but Emily is seeing light everywhere she looks. She barely feels the contact of her feet on the pavement.

In Sunset Beach Park, Chantelle comes running from a side path and joins Emily. She's wearing a body-hugging white singlet and full length tights. No hat or gloves.

"Hey," Chantelle shouts. "Look at you."

"No, look at you. Aren't you cold?"

"There's a big old furnace burning inside me, Em. But it seems you got one too. Is something wrong?"

Emily doesn't know where to begin, and the slight hint of nastiness in Chantelle's question makes her wary of saying too much. She's still not quite sure what happened last night, except that it was simply divine, and long overdue. Getting intimate with Jed was like being injected with energy. Something that went beyond physical, beyond muscles and bones and perfectly interlocking parts. It was synchronicity. Harmony.

"Hello? Talk, woman."

Emily can't keep herself from smiling. "You'll think I'm crazy."

"Too late for that."

"Well, I went up to Whistler last weekend. And you won't believe who I ran into up there."

"Not mountain boy?"

"I couldn't believe it," Emily says. "I rented some skis and there he was. Standing on the tracks, with this deer slung over his shoulders."

Chantelle laughs. She even stops running and doubles over because she's laughing so hard. But it's very much a sarcastic, condescending laugh.

"It's true," Emily says, looking at Chantelle curiously.

"Sure, Em. I believe you. You can't make up stuff like that."

They start running again. Neither talks for a while.

Emily is amazed at how easy running is today, when yesterday it was such an ordeal. She has no trouble keeping up with Chantelle's usual brisk pace.

"And?" Chantelle asks at last.

"And what?"

"If that was last weekend, why are you grinning like an idiot this morning?"

"I gave Jed my address in Whistler and he skied off into the forest. I couldn't invite him back to my hotel."

"Because of the conference."

"Right. And Jed wouldn't have come anyway. But then, last night, he knocks on my door."

"And the sparks fly," Chantelle says snidely. "The beautiful magic happens. All those bottled up hormones and feelings from your teenage years finally let out."

"Yeah. It was ... wonderful."

"Great. So you landed the big one, but you won't be able to hang onto him."

Emily grimaces a little. "Why not?"

"Because he's a loner. A solo flyer. There's no room for you."

"I know he doesn't like the city, but we'd find a way to make it work. He goes tree-planting in the summer. Up on the Queen Charlotte Islands. Then he spends the winter in a remote cabin somewhere, living off the land. Or trying to."

"Can't really get domestic with a creature like that," Chantelle says.

"We'd figure it out. And I think it would be very romantic. A cabin in the woods. Just the two of us."

"You really think you could do that?"

"If he was the one, then sure. Why not give up everything for him? Escape the world. Go wild."

Chantelle scoffs loudly. "You wouldn't last a week."

Emily agrees, but doesn't reply.

They run for a while in silence, until Chantelle says, "We're getting way ahead of ourselves. Jed's probably just a one-night stand. A typical man, despite his natural upbringing. And I won't let him take my favourite running partner off into the woods. Where is he anyway?"

Emily shrugs. "When I woke up this morning, he was gone."

"See? The guy's an enigma. Fucks you and leaves without saying a word."

"Hey, that's not true. We were up most of the night talking."

"Oh, yeah? About what?"

"Everything. About when we were kids and all the skiing we did together. He told me about his life, all the places he'd seen. You've got Jed totally wrong."

"What about girlfriends?" Chantelle asks. "Maybe he's already got a harem in his cabin."

"No way. Jed's not like that. He prefers solitude."

"A lone wolf. Where do you fit in with that?"

"I don't know yet."

"So, with all your deep and meaningful talking, you didn't talk about that? About the future?"

"Why? The present was so nice. Why complicate things by looking ahead? Why ruin it? For me, and I think for Jed too, it was all about enjoying the moment. We'd finally found each other again."

"Well, bully for you," Chantelle says.

Again Emily doesn't reply. In all their runs together, she's never caught Chantelle in a mood like this.

They reach the north end of Stanley Park and start heading back.

Emily thinks she could run forever. Her legs feel fresh, and her breathing is deep, controlled and regular. There's the strange sensation of covering a lot of ground with each step, the world around her becoming more and more blurred.

Past the hazy, shadowed outline of Brockton Point Lighthouse, the totem poles near Deadman's Island, the yacht club and marina.

She doesn't even try to put one foot in front of the other. She lets her body complete the motion. And she notices that Chantelle is the one struggling to keep up.

The seaside route back and over Burrard Bridge. Onto Whyte Avenue and up to the entrance of her building. Once there, Emily thinks she could turn around and do the whole thing again.

"Great run," Chantelle says.

"Sorry I didn't say much. Was totally in the zone."

"At least one of us has the good juice this morning."

As Emily has never invited Chantelle into her apartment, she's careful not to push too hard: "Speaking of juice, would you maybe like a glass?"

"Sure."

Heading up the stairs, Emily feels the pain in her legs. But it's a good kind of pain.

Inside, they both kick off their running shoes. Emily goes into the kitchen. Chantelle looks around, taking in the apartment, then follows.

"Orange juice?" Emily asks. She finds it strange to have Chantelle in her apartment, that she's maybe letting her get too close.

"Sounds good." Chantelle picks up the maple leaf and twirls it by the stem before putting it back on the counter.

Emily pours two glasses.

"What's your plan for the weekend?" Chantelle asks, sipping her juice.

"Well, I was going to drive to Nelson, to get my cross-country gear out of storage, but ... "

"Forget it. Jed's long gone. Don't sit around waiting for him."

Emily takes a drink, then says, "I think I'll go anyway. Spend the night there. It's a long drive."

An awkward silence follows, and it's broken by Chantelle: "I never tried it."

"What?"

"Cross-country skiing."

"It's easy. Watch."

Emily places her right hand on the stove and her left hand on the counter. Still in her socks, she slides her feet backwards and forwards.

"Copy the movements, like you're on cross-country skis. Try it."

Chantelle stands opposite Emily and attempts to mirror her movements. Emily sees that Chantelle has lovely shoulders, tanned, slender and firm.

"Like this?" Chantelle asks.

"Slower. Smoother. Glide your feet. Try not to rush it." Emily closes her eyes. "Let your body do it. Back and forward. Smooth and slow."

Emily can hear Chantelle breathing, can feel the transfer of weight on the laminated floor.

There's a knock on the door.

Emily doesn't move.

When the knock comes again, Emily drifts past Chantelle and goes to the door. She lets Jed in. They kiss.

"Been out running?" Jed asks.

"I have. With Chantelle."

Jed follows Emily into the kitchen.

"Was someone at the door?" Chantelle asks.

Emily nods. "Jed."

"What?" Jed asks, smiling curiously through his beard.

Emily turns to him. "Huh?"

"You said my name. Why?"

"Where is he?" Chantelle asks.

"Standing right here," Emily says, feeling suddenly dizzy. "Go ahead. Introduce yourself."

Chantelle and Jed speak in perfect unison: "Who are you talking to?"

Emily reaches for the counter to steady herself, misses, and collapses to the floor.

***

The phone rings.

Emily opens her eyes. She finds herself lying on the sofa. Her head hurts.

She reaches behind her and grabs the phone.

"Hello?"

"Hello, Emily," says the familiar sing-song voice. "This is Patricia."

"Hey."

"How are you, my dear?"

"Good. Is everything all right?"

"Just fine, just fine. Listen, my dear, what are you doing today?"

Emily blinks a few times and sits up. "Um. Hmm. Nothing. Had a long run this morning."

"What a tough girl you are."

"Yeah." Emily gets to her feet and adds, "But I've got nothing on today. I was going to drive to Nelson."

"Excellent. You can stop by on your way. I really need to talk to you Emily. Today."

"Are you at the farm?"

"Yes indeedy. And that's why I need to talk to you. In person."

"Okay. But it'll need a while." Emily checks her watch. "If I leave soon, I guess I'll be there around early evening."

"Take your time, my dear. You can stay the night with us."

"I don't want to impose."

"Oh, I insist."

"Okay. I'll see you soon."

"Drive carefully."

"Bye."

Emily quickly puts an overnight bag together and packs some lunch.

As she finishes her glass of orange juice, she wonders where Jed has gone, because it could only have been him who carried her to the sofa.

She sits down at the table, eats the lunch she packed and waits.

The only conclusion she can come to is that she ran too hard and far on an empty stomach and passed out on the sofa. She'd dreamt the scene with Jed and Chantelle. Her worst nightmare really, because there's no way any man would choose her over someone like Chantelle. Jed wouldn't be able to resist, and Emily would lose him.

An hour passes. But Jed doesn't come back.

So she starts the long drive to the Okanagan. The GPS directs her out of Vancouver and onto the Trans-Canada Highway. She drives cautiously, keeping to the speed limit, and plays with the radio, searching for songs she likes.

She thinks it's good to get out of the city.

Jed is foremost in her thoughts; their wonderful night together and how they had relived so many stark memories. Jed remembered everything. She wants so badly to see him again. To touch him and have him close.

She finally gets to Merritt and turns right onto the 5A, towards Kelowna. There's snow on the side of the road, ploughed and piled up, but the highway is dry. This reminds Emily to get the winter tires put on her car.

She continues to drive carefully, and wonders what Patricia wants to talk about. What's so important that has to be said in person, on a Saturday, 400 kilometres from Vancouver? Will Tone be there? What does he look like?

It's just getting dark as she pulls into Penticton. The GPS directs her through the town, to the east side of Okanagan Lake and up past the wineries and apple farms to Greyback Mountain Road. She's never been to Patricia's farm, and would never have found it without the GPS.

She heads up a narrow side road, unploughed and undriven since the snow fell. The car slips and slides in the slush, getting nearly sideways as she tries to keep control. At one point, she gets stuck in a drift of snow and has to rock the car back and forth to get out.

It's a relief to park next to Particia's two-door SUV and turn the engine off. She's exhausted from the drive.

The sensor lights switch on and Patricia comes out to meet her. She's wearing a long coat made of what looks like alpaca wool and pink moon boots. Her greying blonde hair is loose and she appears to be make-up free. This is a stark contrast to the almost vaudevillian version of a paediatrician that Emily has seen at the practice for the last six years. She thinks Patricia was always a bit more clown than doctor, and maybe that was why all the kids loved her so much. That and the lollipops.

"Welcome, welcome," Patricia says. "How was the drive?"

"Long. I'm glad to get here in one piece."

To Emily's surprise, Patricia hugs her.

"It's so good to see you," Patricia says, even though they saw each other yesterday. "My dear, thank you for driving all the way up here."

Released, Emily smiles and looks around. The snow on the trees is holding the last of the daylight, but she can't see much other than the house, which looks far too big for two people, and isolated too.

Emily thinks it would be scary to live on the farm alone, especially in winter, when a big snowfall could cut off the access from Greyback Mountain Road. And who knows what kind of animals are wandering around out here.

"Come inside," Patricia says, leading the way. "Warm up by the fire. Are you hungry?"

"A little."

"Good. I made quinoa and squash soup."

Emily places her overnight bag under the coat rack, just inside the door and next to the orderly pile of Tone's shoes and boots. Patricia breezes through the house, her big alpaca coat billowing behind her.

"Make yourself at home," Patricia says. "We'll eat by the fire."

Emily goes into the living room. There's a big fire going. Next to the fire is a stack of wood, symmetrically cut; the kind of wood that gets ordered and delivered. There's also a large canister of lighter fluid. Above the fireplace, the mantle is free of photographs. Emily had hoped to see what Tone looks like, if only from a photo. But there are none, just as there are no photos on Patricia's desk in the practice.

The huge TV is flanked either side by shelves full of DVDs.

Emily finds it all rather impersonal, like the shared living room of a bed and breakfast. She had expected something different.

Patricia comes in with two bowls of soup.

"Where's Tone?" Emily asks.

"Oh, you know him. He went to Apex to go back-country skiing. He should be back later. We'll save him some soup."

"You have it very comfortable here."

"I know."

Patricia hands Emily a bowl. It's hot.

"Thanks."

111

"We've got it really good here. Which is why I wanted to talk to you."

As it's too hot, Emily puts the bowl down on the coffee table. The soup doesn't look terribly appetising; like murky mop water with bits of old yellow sponge.

"My dear, I'll get right to it," Patricia says. "I'm out. I've decided to move up here permanently. I've had enough of the city and I don't want to be away from Tone anymore."

"What about the practice?"

Patricia blows on her soup and says, "It's all yours, if you want it."

"You want me to buy you out?"

"Yes indeedy. And I want you to take my place in the Paediatrics Society as well. They loved your presentation by the way. You got great feedback. They want you to submit a paper for the journal. On the same topic."

Emily can't really believe it. "That's amazing. I'd be happy to."

"Good. It will make the transfer easier. I can pass you the reins and retire to the farm."

"I guess I should say congratulations."

"To you too."

Emily starts in on her soup. Despite its appearance, it's actually quite tasty.

"Are you giving medicine away for good?"

Patricia shakes her head. "I could never do that. I'm going to open a small practice in Penticton, just three mornings a week. It's more about living up here, being with Tone and enjoying the quality of life. I think I waited too long as it is. Should've moved up here years ago. Life's too short to be unhappy."

"Yeah."

Emily stares at the fire. The warm soup feels good inside, but it makes her more tired.

"You should be thinking the same way," Patricia says. "Are you happy?"

"Sure."

"I bet I just made you happier. You've got your own practice now. My advice to you is to get a young doctor in there, someone you like and admire. Then, you give her all the rotten patients."

"Ah, like the kids with lice?"

"That's right. Meanwhile, you can take the nice kids. Spend all your time talking about imaginary friends and hand out lollipops at the end. You'll become everyone's favourite."

"So that's how you did it," Emily says.

"And now you'll do it too. You can have more time for yourself. Like I did, by taking Fridays off and coming up here."

"I was thinking about getting back into cross-country skiing. That's why I'm driving to Nelson. To pick up my gear."

"Well, my dear, if you get a couple of reliable young doctors into your practice, you'll have more time for it."

Emily likes the sound of that, but what she likes more is the idea of palming off the troublesome patients to other doctors, while she gets to work with reduced stress and less exposure to nasty illnesses.

No more anti-lice shampoo, she thinks.

Patricia puts down her empty bowl and asks, "So, what do you say?"

"The soup is very tasty," Emily says with a smile.

"My dear, I mean the practice."

"Is it all that simple? I take over and you retire. I've got some money saved, but how much are we talking?"

"I'll show you the books tomorrow. It's all very straightforward. You get a line of credit from the bank. We're doctors, Emily. Paediatricians. The banks never turn us away. Besides, the practice is very successful. It'll be easy. It's just a question of whether you want it or not."

"May I sleep on it?"

"Very smart," Patricia says. "Come on, I'll show you the guest room and you can settle in."

***

It's a very busy week. There's no time for skiing or running. There's also no sign of Jed, except for a map that arrives in the post; a map of Garibaldi Provincial Park with a small cross marked near the east side of the lake.

There's a lot to do. She has to close the practice in order to take care of all the details, as Patricia stays on the farm and doesn't help. She has several meetings with her bank. She interviews a couple of doctors. There's a lot of paperwork to do. Determined to put her own stamp on the practice, she decides to renovate, and brings in the same band of Russians who painted her apartment and pays them cash. They paint the whole practice in forty-eight hours, and do a fantastic job.

By Friday, having moved into Patricia's huge office, Emily starts to feel that the place is hers.

It's a really good feeling.

She goes home and decides to take a celebratory run. From the Seaside Bicycle Route, she takes the path past Granville Island towards Charleson Park. She's never gone this way before, but is feeling adventurous today. Just feeling really good about herself. She senses that a new stage of her life is beginning.

She runs with ease, breathing rhythmically.

She can't really believe she has her own practice. Now she'll definitely be attending the next reunion.

As she gets to the hazy, blurry expanse of Charleson Park, Chantelle comes sprinting towards her, with the intent of someone on the attack. Emily stops running.

"There you are," Chantelle shouts, stopping just in front of Emily. "Where have you been, you selfish bitch? I've been looking everywhere for you."

Emily tries to keep some distance between them. "I'm sorry. I've been just super busy."

"So busy you don't even need me anymore."

"That's not true. You've been a wonderful friend, Chantelle."

This makes Chantelle even angrier. "Don't patronise me. And don't talk like I'm already gone."

"Go away," Emily says, taking a few steps backwards and evading Chantelle as she tries to get near her. "You're not real."

"I'm not real? I'm not real?" The nimble Chantelle manages to slap Emily in the face. "Did you feel that?" A slap on Emily's shoulder, then another in the face. "What about that?"

Chantelle trips Emily up and gets her on the ground, face first. She sits on top, takes a handful of Emily's hair and pulls. Emily screams from the pain.

"If you weren't so ugly, I'd take you over. But I don't want to be you."

"You're not real," Emily shouts. "This isn't happening."

"Of course, I could become you, but then I would need a whole lot of cosmetic surgery to look beautiful. I'd need implants too."

Emily struggles, but then she closes her eyes and holds her breath. She thinks of lice and pushy parents and having to sign prescriptions for Ritalin.

The grip on her hair starts to loosen.

She thinks about the big office and taking Friday's off and skiing with Jed. She decides to stop running altogether, and to only go cross-country skiing with Jed.

"No," Chantelle shouts. "Don't leave me, you bitch. I need you."

The weight gets lighter on Emily's back. She can hear Chantelle's protesting voice trailing off.

When Emily opens her eyes, she doesn't try to calm her breathing. If anything, she's happy to wheeze and gasp. She gets to her feet and walks all the way back to Kits Point, looking behind her every few steps to be sure Chantelle is not coming after her.

***

It snows all night. In the morning, Emily takes her car to the garage and gets the winter tires put on. She drinks several cups of complimentary coffee while she waits.

Out of Vancouver, she takes the highway towards Whistler, stopping in Squamish for some lunch and supplies, then taking the turn-off to Garibaldi Lake. She goes as far as the road allows before skiing the rest of the way, navigating with the map Jed sent her.

She finds the cabin. Jed is sitting on the porch, waiting.

Milo

The wave sucks up a lot more water than Milo expected. As he pushes into his stance, he sees the shadowed outlines of rocks, seeming to get nearer as more water is drawn into the wave. But there's no turning back now. He has to show those young guys he knows what he's doing, that he belongs out here. No, more than that. This is his break. Through countless summers, he lived at this beach. Before school, after school, skipping school. It was always his break, and if this collection of wasted youth think they can force him off, then he'll show them.

It's been over two decades since he surfed here, but he hasn't forgotten a thing.

As he heads down the face of the wave, he knows there's too much water behind him. He braces himself, taking a deep breath.

The heavy dumper wipes him out. Badly. His old board surrenders under the weight of the water and breaks. He's sent spiralling under, spinning, limbs flailing. He shuts his eyes and blows a bit of air out of his nose to stop the water from going up it.

The wave has some serious follow through, and he spins and spins in the churned wash. His first thought is of all the wasted youth laughing at him. The surfers waiting for sets, and the unemployed time-wasters on the beach, those guys who can't surf, but sit there all day watching for lack of anything constructive to do, pointing and laughing. Sure, it's his first day in a long time back at the beach, but those guys have a pathetic permanence that suggests they've been sitting there for years. Just sitting there, laughing at whoever screws up, stubbing out cigarettes in the sand, trudging up the beach with their empty bottles to get the deposit refund and buy more cheap beer. No education, no real drive to make something of themselves. Maybe a part-time job bartending or stacking supermarket shelves. Maybe a kid tucked away in a ratty apartment back off the beach; a kid seen once a week.

He lets himself get spun around, wondering what's happened to this place. Twenty-odd years ago, he and his buddies camped on this beach, surfed and surfed until their hands were all shrivelled and wrinkled, and their hair turned pale yellow from the sun and salt and stuck together in clumps from lack of washing. They watched endless sunsets. They sat around fires made from dried-out driftwood, happy, relishing their youth. They talked about the future. Talked realistically, too. What they were going to do. What they would become. But none of them had over-reached. Sure enough, they had all gone on to make something of their lives, and had drifted apart. But that was the deal. Kids became adults, and that meant a definite change. Priorities changed. They'd had their time in the sun. Some went off to university. Some got jobs. A few of them followed older brothers and sisters into the family business. That's what Milo did, joining his father and uncle in their construction business.

He thinks the wasted youth on his beach are attempting to stay kids forever, shirking the responsibilities of adulthood, fully caught up in their own selfishness. His anger makes him kick out at the water, to reach for something to hold onto. Steady himself, get control.

But he's still spinning, still getting churned by the water. Because the waves have changed too. They never used to suck up water like this. It used to be a smooth, soft break, churned up only by the storms that sometimes rolled in. He knows it's the pier that was built in the middle of the beach. That long pier with the cafe at the end and all those little stalls selling crap to tourists. The pier that the city really didn't need. It changed the geography of the beach, causing waves to curl, suck up more water and break unexpectedly. That's where all the wasted youth is surfing, riding the curlers from the point of the pier, with all the tourists watching and taking photos. There was no chance getting a wave there, with those very old kids lining up and blocking the entry point, boxing him out and laughing at him.

So, he'd paddled away and caught his first wave in the middle of the bay. And it had turned washing machine on him, dragging him down. Because of that freaking pier.

Down, down, to where the water's no longer churning. He keeps his mouth and eyes shut, because a buddy on the city council once told him they pump sewage straight into this bay, which is why the poles of the pier are covered with greasy brown sludge. And the wasted youth, too stupid to realise or care, surf amongst it all. Not that it would help, opening his eyes, because he can't really see without his glasses anymore.

Milo is middle-aged, feeling himself fading. He's climbed the hill and is now coasting to the finish, towards the dreaded number fifty-nine. At the same age, his father died, and his father's father, and his uncle Ernesto, and his great uncle Jorge. They're all buried near each other, headstones branded with "Age 59." Milo fears the same fate awaits him, but he had always thought he would be the one to break the trend.

Still, these last few weeks, he's been overwhelmed by the sense that his time may be running out, that he has missed out. Because there was never time for anything other than the family business. Learning the ropes, night school classes in business and management, balancing his ideas and priorities with those of his father and uncle. Milo had been against building the pier, but it was too lucrative a project for them to pass up.

One project, then another, and another, but the company never seemed to have enough money. Every year was like some small battle for survival. His father making him be the one who fired people when times were bad, as part of his learning experience. His father dying, and Uncle Ernesto following him two years later. The company suddenly in Milo's control, which was what he had always wanted, but then realised he didn't want at all.

In deeper water, he's got control of his limbs. He's calm. There's nothing left to do but climb to the surface, then get to the beach and go home. End this misguided adventure, this attempt to get back to good times, to the glory of youth. It's over.

After seeing all that wasted youth on the beach, Milo doesn't want to be young again. He'd been wanting that desperately these last few weeks, but it's passed. He has the company. He has his family. He won't force his children into the business. But he needs to find a way to reconnect with them.

He feels down his right leg to his ankle and gets a grip of the leg rope. That's the way up, he knows. Climb the leg rope. The board is broken, but it's also at the surface. He keeps his eyes shut and pulls, one hand over the other. His body straightens, and he kicks a little for extra power. His lungs start to hurt.

He wants to get to the surface.

It was foolish to think he could go backwards in time. Sell the company and buy a flash sports car. Move out of the family home and into a beachside apartment where he could surf every morning and screw younger girls. Look up old buddies and organise ambitious surf holidays on the other side of the world. Foolish to think he could return to the place where he was the happiest. It was fear, panic. Every year getting closer to fifty-nine. The constant sensation that he had wasted his life; sacrificed his own desires and wants for that of his family.

It really hurt when his father died. Not because he loved his old man, but because so many people had come to the funeral. Even the people Milo had fired. He discovered his father had been incredibly generous over the years, paying high wages and donating money to social organisations; he'd had the company build a school football field for free. From all those people, dressed in black, Milo had learned so much more about his father, and it made the loss cut even deeper. From that point on, Milo had tried to honour his father, attempting to be as generous and perhaps forge his own legacy, but the current economic climate didn't allow for it. It was hard enough keeping the company going, paying his own bills and sending a daughter to private school and a son to university.

The leg rope feels surprisingly taut in his hands, like it may snap. He assumes the board is caught in more whitewash at the surface, or is getting pulled by the waves; the pier creating currents he's unfamiliar with, and waves that suck up lots of water.

There was a time he knew every inch of this bay, the pattern of the tides, the ripples in the sand. When there was no surf, they went out with masks and snorkels, exploring the rocks and crannies, having contests to see who could stay under the longest. Milo had been good at that, holding his breath, staying cool and calm under water while the others struggled and shot for the surface.

There's something else he's lost. His lung capacity. Because he's really starting to struggle. He knows he must be close to the surface, so he keeps on pulling. But he stops kicking in order to save his strength.

He thinks about all those years working with cigar-smoking Uncle Ernesto in the small office, wondering if that wrecked his lungs. His father preferred to work on-site, to get his hands dirty and operate the cranes, a preference that eventually led to his undoing, at age fifty-nine.

The sadness makes Milo stop climbing. That regret of not truly knowing who his father was, and having spent so much time resenting him. The trouble of communicating which his father passed on to him, but Milo's son won't have a similar enlightening experience, because they surely won't turn out in the hundreds to honour Milo when he dies.

He starts climbing again, with renewed vigour. Because there's still time. He hates himself for having been so selfish, wanting to make changes in order to be free of his burdens. He should be fixing his life, not running away from it. Going down when he should be going up.

There's time, he thinks. Lots of time. That fifty-nine business is ludicrous.

His lungs are aching. It feels like they're compressing. But he continues to climb.

Because he knows exactly what to do now. Get to the surface, go to the beach and start talking with the wasted youth. They're not pathetic. They're not wasted. They just don't have any opportunities. He can get them working. A youth employment program. Community projects. State funding. And not piers that wreck bays or unsightly high-rise apartment complexes. Stuff that actually makes a difference. He could use his connections on the city council to get more projects. Playgrounds and hospitals and retirement homes.

Then the people would come to his funeral. Then they would tell his son what a great man he was.

And he thinks it might just be the direction needed to turn his company around. Get more publicity, do good work for the community, make a difference to the youth unemployment rate. Make money from it all and win new projects. Maybe even look into green technologies, solar panels and wind turbines. Then he'll have something to talk about with his son. The eco angle might lead to more funding opportunities, too.

Generosity of a different kind, Milo decides. A new legacy for the family.

So he pulls, thinking it's also time he got back in shape. Running, cycling, or something like that. But no more surfing. Not here.

He can't hold his breath any longer. He needs the surface. Wants it. Because there are so many good things to do, so many changes he wants to make. Go running with his wife. Talk green tech with his son, and bring him into the family business somehow, continue the tradition. Live really healthy so he passes age fifty-nine and ends the curse, saving his son from it as well.

The wasted youth on the beach are waiting for him to give them jobs and hope.

The bay is waiting for him to implement a new sewage solution.

The pier is waiting to be destroyed, for the benefit of coastal preservation.

The curse is waiting to be broken.

Climb, Milo.

He's getting dizzy.

His hands start to shake. They slip on the leg rope, sending him back down a little. But he kicks hard, knowing he's almost at the surface, just about to burst out of the water and take in a deep, glorious breath.

He can start again. Live another forty-four years. Not fifteen. He'll get himself healthy, live well and live long. He was an idiot to think the solutions were elsewhere, that he needed to be young again in order to defy the future. To be happy and free.

He is happy. He's got it all. And he's going to make things even better.

He feels the knotty join of the leg rope, where it connects with the board, and is filled with such utter elation that he wants to scream for joy. His whole body seems to buzz when he feels that knot.

The surface is centimetres away. Fresh air. New beginnings.

One final pull.

He lets go of the rope and touches the board. He feels the broken end, and reaches past it, expecting to break through the water. But his hand hits something cold and hard. It's round, metallic, a kind of pipe.

He follows the outline of his board with his hands, feeling that the piece is actually rather small, just the end of it. He pulls at it.

There's rock on one side, the pipe on the other. The board doesn't move.

Frankie

There were seventeen men in the container. It stank. It was almost dark. The only light was coming from the scattered holes drilled through the top. A line of buckets divided the container in two: the gamblers on one side, the religious men on the other. An inconsistent ventilator churned the fetid air, but made little difference.

A horn sounded.

"Quiet."

All the men fell silent, avoiding each others' eyes, but in the cramped space they had nowhere to look. So each man's eyes fell on his own small pile of meagre belongings: the remains of the food he had been given, the water bottles sucked dry, the threadbare blanket that had been of almost no use and had left them huddling together on the cold floor for warmth.

The horn sounded again.

"We're stopping."

"You can't tell."

"It's been three weeks. We should've made it by now."

Another horn sounded, different and louder than before.

"Quiet."

They waited in silence.

When no sounds came, the gamblers sat themselves back down and started mumbling bets to each other as yet another card game started in bored seriousness. Several of the men had already lost a good amount of the money they intended to earn in the new land. Indeed, some of them bet with risky glee, happily losing large sums that were recorded on the flattened cardboard of food packages.

One of the religious men spoke in the direction of the gamblers: "Quiet."

But they just snarled at him, grinning and keeping their frayed cards tucked under their chins, their bloodshot eyes narrowed to pink slits. A few of the gamblers had had just about enough of those God-loving religious men. No amount of providence, praying or faith would deliver them from this mess. Early in the journey, one of the more disgruntled of the gamblers had tried, when the opportunity had presented itself during the lull as the men slept in shifts, to convince the lone tribal man to kill the leader and thus prove there was no God protecting them. Looking uncomfortable in his western clothes, the tribal man had shrugged. "No weapon," he'd said. The gambler had shown the pencil he had fashioned into a tiny spear by painstakingly grinding one end against the metal floor. The tribal man had shrugged again, but then looked closely at the pencil and had begged the gambler to teach him how to write his new name. The gambler had then put the spiky pencil away, taken a stubby, chewed one from his pocket and obliged the tribal man.

The card game continued. One religious man had his hands clenched tightly together in prayer.

There came a loud, metallic thump and the men were thrown slightly off balance. As they recovered, they looked at each other, wanting to believe they had made it, that their prosperous new lives could begin. They would get their papers, as Frankie had promised; his partner would sort everything out, get them working legally and help them get settled.

"We're here."

"Thank you, Lord, for delivering us to this new land safely."

"Your Lord had nothing to do with it. This ship has a captain you know."

"But we made it, all in one piece."

"You only just. Another day in here with you lot and we would've made you a sacrifice to your God."

The gamblers chuckled to each other but soon returned to their cards. They had spent the whole journey betting, winning and losing, sometimes fighting, and now with the trip seemingly coming to an end, they didn't know how to stop.

"Who says we've made it anyway?"

"It's been three weeks. Frankie said it would take less than that."

"And he also said there would be delays and that we should wait until his partner comes to let us out."

"Maybe your Lord will be on the dock to open this crate and he will give us passports and jobs and blonde wives who are completely hairless, you know, heh-heh, down there."

The gamblers smiled greedily, looking at one another for confirmation and support, for hope.

"The Lord will provide for those who are deserving."

"And hopefully the strength to sit here and wait for him to open the door."

"Yes, Frankie said to wait."

"Frankie is not God."

The card game was finished, the wins and losses duly recorded. From the tight confines of their circle in the back half of the container, the gamblers stood up as one. They approached the line that had been marked out on the first day of the journey, the line made by the now foul and almost overflowing buckets; the line that had maintained a vestige of order and sanity as the walls seemingly crawled an inch inward with every passing day.

There was another loud thump and all the men looked upwards to the direction where it had come.

"At last."

A few of the religious men cheered and started packing up their belongings, with their rubbish trodden beneath them on the floor. The gamblers stood close to the buckets.

"If we're here, then we can open the door."

"It's just a matter of time before someone lets us out."

"He's right. Frankie said not to open the door. If the police find us then we'll go to prison."

"Or get sent back."

"I'm not going back."

"I would rather go to prison."

On this point, all seventeen men were in agreement.

"We have to wait, but we should be ready for them when they come. Pack up your stuff."

"We don't even know for sure if we're here."

"I know it."

One of the religious men put another on his shoulders and lifted him towards the coin-sized hole drilled through the top corner of the container. He put his face close to the hole, so that a circle of sunlight lit up his dark brown nose and pink, chapped lips.

"I smell diesel."

"That's just the ship's engine."

The man put his mouth towards the hole. "There's no draft."

"That means we've definitely stopped."

"All those noises were the sounds of the freighter docking."

"Can you see anything?"

The man tucked his head into the top corner of the container and tried to look through the hole.

"Blue sky."

"You're always looking to heaven. Let us see."

The gamblers stepped over the buckets and towards the other end of the container. Now, all the men were cramped into one half.

"You crossed the line."

"What're you going to do about it?"

"We've come all this way and now you want to fight? What will Frankie's partner think when he opens the door and see us trying to kill each other?"

"He'll see what energy we have and give us jobs that pay big money."

"Or he'll shut us back in and send us home."

"Look, we don't want to fight. We just want to look through the hole."

The religious men divided, like a guard of honour, and let two of the gamblers walk towards the end. The one that got on the other's shoulders had a smaller head, and he was able to get his head deeper into the corner of the container. He squinted one eye shut and pressed the other against the hole.

"We should've let him look from the beginning."

"What can you see?"

The man moved his head slightly, trying to broaden his view. "Containers."

"On this ship?"

"I can't tell."

"Frankie said we would be stacked on top. So we'd get some air."

The metallic clanging noises made them all freeze. The noises echoed inside the container. Something was hitting the sides and the top.

"What's that?"

"Quiet."

Whispered: "Can you see anything?"

Again, the man tried to move his small head to see more through the hole. "Containers. Blue sky."

But then the container moved and the man holding the other man lost his footing. Both fell to the floor, causing the container to tilt slightly. The other men spread their legs to keep their balance and footing. The container spun very slowly in the air. The gamblers jumped over the buckets to balance its weight.

"We're moving."

"We're being lifted off."

"Quiet."

There was a loud creaking sound as the container moved through the air. In their groups, the men looked at each other, all of them wanting this to be the end, hoping they were just a few minutes from taking their first tentative steps into this new land. They had so many dreams they wanted to come true, and now looked at each other for confirmation. At the start of the journey, they had spoken so much about the future, had looked up at the light holes like they were stars in the night sky. They had talked about what kind of jobs they would have, how they would spend their money, how after a year or two, they might go back home with a new name and show everyone how they had made it. That was the real dream, going home, because they all knew they would never be able to do that. Frankie had told them, smiling and showing the gold in his molars, that this journey would be like dying and going to heaven; you would be in paradise, but you wouldn't be able to see your family and friends, or visit your old world again. For many of them, the choice had been easy; raising the money had been hard.

The container landed with a thump. The impact tipped one of the buckets over so that the contents sloshed and rolled across the floor. The religious men leapt out of the way to avoid it, pushing themselves against the wall, as most of it went onto their side of the container. They picked up the remainder of their belongings to keep them from getting covered.

"Still think God is on your side?"

Laughter.

"Shut up. Why don't you get the little guy with the monkey head to have another look through the hole."

"I don't have a monkey head. You apologise or I'll tip one of these buckets over you."

"Forget it. We'll look."

But the man with the small head moved forward. He stepped over the buckets, then tip-toed through the mess to the corner where the religious men had crowded close together. But none of the other gamblers came with him and he reluctantly got onto the shoulders of one of the religious men and pressed an eye against the hole.

"Well?"

"Containers. Thousands of them." He moved his head, smiled, and came back down. He returned to his group. "I saw a crane."

"We're on the dock."

Some of the men cheered; a few even danced a little.

"We made it."

"I can't wait to get out of this stinking prison."

"Let's open the door."

The religious men crowded their end of the container; the end that had closed them inside and the end that would open again to let them out.

"Frankie told us to wait."

"Just open the door so we can look out."

"And get some fresh air."

"I've never been in a place that stinks this much."

"Open the door."

"We can't. It will ruin everything."

"Why? We made it. They can't send us back now."

Some of the religious men were looking uneasily at each other, and at the steel door behind them.

"Frankie said to never open the door. We've come this far. Another hour or two won't kill us."

"I can't wait any longer. Open the door."

"We need fresh air."

"I'm hungry."

"Don't worry. The people here are so fat, we'll have no trouble getting food."

The gamblers started to pack up their stuff. They put their things in plastic bags, careful not to rip the sides, and drained any remaining drops of water from their bottles. They stood together, close to the line of buckets, ready.

"Open the door."

"But Frankie said not to."

"Maybe his partner doesn't know which container we're in."

"There are thousands of containers here. How can they know where we are?"

"Right. If a few of us get out, they'll see us."

"They know which one it is. We just have to wait."

"No, we have to get out. Then they'll sec us and give us food and money and women."

"Yes."

"No."

"The longer we wait, the less chance they will have of finding us."

"Lord, give us patience."

"The Lord's not here."

"Open it."

The gamblers stepped over the buckets and walked towards the door. The religious men were forced into a tight huddle around the doorway. They shared quick looks, their eyes betraying their fear.

"We should wait. That was the deal."

"We paid a lot of money for this. It's time we took control."

"We don't even know if we can open the door from inside."

"Get out of the way so we can have a look at it."

The gamblers moved forward and, slowly, the religious men moved as well, shifting to the side. Glances were exchanged and shoulders passed tremulously close to each other. The religious men stepped over the buckets and watched the gamblers examining the door.

On one side, there were thick hooks firmly latched around a wedge of metal, at the top and bottom. There was a long shaft that connected the top hook to the bottom; if that shaft was turned, the hooks would come free from the wedges and the door would open. A few of them wrapped their hands around the shaft and tried to turn it, but the hooks were stuck.

"It has to be opened from the outside with a lever."

"So we have to wait then."

"I can't take it any longer."

"The Lord will provide."

A few of the religious men, happy to be away from the spilled excrement and feeling weak, sat down on the floor with their backs against the wall. One of them felt the heat of the sun warming the cold metal against his back. He closed his eyes and smiled thinly.

"No chance."

"Just wait. Frankie's partner will be here soon."

"Our world is out there waiting for us."

"Have a little faith."

"Faith is getting us nowhere."

"We need to lubricate these hooks, to make them move."

"Ask your God for some oil."

A few of the gamblers laughed.

"All we have is shit."

"Use that then."

The gamblers looked at each other, wanting it to work, but not wanting to be the one who would pick it up. They stood in silence looking down at the mess on the floor. The tribal man stepped forward and bent down.

"I'll do it. I just want to get out of here."

He took it in his hand and smeared it against the bottom hook, trying to force it between the metal and getting it under his fingernails in the process. He did the same with the top hook. The job finished, one man generously offered a rag, perhaps covered with other stuff just as bad, for the tribal man to wipe his hands.

The gamblers crowded around the door, each of them sliding their hands around the shaft.

"What if Frankie's partner comes?"

"He'll get here sooner when he sees us."

They counted together: "One, two, three," and turned the shaft. They realised then how weak the journey had made them. But the shaft had moved a little and after a pause to catch their breaths, they tried again.

"What if the police are waiting outside?"

"It doesn't matter. They can't send us back."

"They don't even know where we came from."

"We could tell them."

All the gamblers stopped.

"Frankie said to forget your name, your family, where you come from, everything."

"Frankie also said to wait for someone to open the door."

"Well, where is he then?"

"We're still here."

They counted again. The shaft moved a little more.

"Come on, keep turning."

"We've almost got it."

The religious men were standing now, their eyes wide. Though they had not been as vocal as the gamblers, they had their share of hopes and dreams and goals, their heads filled with fairy tales about the untold wealth of this promised land. Yes, they wanted to open the door and get out; to be born again as a new and prosperous individual, one with a future.

The gamblers grunted as they strained with the last of their strength. The shaft creaked and they groaned, but then the door opened a crack. One man, overcome by the possibility of freedom, charged with his shoulder against the door to open it further. It flew open and banged against another container. Bright sunlight streamed in. The men squinted at the light and held their hands in front of their faces.

When their eyes had adjusted somewhat, they saw a man silhouetted in the doorway. On seeing the man, the gamblers stumbled backwards, stepping into the mess of the overturned bucket. One of them tripped over and landed in it.

The man looked at the shadowed faces and scrunched up his mouth in disgust at the smell. He covered his nose and put a phone to his ear: "Yeah, Frank, I've found another one."

"Frank. Frankie."

The seventeen men chorused: "Frankie, Frankie."

One of the religious men, who spoke English, stepped forward. "We friends of Frankie."

"Hey, get back inside. All of you, stay inside."

"You friend of Frankie?"

"Yeah, but he's not your friend."

"Frankie send us here."

The man shook his head. "He'll laugh when he hears that. Where are you lot from?"

No one answered. They pretended not to understand the question.

"Country? What country? You know, it would make things a lot easier if you came with passports or some kind of ID."

Again, no one answered. So, he grabbed the two doors in his hands.

"Wait."

"Stop."

"Quiet. Frank will be here soon. There's another crate of you idiots on dock seven. Jesus, two in one day."

The door was slammed shut and locked.

Shannon

Unfittingly for the digital age, it started with a letter, a reckless late-night confession that Shannon wrote to Jake, which was never meant to be read, because Jake was together with Suzi B and Shannon feared her wrath, but which somehow fell into the hands of Suzi C, who showed it first to Suzi B, then to Danni, then to Marni, and for a while the whole school was reading the letter, causing utter embarrassment for Shannon and an undefined illness that kept her away from school for weeks, until she made a silly goodbye video and posted it online, and then tried to commit suicide with sleeping pills and failed at that, and woke up in hospital where a few doors down Suzi B was in a coma after a horrific horse-riding accident, about which rumours circulated of a revenge-seeking Shannon somehow contriving to manipulate the horse in order to cause the accident, even though she was at home the whole time, yet Shannon recovering in hospital was quietly pleased to hear about Suzi B's mishap and thought that, hey, karma can be a bitch, and was surprised to be feeling pretty good that Suzi B was a potato and would never recover and would instead turn rotten and soft and grow horrible roots like potatoes do, then die, so Suzi C became just Suzi, and together with Danni and Marni made life absolutely miserable for Shannon, school day after school day, and in response Shannon tried to turn herself into a defiant outcast, a scary emo punk-slut with straight A's who savoured each morsel of hate delivered to her by Suzi, Danni and Marni, storing them all away for later use.

As everyone knows: high school is hard.

Except that after skipping the prom and graduation day, Shannon moved away and other things filled her life, including her reinvention as an engaged, almost wholesome university student, with enough going on that the traumas of high school receded into the background, to the point they seemed like events that had happened to another person, as Shannon found happiness with a steady string of boyfriends and enjoyed the wonderful trappings of a student life funded by her divorced parents, who were intent on rewarding her for casting aside that awful emo punk-slut phase, despite said phase being the detonator that blew the shaky foundations of their marriage to pieces, and were just so damn pleased and proud that Shannon had got it together and was on the way to a normal life, graduating with honours, doing the required internships and taking a job in the marketing department of a children's and young adults' publisher, moving into editorial after five years of donkey work without getting pregnant and needing maternity leave.

But then a letter arrived, forwarded to Shannon by her mother, who still lived in their old house and was actually dating Shannon's father again, the contents being an invitation to her 10-year high school reunion, dismissed by Shannon at first, but then removed from a garbage can and flattened out, because Shannon resolved to go and to take her latest squeeze, Morton the published YA author, with her, just to show all those bitches and bastards how incredibly awesome her life was and all that high school crap was well behind her, enough for Suzi, Danni and Marni to be, like, totally jealous of and drool with envy over Shannon's bohemian-hipster-writer boyfriend, so that Shannon could hammer the final nails into her coffin of teenage trauma and bury it.

Except that Morton couldn't make it and Shannon thinking she was tough enough to fly solo at the reunion and not get shot down was a stretch, because people seldom change, and Shannon was left completely vulnerable and at the mercy of the spiteful whims of the cliques and groups that endured ten years on, with only a handful of her peers having moved away from the town and Shannon the sole escapee to bother making the journey back home to relive all those wonderful high school moments and catch up with long lost friends, hah, and the cliques went at her with a bitter relish that had festered and grown with time, and almost everyone present looked pretty old, with the ten years seeming more like twenty, because all the stoic locals were married and/or divorced and had kids and mortgages and pathetic suburban secrets, and had latched onto priorities more in tune with how life was half a century ago, all the while hanging on grimly to the vestiges of perceived high school glories, with a large display board celebrating their mediocrity via a collection of photos and memorabilia, including a hideous photo of emo Shannon and an enlarged photocopy of her infamous Jake letter, despite said letter being the most interesting and creative item on the board, so the juvenile mocking and teasing started again, like it had never stopped, with Suzi, Danni and Marni going at Shannon with such vile malice that Shannon ran for the door, went to her mother's house and cried on her bed, the way she had done after so many days at school.

But this time it was different, because Shannon was different, and there wouldn't be any sleeping pill cocktails or dying her hair black or painting her face vampire white or shagging anything with a pulse, for her life was far better than that of Suzi or Danni or Marni, and if they needed to elevate themselves by stepping on others then good for them, because Shannon had evolved beyond such behaviour, and she didn't need any of them, nor did she have to see them again, nor was there any need to lash out in noirish protest, as it was pretty clear that their lives were miserable enough, still stuck in that little town which they'd never left and never would leave, living on the residuals of high school rule, and they were twenty-nine going on dead while Shannon lived it up with her fabulous publishing job and her hipster boyfriend and the even more hipsterish boyfriend who would eventually succeed Morton, so that the morning after the disastrous 10-year reunion, Shannon could simply have an awkward breakfast with her dating parents, then drive back to her real home and her awesome life.

Except that she didn't.

Instead, Shannon took a couple of days off and stayed in the town, secretly following Suzi, Danni and Marni around, learning that Suzi had married Jake and that they had three ugly kids and that Jake had morphed from a teenaged hunk into a cheese-skinned and already middle-aged blob, completely unworthy of the cheapest bulk-printed Valentine's card let alone the poetic and romantic musings of a lovelorn teenager, and also learning that Danni and Marni were both divorcee mothers who ran a kids clothing shop, new and used, called MaDs, and who had made an exceedingly amateurish children's book in which Danni had done the scrawls that were passed off as illustrations and Marni had written the incredibly dull cat story and which they'd printed themselves and were selling in their shop, to little success, which is why devilish Shannon's last act before leaving town was to brazenly go into MaDs and place her business card on the counter, saying that they should submit their book to a real publisher and that she would do all she could to help them succeed, causing Danni and Marni to gush with cringe-worthy gratitude, using the kind of appreciative words which Shannon didn't think Danni and Marni even had in their vocabularies.

That led to another letter, received a week later, written on perfumed, plum-coloured paper with a floral trim, with spelling and grammar errors peppering each paragraph as Danni and Marni outlined their tired story of a cat going on an adventure with two friends and divulging extensive biographical information that actually made Shannon feel even more sorry for Danni and Marni and their pitiful lives, but this didn't stop her from dumping their book in the recycled paper bin and writing back to them using her publisher's head of rejection, Angela O'Neill, who didn't exist and who sent all her publisher's rejection letters and emails to aspiring writers and who made it very easy for nasty replies from said writers to be flagged as junk or thrown straight into the recycling bin, and Shannon felt so good writing the rejection letter, in which she was openly critical of the book, stating that Danni and Marni had no talent whatsoever and should give writing and drawing away, she felt so warm inside that she attempted to deliver a few other small acts of revenge against Suzi, Danni and Marni, and these were much more satisfying than any roll in the hipster hay, with revenge far from being the cold, empty dish her parents had warned her about, but was rather a sizzling all-encompassing buffet of bliss that filled every inch of her being.

Except that her dalliance with revenge became like one of those brief, wonderful holiday romances which are full of fire when they happen, but burn out just as quickly.

After several consecutive weekends spent in her home town, hell-bent on throwing spanners into the lives of Suzi, Danni and Marni, and succeeding gloriously yet feeling less pleasure with each act of revenge, it dawned on Shannon that Suzi, Danni and Marni already had lives that were pathetic and minuscule and worthless, and that there was no revenge she could enact to make things worse for them, leading Shannon to conclude that, hey, karma can be a bitch, and that peaking in high school was just about the worst thing a person could do, and if she kept trying to further ruin the lives of Suzi, Danni and Marni, then karma might come back and be a bitch to her, and so now that her parents had sold the house, remarried and moved to the coast, there was no reason for Shannon to go back and mess with the three women's lives, because life had already got revenge for her.

But Shannon really wanted to bury her coffin of high school trauma, to get closure, and this resulted in a final letter, a falsified early-morning confession which Shannon wrote to Jake, outlining how fantastic the last few years had been, with their erotic trysts in hotel rooms and the rare yet wonderful weekends away together, and how sad she was that Jake wanted to end it because he'd met someone new, with Shannon sliding the letter into a pink envelope and addressing it simply to "Matthews" to ensure that Suzi would be the first to open it, because Shannon knew that dominant Suzi opened all the household mail.

Brian

The walk to the cemetery is quiet. It's too early for anyone to be out, but he sees lights on in some of the houses. Curtains have been pulled open and televisions switched on. Kids are up. Parents are trying to get them ready for school.

Brian smiles, glad not to have to teach anymore, to be dealing with those little brats. He's actually appreciative of all the parents behind those doors and windows; the heartless, rumour-spreading bastards who hounded him like some paedophilic demon.

Brian whistles as he walks, a bouncy, childish tune unfitting of the gloomy dawn. He knows the fog will lift, probably around lunch time, when the breeze blows in off the river. But now, the town is swimming in soupy grey, as if the clouds are coming out of the ground rather than down from the sky.

The smoke rising from hell, he thinks. No, it's a cloaking device. Hiding the problems, disguising the secrets, slapping a coat of paint over the cracks. Make all the mistakes disappear. Ignore the loss and pain. Drink your problems away. Never try to repair the damage. Never forget and never forgive.

The priest talks about this every Sunday, selecting Bible passages that urge people to forgive the sins of others; that forgiving is the most generous and caring thing a person can ever do, and that admitting your weaknesses, frailties and mistakes brings you closer to God. And he inevitably calls upon the congregation to stand and sing, hymns about shepherds and flocks and forgiveness and acts of kindness, and they all sing along. From his back-row pew in the church's right-hand corner, Brian sings as well, and he believes his fine baritone smoothes out the croaky gaps in the town's collective voice. He and Father Dougald, soulfully and skilfully carrying the tune while the rest of them struggle along, caught up in their own intricate web of problems, wishing they were doing other things, singing other songs. And with the amens said and the hands shaken, and the priest standing at the door and still banging his forgiveness drum, Brian takes his position just outside the church door, so that they can all scowl at him on their way out, or just plain ignore him.

Brian is not interested in anyone's forgiveness, because he did nothing wrong. There is nothing to forgive.

He reaches the cemetery and heads towards the small gardener's hut. The sign above the hut's door says "Plot Manager." This is Brian's official title, but he much prefers to call himself a gravedigger. He thinks it lends him the sinister, mysterious and devious qualities already bestowed upon him.

Let them say I'm sinister, he thinks. Because one by one, they will all end up here.

He removes the nasty note taped to the door, balls it up and throws it in the paper recycling bin.

He gets his tools together. This morning, he's starting on the Willison plot; or rather, adding to it. Maureen Willison, Mo to her friends. A key member of the town's special collection of widows, and part of the clique of bakery biddies who were so damning in their conviction regarding the fate of the two boys who went missing. It was Brian, the kids' teacher, they decided; that rather strange outsider who lived alone, had no girlfriend or friends, and spent all his free time in his garden. It could only be him, and from there the rumours spread like a contagious disease. Fellow teachers became accusers. Once flirtatious single parents left horrible letters in his post box. No one talked to him; not even a simple good morning in the hardware store where he went for gardening supplies. And there wasn't a shred of evidence; the locals simply blamed him.

He places his tools in the wheelbarrow. He also takes a ball of twine and some wooden markers, to ensure the plot is exactly the right size. Some joker has let the air out of the wheelbarrow's tire and he spends a few minutes pumping it up.

He's still whistling as he pushes the wheelbarrow up and down the cemetery's lanes, towards the special section reserved for the missing miners; the section that was added to the cemetery twenty years ago. The fog is heavy enough for him to only just see the outline of the church on the hill. He assumes the priest is up and already downing his breakfast whiskey.

The death of Maureen Willison has put a spring in Brian's step. Because this grave, even more so than others in recent weeks, will be an absolute joy to dig. He's also feeling the excitement of the hunt. What will he find down there?

He has the regular maintenance and gardening tasks to do, but it's the Willison plot that got him up early this morning. He was looking forward to digging it so much, he could hardly sleep; he had to play the mandolin until his fingers hurt and he couldn't keep his eyes open any longer.

Maureen Willison, retired substitute teacher and vile head of the Parents & Teachers Association. A volunteer member of basically every organisation in town, and a serial spreader of rumours. A squid of a woman, with a tentacle that seemed to reach every household and place of business. Maureen Willison, now deceased and being dolled up for display, who hit on Brian at the school Christmas party during his first teaching year and then systematically tried to ruin things for him when he turned down her fumbling, almost geriatric advances; who touched his cheek with a hand that was slightly arthritic in winter.

The memory makes Brian smile, because the bitch is dead.

It takes a good ten minutes to reach the cemetery's special section and the Willison plot. The headstone reads: "Wilbur Arthur Willison. In beloved memory. Your light shines brightly while we stand together in darkness."

His task is to dig the plot next to Wilbur's. His personal objective is to get close enough for him to access the coffin.

Brian begins by measuring the grave, putting the stakes in the ground and using the twine to mark out the required rectangle. He's conservative in his estimate of how close Wilbur's coffin might be, as that plot was dug well before his time. But once down deep enough, it won't be hard to tunnel a little to the left, just enough to tap the coffin. He assumes Wilbur's coffin is around four feet deep, like the others.

He gets to work, using the expensive shovel Father Dougald gave him as a welcome present.

The dirt is soft and spongy. He takes out large sections of grass and places them carefully to the side. The dirt goes in a neat pyramidal pile next to the grave.

As he works, Brian lets his mind wander. The thoughts come and go. He feels the usual resentment, the hate, but he's also developed a certain acceptance of his situation; he's thankful for how he ended up standing in this grave with a top-of-the-range shovel in his hands. He can't offer the forgiveness Father Dougald demands, but he is able to manage gratitude. And there is the satisfaction that they eventually all end up here.

Around mid-morning, the priest wanders down from the church, carrying his tartan-patterned thermos and two mugs.

By this stage, Brian's shoulders are about level with the ground, meaning he's around five feet under and presumably close to Wilbur's coffin. He pokes at the side of the grave with his shovel, gently scraping the dirt away, until he hears the scratch of metal against wood. He shovels some dirt back into place, so the grave is uniform again and the coffin hidden, and climbs the short ladder out of the grave.

He takes off his gloves and wipes his brow with his handkerchief.

"Good morning, Brian," the priest says.

"Morning, Father."

"You've had an early start."

"I think the quiet of the morning is the most suitable time for this kind of work."

The priest looks at the grave. "Indeed. Maureen is such a loss. For the community, her loved ones."

"Yup. A huge loss."

"So sudden." The priest pours two cups of black tea. "Generous of spirit was our Mo, and of voice, but not exactly generous of purse."

"What do you mean?"

"Well, perhaps she thought she gave enough to the community, but whenever the collection plate was passed around, she never put anything in."

Brian takes the cup handed to him. "Is that right?"

Father Dougald chuckles a little, the morning whiskey having put him in good spirits, his bulbous nose already red. "They think I don't notice these things, but I notice. You can see it weighing on their conscience afterwards. Their guilt, from their penny-pinching."

"More of a taker than a giver, eh, Father."

"Not that bad. I'm sure she had her reasons."

After a sip of tea, Brian says, "Guess she thought some of it might reach me."

"That's an awful thing to say." But the priest is smiling. "Your situation hasn't stopped others from giving."

"They're giving to the church, not to pay my wages. For them, I don't even exist."

"Oh, I'm sure you're in their thoughts. Much more than you think."

"I didn't do it," Brian says flatly.

"I know. I know." Father Dougald pats Brian gently on the shoulder and starts to walk away. "Best get finished, Brian." He looks at the sky and adds, "Before the heavens open."

Brian looks upward. He doesn't think it will rain. At least, he hopes it won't, because that would mean going all the way back to the hut to get a tarp. And right now, all he wants is to search Wilbur's coffin.

He finishes the tea, pouring the dregs into the dirt and waiting for the priest to make his way back to the church. Going slowly up the hill, Father Dougald stops and takes a small flask from his pocket. He has a drink, then continues.

Incredible man, Brian thinks as he heads back down the ladder. Even with the drinking.

It was Father Dougald who came to Brian's rescue when things were really grim; when Brian's house was getting vandalised and his car was set on fire; when the police were deemed too slow with their investigation and the town set about exacting its own form of justice. The people were angry, distraught, because yet another tragedy had hit them, and they needed an outlet. A focus. It was the teacher. That Brian guy who lived alone and was obsessed with his garden. It had to be him, because it couldn't possibly have been anyone else.

Brian was vehement in his innocence. The police cleared him due to the complete lack of evidence, but the damage was done: forced out from his teaching position, evicted from his house. Only the priest showed some support, taking him in and giving him a job. Father Dougald advised Brian to leave the town, to take a job elsewhere. Leave the country even, start anew; Brian was plenty young enough to do such a thing. But Brian had stayed. For him, leaving would have been an admission of a guilt he didn't have, and proof that everyone was right.

They ignore him. They hate him. They do not forgive. They do not apologise or show regret. If one of them dies, he digs their grave, just as he is doing today.

Brian scrapes away the dirt, exposing Wilbur's coffin. Again, his lazy predecessor had dug barely a four-foot grave. Brian assumes there had been too many graves to dig at once, what with thirty-nine miners to sort of bury, to go the full six feet down.

During the last three months, he has managed to dig up nearly all of those graves. Once, like today, a wife had to be added, meaning a new grave dug. But for all the others, Brian had come out in the middle of the night to tap the coffins.

It had begun by chance, when he was digging his first grave, for the miner's widow. A novice then, he accidentally drove the shovel into the miner's corpse-less coffin, exposing the treasures inside. He took it all, and then started hitting the other coffins. He had found some remarkable things inside. Things of value, which had increased in value over the years, and which he sold online. His treasure-hunting had resulted in a small fortune, sitting in a Standard's bank account on the island of Jersey and earning good interest.

Sure, there had been no bodies to bury, but Brian still didn't understand why the locals had filled the coffins with items of such value. Watches and rings and cuff links. Musical instruments and antique weaponry. First edition books and gold-plated fountain pens. Certainly a few photographs and an old suit would have sufficed. Brian assumed that the wives hadn't really known the value of the items placed in the coffins. Without a body, they attempted to fill the space with what they thought were mementos, but which turned out to be very much worth a few hours digging in the dark. One foolish widow had even buried money, in the form of valuable coin collection.

Brian moves more dirt, exposing a side of the coffin. It's enough for him to cut away a piece. With his small, cordless circular saw, normally used for cutting roots, he removes a rectangular section about forty by twenty inches. Several empty liqour bottles fall to the dirt, as well as a few small items. Photographs and papers. There's a greasy old comb, with a few strands of hair in it, and a rusted straight razor.

Brian knows the story well. Wilbur Arthur Willison, a good twenty years senior to his second wife Maureen, had been a promising footballer; a teenage member of Manchester United who played a handful of games before injuries stopped him. His football career over, Wilbur, came back to his hometown and went to work in the coal mine, where he toiled for over three decades. He would have been close to retirement age when the accident happened. A mainstay of the community, one of the town's few heroes, Wilbur was considered the greatest loss out of the thirty-nine miners, and his grave occupied the central position in the cemetery's special section.

Brian is banking on there being some football memorabilia inside; some mint condition Red Devils shirts that he can sell to collectors. He bends down, takes a torch from his pocket and looks inside the coffin. He can barely breathe he's so excited. But there are mostly more empty liquor bottles; Maureen having paid homage to her alcoholic husband in this fashion. He does pull out a pair of old boots and a few obscure jerseys, but they don't look to be worth anything. He'll have to do some research later, on second and third division clubs of that era.

Brian assumes Maureen was clever enough to sell anything of value, including any Man United stuff, in order to fund her twice-yearly jaunts across the Channel to Saint Malo.

It's very disappointing. Just another drunk, he thinks, feeling slightly sympathetic towards Maureen.

Apart from the jerseys, he puts everything back in the coffin. The cut-out piece gets replaced, with some tape to hold it. With the dirt shovelled back across, the coffin is hidden again.

All excited for nothing, Brian thinks, and he goes back to digging.

It's hard work now, being almost six feet down and having to heave the dirt up and out of the grave. But he's almost finished.

His shovel work is impressive as he squares the corners, making the grave neat.

He wonders if it's worth breaking into Maureen's house. No, that woman left nothing behind.

The spirit level shows that the grave is not quite flat. He removes a bit more dirt from the top left-hand corner, putting him close to Wilbur's headstone, if he looks up, and that ridiculous "Your light shines brightly" quote.

He's scraping dirt away from the corner when the shovel hits wood. With his gloved hands, he sweeps the dirt aside, revealing a broad flat section, the wood rotted and cracked. The planks are different from the wood of a coffin. He digs into Wilbur's grave a little, and the planks continue.

With a section about a metre square exposed, Brian stands up straight and looks at it. He steps back, thinking that the ground might collapse underneath him. Then, he edges forward and finds the edge of the wood with his boot, just to be sure he's standing on solid ground.

It's a tunnel, he's certain of it. Some kind of passageway.

He climbs the first rung of the ladder and pokes his head out of the grave to see if anyone's around. The cemetery is deserted.

He takes his hand-held saw and cuts out a section he'll be able to fit through.

While the wood has rotted on top, where it was exposed to the dirt, the panels are thick and solid. The saw's circular blade is more suited to slicing cheap coffins open and is not quite large enough in diameter to cut all the way through these planks. He's forced to stamp down on the section with his right foot. He keeps his left foot in the dirt and steadies himself with the walls of the grave, stamping and stamping until the section gives way. It thuds in the darkness below. To Brian, it doesn't sound like it falls very far.

A small cloud of yellowish dust comes out of the hole. Brian swats at it with one hand while he lowers the ladder down with the other. The top two rungs of the six-foot ladder stick out of the hole; he'll have to crawl or crouch if he wants to explore what's down there. But to do that, he knows he'll need to be better prepared. And he'll have to wait until night time.

He pulls the ladder out, places it next to the wall of the grave and climbs out. He jogs to the hut to retrieve a tarp, and jogs back to the grave. With this set up, Brian stops for lunch, taking a seat on a bench with his back to the obelisk memorial, where the miners' names are engraved in the stone, with Wilbur Willison at the top of the list.

He eats his sandwich slowly.

The fog has cleared. He looks over the cemetery's expanse, with its trees, both young and old, its orderly rows of headstones, the grass neatly trimmed and not a weed in sight. He considers this the most beautiful place in town, more landscaped garden than graveyard, especially since he took over. It's a wonderful spot to rest. Peaceful and cared for. Yet, underneath is some kind of passageway.

Brian starts making a mental list of what he'll need. A headlamp. Knee pads. Possibly some kind of breathing apparatus. Glow-in-the-dark spray paint so he can mark his way. A large duffel bag that he can fill with whatever he might find. A compass. A notepad and pen so he can map the passageway. Maybe an axe and some other tools. A contour map of the area, preferably dating back to when the mine was operational.

It will require a trip, to the big chain hardware store an hour's drive away; where students and hapless young adults work, and none of them know him, nor will they cast nasty, suspicious looks as he loads a trolley with all that gear. Unlike in the local hardware store, where they never say good morning and where they treat any purchase he makes as a precursor to another double murder. But even with the awful treatment, Brian still frequents that store, buying all his regular supplies there, though the chain store is considerably cheaper. It's because he wants to keep reminding them, in the same way he wants to remind everyone in town, that he is still here, that he is not guilty, that he feels no shame, and that one day he will dig their grave.

The list gets too long to keep in his head, so he writes it all down.

After the disappointment of the morning, Brian is again buzzing with the excitement of the hunt. This has the feeling of an expedition.

***

Brian likes the cemetery at night.

It's very dark, with the only lights coming from the big recycling plant on the outskirts of town. The only noise as well.

There are rabbits on the grass, nibbling away. He hears the soft hoots of owls. It should be a scary place, this cemetery in darkness, but Brian finds it rather inviting. He's spent quite a few nights out here, tapping coffins and pilfering them of goods. Other nights, when he can't sleep and playing the mandolin doesn't succeed in calming his over-active mind, he wanders down the river to the cemetery and strolls around. He walks on graves and sometimes takes a piss in any recently filled flower vases. One time, he found Father Dougald asleep on a bench, his small flask open in his right hand. Brian had used a wheelbarrow to get the priest up the hill to the house behind the church, and had helped him into bed.

The gear is very heavy, especially the breathing apparatus, which he ended up hiring rather than buying. He'd lied to the man at the counter, saying he was fumigating his basement. The man said the tank should last about ninety minutes, which doesn't give Brian a lot of time; he left the second tank at home, as it was too much to carry. The apparatus has a full face mask and shoulder straps, so it can sit on his back like a small backpack.

The tarp is wet. Father Dougald had been right about the rain, but it had only been a brief shower, when Brian was having an evening nap.

Down in Maureen's grave, he kneels in the dirt to slip the breathing apparatus over his shoulders. With the mask securely in place, he gets the air flowing. He surprises himself with how relaxed he is. There's something about the mask that actually feels good; that he's hiding from the world and no longer breathing the same air as everyone else. It's also isolating, and comforting.

With the headlamp on, and the knee pads, and the duffel bag over one shoulder, he checks all his gear one last time before lowering himself down the ladder. It's awkward, because of the weight, but his back and shoulders are strong from shovelling so much dirt the last three months.

He uses the glowing spray paint to mark the wooden wall with an arrow, pointing in the direction he's about to start. According to the compass, he's heading east, away from the town.

The passageway looks old and rather makeshift. It's fully panelled with wood, except for the dirt floor, and reinforced with cross beams at intervals of about two metres. But even with that, Brian thinks there's something haphazard about it. A rushed job. Almost like the tunnel built by prisoners trying to dig their way out. He's curious about where the passageway ends in the town, and decides to explore a bit in that direction later, if he has enough air left.

Brian crawls forward. He takes his time, not exerting himself or wasting air. The passageway itself is fascinating; that once upon a time, a group of men built this, and that if only his predecessor had dug a deeper grave for Wilbur Willison, then he would have found the passageway and, if Brian's assumption is right, the men who were still alive perhaps could have been rescued before they were all symbolically buried in half-empty coffins only four feet down. And that the mine might not have been closed and the town wouldn't have turned to landfill and recycling in order to stay prosperous.

Behind the mask, Brian smiles. Not for the first time, he wonders why this town seems cursed. Once, the locals here stole from the earth. Okay, that was the industry. Then, when the earth got revenge, trapping thirty-nine men down in the mine, the town decided to fill the earth with garbage instead. But that's also industry, taking the garbage deliveries from nearby towns and dumping it in the large holes and tracts left over from the abandoned mines. And expanding into recycling as well, making good money from it.

Yet Brian is certain the earth will get revenge again. Aware of what gets tipped into the ground, he doesn't drink the local tap water, nor does he eat any produce grown in the town's vicinity.

As he crawls, Brian decides not to waste time drawing a map. It's enough to mark the walls. When he sprays an arrow, he writes the number of minutes it's taken him to get this far, just to be certain he'll have enough air to get back.

Visibility in the passage is poor, and his hands and knees scuff up the dust, making it worse.

The passage starts going downhill.

He wonders when someone last used this passageway. What was it used for? Perhaps it predated the last operational mine. It's a tunnel from, maybe, a century ago.

Eventually, Brian reaches a dead end. A wooden wall. He knocks on it with his fist, thinking it doesn't sound very solid. From his duffel bag, he takes the small axe and starts chopping at the wood. It's dry and splinters easily. After ten minutes of hacking, the space is wide enough for him to get through.

In the open area, Brian gets to his feet. It's a relief to stand up straight. The light of the headlamp slices through the area, but he can't see much. He points it at the ground; it's littered with clothed skeletons. Shocked, he rears back against the wooden wall he came through, hitting it hard enough for a small crucifix hanging there to fall to the ground.

He calms his breathing. He's seen corpses before, but not like this; so many of them.

He finds the crucifix and hangs it back on the little nail.

The mine's makeshift chapel, he concludes. Prayers for good luck before going down to work.

And a potential scene unfolds before his eyes: the thirty-nine men, trapped by some cave in and running out of air, had come to the chapel to die. Yet, behind that crucifix was a passageway they might have escaped through. Instead, they asked God to help and waited to be rescued. Got down on their knees and died.

Brian counts the bodies. There are thirty. He pilfers each one: sliding watches off the remains of wrists and slipping off wedding rings looped loosely around bony fingers. He takes the money as well, and the little trinkets the miners carried for luck. The rabbit's feet and cheap lockets he tosses to the floor, but other lucky charms are of interest, including several war medals, a handful of solid gold crucifixes, some old coins and a few precious stones. The real find is the string of pearls hanging around one miner's neck. It's not terribly pleasant, being so close to these corpses, but the loot is worth it.

He puts it all in a small backpack that then goes inside the duffel bag.

He sprays an arrow on the wall, near the section he hacked out with the axe.

A glance at the air pressure gauge tells him he has just over an hour left.

He's curious about the other nine bodies.

He heads towards the chapel's entrance. Strangely, the door is locked. He uses the axe to chop out a section near the lock and gets the door open. Out of the chapel, he follows a short passage that leads to a main area, the mine's central gathering point, of sorts. There are several doorways connecting to the area and two elevator shafts.

As he looks around, he finds it bizarre that the miners had been trapped so close to the surface, but couldn't be rescued. Sure, it was twenty years ago, he thinks, and communications were different then, but they couldn't make contact from here? They couldn't just walk out? And surely they would be able to breathe here. There must be a ventilation system, or something. This is barely ten metres deep. Probably not even that.

The set-up in the chapel gives Brian the impression of something organised, or of people caught by surprise. A mass suicide, or a mass murder. The way the corpses were all scattered around, the jaws stretched open or the teeth clenched together. The fact that the door was locked. Were they imprisoned? Did they lock themselves in? Or did they lock someone else out?

The nine others.

Brian is overcome by the very distinct feeling of not wanting to be down here. He wonders if the air was poisoned somehow. If it still is.

He keeps the mask on, marks the chapel's door with an arrow and takes the next doorway to his left. It's some kind of supply room, filled with piles of trash: empty cans, water bottles and food wrappers. It has the disorganised look of a raided room.

The next doorway leads down a long passageway. He sprays an arrow and the time and heads down it. He walks slowly, keeping the light straight in front of him. When he stops to get the axe out of the duffel bag and shines the light on the ground, he sees a lot of footprints.

He continues, edging along the wall, axe in hand.

There's a door on the right. He tries the handle, and it's also locked. He hacks it open.

It's the lunch room, or some kind of meeting or changing area, with tables and chairs, and toilets at the back. He counts eight corpses, sitting in chairs or having fallen from the chairs and lying on the ground. He does some quick pilfering, adding more watches, rings and lucky charms to his backpack.

He thinks this room has the look of a murder scene. Eight men taken by surprise, dying suddenly.

That does it for Brian. He pulls the door shut and starts heading back. He almost runs, but the breathing apparatus is too heavy for that.

In the main area, he's about to go through the gruesome chapel when he decides to quickly check the other doorways. One leads into a utility room, where there's a large contraption that looks like a rather archaic ventilation system. On the floor, Brian sees a canister with a skull-and-crossbones on it.

So, that's what happened, he thinks. Someone poisoned the ventilation system.

He wonders if the air is still poisonous. It appears the ventilator is no longer functioning.

The last doorway leads uphill, to what Brian assumes would have been the mine's outside entrance. After ten metres, there's a corpse in several pieces, and further down, the passageway is blocked off.

That must have been the explosion everyone said they'd heard, Brian thinks.

He steels himself to check the pieces of the corpse. He picks up a bony arm first, taking the gold watch from the man's wrist and the thick wedding band from the left ring finger. He finds the other arm; the hand is clenched around an empty whiskey bottle.

The man's torso is against the wall. The clothes have been shredded by the blast. Underneath, Brian sees the remains of a vintage Manchester United jersey.

"Wilbur," he says.

Checking the remaining pockets of Wilbur's coat, Brian pulls out an envelope. There's a letter inside, very formal and official, slightly burned at the edges.

The mine will be closed. All the workers laid off. Too dangerous and not profitable.

Brian's had enough. It's not important why Wilbur the alcoholic got drunk, poisoned the air and killed thirty-eight men down here, or if it was an act of protest that went horribly wrong. He wants to get out.

He feels slightly dizzy. A check of his air shows he has about ten minutes left. He realises that in his panic and fear, and because of his efforts chopping walls and doors open, he's sucked up the air faster than expected.

So, he really needs to get out.

He opens the door to the chapel, but a flicker of light catches his eye and makes him turn. He shines the headlamp down the long passageway.

There's a boy, dressed in ragged clothing, with a torch in his right hand, the light of which is barely shining. He holds a hand up in front of his face, then runs away.

Brian gives his head a shake, sure that he's seeing things. It's the thin air, he decides. The shock. Get out, get out.

He goes quickly through the chapel and squeezes through the gap in the wall. It's hard work, crawling uphill. His lower back hurts. Breathing is difficult. Every time he blinks, he sees that boy silhouetted in the passageway, a hand in front of his face.

Brian has to stop a few times, to keep from passing out. But he makes it to Maureen's grave, where he rips the mask from his face and collapses into the dirt, gasping.

***

The knock on the door wakes him. The clock shows it's just before noon. He staggers out of bed, stiff all over and coughing as he walks, and opens the door.

"Father Dougald?"

"Top of the morning, Brian," the priest says. "Just wanted to check if everything's all right. It's not like you to miss a day's work."

"I know. I'm sorry. I'm a bit under the weather." Brian coughs some more, and it's not a show. He'd slept fitfully, often waking to cough, and tossing from one side to the other.

"Is everything set with Maureen?"

"Yes." Brian clears his throat loudly and hits his chest with his fist. "Excuse me. I think I'm getting a chest infection."

"Would you like me to drive you to the doctor?"

"Thanks, Father, but I'll be fine. Just need some rest."

"Take the day off. You earned it."

Brian nods. "Would you like to come in? Have a cup of tea?"

"Very kind of you, but I'm due to give a talk at the school." Father Dougald looks past Brian, into the cottage, and smiles rather whimsically. "The commemoration day is coming up, as you know. Twenty years it is now."

"Yes."

"Terrible tragedy," Father Dougald says, shaking his head.

"Awful." Brian coughs, then says, "But didn't you tell me once the mine was going to close? That there were rumours going around. Everyone would be laid off."

The priest shakes his head. "Never heard about that, Brian. Probably just rumours. I'm actually rather glad, though. Not because of the disaster, not at all. But because the mine closed. It was terrible for the men going down there every day. It wasn't safe. It wasn't even safe enough for rescuers to go in and search for the miners."

"Did they try?"

"It was far too dangerous." The priest gives Brian a soft smile. "Never mind. Things have a way of working out. The town's done very well with waste removal."

"And recycling."

"Yes, that too." Father Dougald turns and walks away. "Get some rest, Brian," he says over his shoulder. "I'll need your strong shoulders tomorrow. To put Maureen safely in the ground. And be sure to clean that mess off the door."

Brian looks at it. "Child murderer lives here" is written in thick red pen. It's been there for a week. If he cleans it off, some joker will just write something else.

He sighs and watches the priest walk slowly down the street. Sure enough, Father Dougald stops after a while and takes a swig from his flask.

The funeral, Brian thinks. Tonight would be the last chance to go down into the mine. Or he would have to tap the passageway from another point.

He's not sure he wants to go back down.

But, the boy.

Brian's tiny cottage, the priest's garden house, is on the outskirts of town and close to the river. When evicted from his old house, his ex-landlord had given him an hour just after dawn to collect whatever he wanted to take with him before the house was bulldozed and the garden destroyed. In its place, an office complex was to be built for the ever-expanding landfill business. It meant that Brian had few belongings when Father Dougald handed him the keys to the garden house; only what he could carry, as his car had been set on fire. It amounted to a bag of clothes, his mandolin and two small boxes. The few delicate items he'd wrapped, but he never bothered unpacking any of it, these mementos from another life. He donated most of the clothes to charity and left the boxes in the closet.

He goes to the closet now, because he'd wrapped those items in newspaper. At the time, the paper was full of stories about the missing boys.

He flattens out the newspaper, casting the items aside. And there they are. Quintin and Clint. He looks closer. Clint O'Connell. Quiet boy, good at maths, a slow reader. He and Quintin were inseparable friends. Clint and Quint, always sitting together, always playing football at recess. In scouts together. Both were altar boys. Good kids. Never any trouble.

Brian had known them as students in his class, but had never taken it further. He was once told by the principal that his predecessor had been dismissed for being a little too touchy-feely with some of the students. Which was why Brian had made a concerted effort to keep his distance.

He saw Clint last night. He's sure of it. But he wonders how Clint could have survived down there for three months. The deadly air. Lack of sunlight. Lack of food.

The storage room, Brian thinks. They raided it, to survive. And it could mean both boys are still down there. Clint had that old torch, too.

Brian stands up quickly and gets to work. He replaces the empty tank of the breathing apparatus with the full one. He collects his gear, adding some rope, a roll of tape and a bottle of water. He's all set to head out the door when he realises he'll have to wait for night.

***

It's a brisk, sunny afternoon. Brian dresses warmly and sits by the river.

It's peaceful, with most of the locals preferring indoor entertainments after school and work.

But Brian is restless. He wants to go back into the mine. He intends to bring Clint and Quintin back and clear his name. Then, he will leave this cursed town.

The sun sets slowly.

Brian spends an hour playing his mandolin, trying to distract his mind from envisioning Wilbur's drunken last moments: the poisoned air, the botched explosion, all those innocent men dying.

Back in the house, he drinks a pot of tea and focuses on the task at hand. The positives. He also tries to eat something, but he's too nervous. The excitement of the hunt. The ultimate treasure. But how will he find two boys in what is potentially a labyrinth of passageways, with only ninety minutes of air?

Clint had no mask on, Brian recalls, getting a flash of the boy with the hand in front of his face. They're down there, breathing, so they must be somewhere safe. Maybe the air's not poisoned anymore.

Brian kills an hour writing a letter to Father Dougald, explaining the passageway he found and the kids being down there, just in case he doesn't make it back. He leaves out any mention of the thirty-nine corpses, or what Wilbur Willison had done; the town's hero actually being the town's villain.

He leaves the letter on the kitchen counter and with it close to midnight, gathers up his gear and walks to the cemetery. Like last night, he takes the route along the river, skirting the town.

He's nervous, and angry. How things could have been different. Three months, spent digging. All that time, he was the hunted. The hounded. They never let him be. Never forgave. Never even listened. The only words spoken to him were accusations and insults.

And he's aware now of how miserable his life has been these last few months. No. Going further back, to when he accepted the teaching position and moved to this town. And even further, to becoming a teacher, which was only what his mother had wanted.

Brian had wanted other things. The world, adventure, exploration.

He thinks the two boys stuck down in the mine are a bit like him; because that was the kind of thing he'd done all the time as a kid, explored unknown places, going into caves and abandoned houses. What was down there? Why was everyone so scared of this place? Brian had wanted to know.

Tonight, Brian wants to know why the kids went into the mine. He wants to know how they survived, and why they couldn't find a way out of a place they'd found their way into.

By the time he gets to the cemetery, Brian has found his focus. He doesn't use the lanes. He walks straight across the plots to the cemetery's special section. The blue tarp is still hanging over Maureen's grave, like it's an excavation site. Six feet down, he gets the breathing apparatus on, secures the mask and puts the headlamp and knee pads in place. He's still stiff, but he crawls quickly down the passageway. Through the chapel, axe in hand and not looking at the floor, then along the passageway to where he saw Clint. Further down, he starts marking arrows again.

He's struggling with his breathing, and has to cough a few times, which fogs up the mask a little, but he's not willing to take the mask off and risk breathing poisoned air.

The passageway forks. He sprays an arrow and goes right. He walks for about ten minutes, then the way is blocked. The passageway has collapsed. Through the splintered wood, he sees rubbish.

Landfill, he thinks, and he turns back.

It's something he hasn't considered: the compressed garbage getting rammed into the earth, collapsing passageways, filling the mine. Maybe the kids were unlucky, and got blocked in by new landfill.

At the fork, he marks a cross on the right passageway and an arrow on the left. There are footprints in the dirt. It's then he fears that the boys have already found their way out, using the passageway to Maureen's grave.

He checks his air. One hour left.

When he aims the headlamp forward again, Clint is standing there.

Brian stumbles backwards against the wall. His hand tightens around the axe.

Clint stares at him.

The boy's face is dirty, as are his hands, and his clothes are falling apart.

"Clint," Brian says. He has to shout because the mask muffles his voice: "Clint! There you are. You're alive."

Clint nods slowly.

"Where's Quintin?" Brian asks. "He's down here with you. Where is he?"

The boy looks down at the dirt. Then he steps closer and peers through the yellow-tinted mask.

"Mr Fitzgerald?"

"It's me," Brian shouts, but he doesn't dare take off the mask. Up close, Clint looks pale and sickly. Brian takes a few steps backwards. "What happened?"

Clint appears confused again. "What day is it?" he asks.

"It's Wednesday, the … it doesn't matter what day it is. You've been down here for three months. Now, go get Quintin. We're getting out of here. I've found a way out."

Clint doesn't move.

"Come on. I'm here to rescue you."

"But. Mr Fitzgerald? There's just me."

"What happened to Quintin? Tell me, Clint."

"He's gone."

"What? Gone where?"

Clint starts to cry, the tears streaking through the dirt on his face. "The rubbish. He got flattened."

"What?"

"It came from nowhere. We were just exploring, Mr Fitzgerald. We found this cave. And then Quintin got buried."

"And you got stuck in here. Oh, God. You poor boy."

It's disappointing that Quintin is dead, but Brian has Clint and that will be enough to clear his name.

"Let's go, Clint. I'll show you the way out."

Again, the boy doesn't move.

"Now!"

Clint shakes his head. "Not going back."

"What?"

"Not going back. All bad. I'm staying here."

Brian raises the axe a little. "You're coming with me, Clint. You're not safe down here. This place could cave in at any moment."

"No. No church. No garden work. Staying here. No more being an altar boy. Safe here."

Clint tries to run, but Brian grabs him. The boy is too weak to fight, and he's very thin. Brian easily turns him around and starts marching him down the passageway, occasionally shoving him in the back with the axe handle. When Clint tries to turn and run, Brian stops him and pushes him forward again. Eventually, Brian has to lift Clint and carry him. The boy protests, kicking his feet in the air and sending one shoe flying against the wall, then passes out from the exertion.

This makes Clint much easier to carry.

When they reach the main area, Brian moves quickly through the chapel and gets into the passageway. It's awkward, dragging and carrying the unconscious Clint back to Maureen's grave, and hard work. At one point, Clint comes to and crawls slowly in a daze, then collapses. Brian continues dragging him. The skinny, malnourished Clint doesn't weigh very much.

Out of the passageway, Brian sits Clint up against the wall of the grave. He slaps the boy lightly in the face, but he's still out. Brian checks Clint's pulse; it's strong. To be sure, Brian ties Clint's feet and hands together, so the boy can't run away, and tapes his mouth shut.

Mask off and breathing apparatus cast aside, Brian runs to the plot manager's hut to retrieve a shovel. Something makes him select an older shovel, and not the one Father Dougald gave him.

Back at the grave, he uses Maureen's dirt to fill in the passageway enough to place the cut-out wooden section back on top. Then, he fills in the remaining dirt, covering up the exposed wood. He sets up the grave, getting it ready for tomorrow's burial, and takes down the tarp.

He collects his gear, hauls Clint out of the grave and carries him back along the river to his small cottage. Brian stays in the shadows, and is very careful not to be seen. At home, he sits Clint on a chair and slaps him lightly in the face.

"Clint? Clint? Wake up."

The boy slowly opens his eyes and looks around. When he sees he's in Father Dougald's cottage, he starts to struggle against his binds, and his screams are muffled by the tape.

Seeing the abject fear in Clint's eyes, Brian puts the pieces together. Clint and Quintin, altar boys, running away. No garden work, Clint had said. No church.

"Dougald?" Brian asks. "He brought you here?"

Clint continues to struggle, but he nods as well.

"Oh, this town," Brian says, pacing back and forth. "This fucking town."

He runs his hands through his hair and paces a bit more, thinking hard. He never should have stayed here. He should've left, like Father Dougald had advised. Father fucking Dougald.

It doesn't matter if his grave-tapping has earned him a good amount of money. He should've packed up and left when he had the chance.

He's no plot manager. He's not even interested in revenge any more, in burying all the bastards. What he wants is to escape. Start again. Most importantly, put this place behind him. He can't keep digging here. The more he digs, the more he finds. And he certainly doesn't want to be buried here.

"Look, Clint," Brian says. "I'm not going to hurt you. Father

Dougald is not coming. I live here. You understand? You're safe here. I saved you, and now you're going to save me. You're going to clear my name, Clint. Okay? By this time tomorrow, I'll be gone. Tomorrow morning, after Maureen's funeral. I'll come back here and let you out. Is that clear?"

Clint nods.

"Can I take the tape off? If you scream, I'll have to put it back on."

Clint nods again, and Brian decides to trust the boy. But the rope will remain. Brian's not taking any chances.

He pulls the tape off. Clint takes in some lustrous breaths and coughs a few times. His face is very pale.

"It was bad down there, wasn't it?"

"Yeah," Clint says, keeping his head lowered.

"How did you survive for three months?"

Clint shrugs.

"How were you able to breathe?"

"It was bad at the start. But I got used to it."

"We humans are nothing if not adaptable," Brian says with a thin smile.

"Mr Fitzgerald, can you set me free?"

"Sorry, Clint. You're going to have to trust me. I can't let you get away. You're my only chance. And I've still got some loose ends to tie up tomorrow."

"I'm thirsty."

Brian gives Clint a long drink from a water bottle. Then, the boy leans forward, with his head on the table, and starts sleeping.

This allows Brian to start cleaning up and packing things away. He doesn't have much, having lived a rather frugal existence the last few months. A half-dozen garbage bags get quickly filled, leaving him with a duffel bag of clothes, his mandolin and the loot he pilfered from the miners.

He's ready to go. He sets his alarm and goes to bed.

***

He sleeps poorly again, coughing a lot, the images of the mine pervading his dreams: the corpses, the passageways, the ragged Man United jersey on Wilbur's bony torso, Wilbur in several pieces and Wilbur's bony hand clutching the bottle.

He dreams of his life as well, as it was before the boys went missing; as it might have been had they not.

He gets up a few times to check on Clint. The boy sleeps soundly, his head on the table.

When the alarm wakes him, Brian's first thought is that his old life was much more miserable than his life is now. He was stuck then, a prisoner of his own comfort and routine, a man on permanent garden leave. He can escape now, with a clean slate. There's a strong temptation just to grab his gear and drive away. But he can't, not with Clint tied up in the cottage. And he certainly can't leave Clint here for Father Dougald to find. So he lets Clint sleep and drives half an hour to return the breathing apparatus, and spends ten minutes filling out the feedback form. Then another half an hour driving back.

Once home, he still has more time to kill. He loads the garbage bags into his car, along with his loot, duffel bag and mandolin.

He doesn't want to be at the cemetery when Maureen's funeral is on, but he is required to fill in her grave today. And he will.

He looks through some of the books on the shelf, the ones about local history. In one book is a map of the town, as it was just before the Second World War.

When Clint finally wakes up, Brian unties him so he can go to the bathroom and wash his hands and face. They have lunch together. Clint's feet are tied to the chair, but his hands are left free. They talk a little, with Clint seemingly glad to be out of the mine. Brian shows Clint the map, and explains his theory about the passageways, that they led to buildings in the town that are no longer there, including the old pub. Brian also tells him about how he was accused of murder and how he lost everything. Clint is sorry, and he promises to make things right. In return, Brian promises to take care of Father Dougald.

"This is what I want you to do, Clint," Brian says. "I'm going to start in minute. I want you to wait for an hour before you untie the ropes from feet. It's really important you give me that hour, so I can take care everything and get out of town. If you start walking around, if people see you, the town will go crazy. Okay? Do you understand?"

Clint doesn't appear terribly keen about being left alone in the cottage, but he nods. "Yes, Mr Fitzgerald."

"Tell your parents the truth. That I found you and that I rescued you. If they ask what I was doing down there, tell them I found a passageway where the old pub used to be and went exploring. Tell them I was determined to prove my innocence and clear my name. You tell them that."

Clint nods again.

"Okay. Good. It will be all right, Clint." Brian looks around to see if he's got everything. "I think I'm ready." He points at the clock on the wall and adds, "One hour, Clint. Deal?"

Brian shakes the boy's hand and tries to smile. The whole plan hinges on Clint waiting, and Brian's not completely sure the boy will.

"All the best, Clint. Just tell the truth."

"Yes, sir."

"Your parents will help you. They're good people, despite everything."

Brian doesn't bother looking around the tiny house and reminiscing. He wants to get out. He leaves the keys on the kitchen counter and pulls the door shut. The graffiti is still there.

Driving away, he checks the rear-view mirror to see if Clint runs out of the cottage; he doesn't, and it's a relief. Brian starts to believe things will go as planned.

At the cemetery, he sees Maureen's mourners getting into cars and driving away. He parks and waits until they're all gone; it looks like the whole town was in attendance. Through the cemetery trees, he spots Father Dougald walking up the hill to the church, flanked by two of his altar boys. The priest has an arm around each boy.

"You bastard," Brian says.

With everyone gone, Brian takes the half-dozen garbage bags and carries them to Maureen's grave, where he drops them inside. Then, at the hut, he shovels some dirt into a wheelbarrow and takes this to the grave, piling it up on the side. It takes four wheelbarrow loads before Father Dougald comes wandering in the direction of the cemetery's special section.

Brian leans on his shovel and waits for him. The cemetery is deserted, with all of Maureen's mourners on the way to getting sauced at her wake.

"Morning, Brian."

"Father."

"Nice service, this morning. A lot of tears, let me tell you."

Brian thinks that Father Dougald doesn't appear to have shed any.

"I bet," Brian says.

"Wilbur and Maureen are together again." Father Dougald walks forward to look into the grave. The blue garbage bags surprise him. "What's this?"

"Landfill."

And Brian raises the shovel Father Dougald gave him and whacks him in the back of the head with it. The priest falls on the bags, deflating them. Brian looks around to be sure no one has seen him and starts shovelling in the dirt.

But Dougald isn't dead. When the priest starts squirming slowly under the dirt, like a massive worm, Brian whacks him in the head again and keeps shovelling, until the grave is full and Brian can put in the squares of grass he cut out two days ago. He doesn't waste time making the plot look new or watering it; the grass will grow and set all on its own.

Brian waits a few minutes, just to be sure a hand doesn't poke out of the grass.

Satisfied, he takes the shovel with him and runs to his car, putting the shovel in the back.

He takes the riverside road out of town, starting the long drive to Weymouth, where he can take the ferry to Jersey.

He wonders who the locals will blame for Father Dougald's disappearance.

They'll probably point the finger at me, he thinks.

But Brian really couldn't care less. He's gone.

Just before passing the cottage, he sees Clint walking along the river path towards town. Brian honks the horn and waves. Clint waves back.

Marty

Friday.

Marty is driving home. The rush hour traffic has petered out, leaving a steady flow of cars rather than the usual bumper-to-bumper congestion. It's one of the benefits of working late, and she frames that narrative with her as the smart one, the strategic thinker and diligent worker, patiently waiting for the traffic to clear before starting for home.

Not someone chained to the desk. A person merging with a computer. Someone scared to be seen leaving too early. That's not the narrative she wants.

Her phone rings. She presses the little receiver symbol on the steering wheel.

"Marty speaking."

"This is Janice. I'm sorry to bother you, but I'm having problems."

Marty lets out a disgruntled sigh. "With?"

"The presentation. I can't get the multimedia bits inside. I keep losing them."

"The whole thing will be useless without the videos and animations."

"I know. I'm trying, Marty."

"The guys I'm presenting to don't really understand words. But pictures they get. Graphs and charts and videos and cartoons. They need to be visually entertained."

Janice doesn't reply. Marty can hear her typing.

"Look. Just send me what you've done and I'll finish it over the weekend."

"But you said you were busy all weekend."

"I am. But this presentation is too important. Email it to me and go home, Janice. Go home and enjoy your weekend. We all work far too much as it is."

"Okay. Thanks, Marty."

Janice hangs up.

Marty pulls into her suburban street thinking it's time to get a new assistant. Someone younger, who's good with computers. She could frame the narrative by telling Janice her abilities could be better deployed in other departments of the company. Yes, Marty thinks, that's the way to tell that story. Get her transferred to some innocuous department like HR or accounting, and help Janice better manage her own personal brand in the process.

She parks in the driveway and scoops up her laptop from the passenger seat. Through the front windows, she can see Avril and Zabrina playing some kind of charades game with Fiona. The babysitter's an aspiring actress and often plays such games with the girls. Marty's okay with it; better than sitting in front of some screen. She watches from the car, briefly. Fiona checks her watch a few times.

Yes, Marty thinks, I'm late. That's what it means to be a Brand Strategist. Long hours, working on weekends, too. And you've probably got more important places to be than in my living room, playing with my kids.

She feels suddenly old, as if life is on fast forward, and that she's reached that awful point where there's no reason to have dreams any more. All she can do now is pave the way for others, encourage the dreams of Avril and Zabrina; provide the means for them and then step out of the way.

Let them dream, Marty thinks, but keep the narrative real.

Fiona has a dream, and it's one she'll probably never reach. Marty knows if Fiona gets some kind of acting break, she'll lose the one babysitter who's actually worked out. Marty hopes things won't get to the point where sabotage may be required, on her part.

She enters the house and it's a blur of greetings and smiles and hugs. Fiona babbles something. Avril and Zabrina talk at once. Avril holds up a spelling test that's got a gold star on it. Zabrina shows Marty a picture she drew; it could be a horse, or an elephant, or a combination of the two. A horse-elephant, which Marty thinks would be the most interesting. A horsephant.

Fiona leaves.

Marty dumps her stuff on the kitchen table and takes a fork from the drawer. She pokes at the tuna risotto Fiona made, not bothering to heat it up or add the necessary pinch of salt. Avril and Zabrina continue talking. The school day, this kid doing something to that kid, the afternoon with Fiona. Zabrina boasts that they didn't watch any TV. And this gets Marty thinking about television. Specifically, about viewer recognition television. VRTV. Advertising that's disguised as entertainment. Advertainment. But branded content is what they're calling it internally. The viewer sits down and the content that's watched gets manipulated by that viewer. It's interactive. And it's evil, profitable and a total invasion of privacy. And it can't ever be worded as a kind of advertising, because viewers would then rebel against it. It has to be entertaining content.

She wonders how to frame the narrative of VRTV, to convince brands to buy into it. She knows end-consumers will require a different narrative to get them watching and keep them watching.

She needs to get started on the presentation.

"Okay," she says. "Time for bed."

Both girls whine, especially Avril. At nine years old, she's starting to expect preferential treatment over her six year-old baby sister.

"Come on," Marty says, herding them towards the bathroom. "Big day tomorrow. You need to be rested for it. Your dad's picking you up at eight."

"I don't wanna go," Avril says. "I wanna spend the day with you."

"Me too," Zabrina says.

"That's really sweet of you. We got Sunday remember. Anyway, you know the drill. Saturdays with dad. I don't agree with it either, but that's how it is. Now, brush teeth, wash hands and jump into bed."

"Tell us a story?" Zabrina asks.

"Didn't Fiona entertain you enough?"

"Please?"

There goes another hour, Marty thinks.

Avril joins in. "Please, mum?"

"I thought you liked reading your own books."

"Your stories are better," Avril says. "When we get them."

"Careful with that tone, Av. Okay, you twisted my arm. Get ready for bed and let's meet in Zabrina's room. Bring a blanket, Av. One for me too."

In the kitchen, Marty turns her computer on and gets her presentation open. The version Janice has sent her is a total mess. She pours some wine into a plastic cup and, after hearing the girls yell out for her, takes this into Zabrina's room.

Avril and Zabrina are huddled in bed together. Avril's got an arm around Zabrina, pulling her close. Marty hopes Avril will always be so protective, that the girls will always be so close.

"Think you can stay awake?" Marty asks, trying to push away her sudden feelings of sadness.

"If the story's good," Avril says.

"Ah, you're putting me under pressure. You get that pushiness from me, you know."

The girls laugh.

Marty sits down on the edge of the bed, then shimmies her way backwards until she's sitting against the wall. She pulls the blanket over her legs. Turning to the girls, she gets a close up of the bunny wallpaper that Greg decorated this room with. He'd done it as a surprise, before Avril was born. Marty hated the wallpaper. Hated it that Greg had just made the decision, and so many other decisions, without asking her. The beginning of the end started with that bunny wallpaper. All these men in her life, at home and at work, deciding things for her, ruling over her. Sure, Greg was long gone, if not completely out of her life, but her work was still very much male-dominated.

She sips her wine, thinking that the plastic cup makes it taste less like wine. "What kind of story do you want?"

"Something fantastic," Avril says.

"With princesses," Zabrina adds.

"A fantasy world. With strange animals and strange people."

"And princesses."

Another sip. "Okay, well, let's say that, yeah, far, far away, in a distant part of the universe, there's a world a lot like this one. Except there are some things that are different."

Marty looks towards the window. It's dark outside, and the window is a blank canvas she can paint her imagination on. The world appears before her.

"It's a planet," she says, "exactly like this one. With all the same continents and countries and oceans and mountains. All the same animals and trees. The only difference is that on this planet, women are in charge."

"What's the planet called?" Avril asks.

Marty continues staring at the window, seeing the planet. It's like the view of earth as seen from space. Then, it zooms in, and she sees the continents, the lay of the land, the city where she lives. Street level. Women. Happy women. Confident, strong and straight-backed.

She has a vague recollection of some weird sci-fi show she saw as a kid.

"Mum?"

"Huh? Oh, what's it called? What do you think? Earth?"

"But it's different," Avril says. "You said it's different."

"It is. It's the woman's earth. Her earth. Herth. That's it. Without the A. H-E-R-T-H. Herth."

Avril smiles. "That's so awesome."

"Yeah. Very awesome," Marty says. She looks at her girls. "And because Herth is ruled by women, life is very different to here. There are no wars. There is no fighting whatsoever. Everyone is looked after. Everyone has what they need. Women hold all the important positions in society."

"What about the boys?" Avril asks.

"Well, yeah, the boys. Okay. So men are part of society, but they're mostly involved in, with, you know, they work and they take care of the household. They do the shopping and the cleaning. They're too small and weak and emotionally fragile to be making important decisions. And the men, the boys, they aspire to be good partners, for the women. They want to be hard workers, and they want to look good and attractive so a woman selects them to be a partner. But there's no marriage. Because there's no religion on Herth. Never was. Yeah, that's good. No religion. There's no need to believe in some higher power. To blame something else when things go wrong. The women have always solved problems themselves. There was never the need to pray for help. To externalise the blame. That's why the planet has always lived in peace. There were never any gods to fight over. Conflicting beliefs to die for. There was no colonisation. No empires and invasions. All of the world's native peoples still survive."

Marty sees that this advanced piece of thinking goes over her daughters' heads and decides to dial it back a little. Zabrina is starting to fall asleep. Avril's trying hard to stay with it, but looks a bit confused.

"Are there any princesses?" Avril asks.

Hearing the word, Zabrina snaps awake. "Are there?"

"No, not in the way we would think about it. But there are special girls. They're not princesses, but they are different from the other girls. Special. A princess is born a princess and there's nothing special about her except her parentage. But these girls, they're special because they really are special. They're smarter, more talented, more beautiful, more daring and brave. And on Herth, there are two such girls. Sisters actually."

"Really?" Zabrina asks.

Marty nods. "They look just like you do, and have your names too. And these two very special girls are going to save Herth."

"From what?" Avril asks.

"What do you think? What kind of trouble could Herth have?"

"Um. Something dangerous?"

"That's good. Like a disaster? A danger they can't see. Something unknown and mysterious. Oh, yes. Herth is in trouble. There are evil forces rising. It will be up to Avril and Zabrina to save the world from this evil. Because a rebellion is coming. A big rebellion. There's one bad person who's threatening to bring an end to Herth's peaceful existence."

Zabrina pulls the blanket up to her chin.

"But the girls don't really know yet how special they are. They don't know about the coming dangers, or about the mission they will go on. They're normal girls, at the moment. They go to school with all the other kids."

"Are there boys at school?" Avril asks.

"Yes, of course there are. But only until the boys, you know, until they change."

"Change? How do they change?"

"Ah, well, let's just say they stay at school until they're twelve years old. Then they leave to join the workforce."

"I don't like boys," Zabrina says.

"Well, these boys are at school for a while, because everyone deserves an education. But the boys are very well behaved. They don't make any trouble for the girls, because the girls rule the schools as well. And it's only girls who go on to university. The boys are needed in the factories and on farms. There's a lot of work for them to do. When they're older, they work for the household."

"Like Fee?" Zabrina asks with her eyes closed.

"Hmm. A bit like Fiona, yes. A man can be a babysitter, but he can also become a woman's partner, if she chooses him. But once chosen, he must do everything she says." Under her breath, Marty adds, "And there'd be no freaking bunny wallpaper, that's for sure."

"What?" Avril asks.

"Nothing. Right, so, I think it's time for you two special girls to have a very special sleep."

"But what about the story? What happens?"

Marty gets up off the bed. "We'll finish it tomorrow."

165

"Oh, mum," Avril whines.

"Come on, Av. Off to bed. Sometimes it's good to wait for things."

Avril slowly gets up. She's careful not to move Zabrina, who's already asleep, and takes her blanket with her. It's Avril who turns the lamp off and Zabrina's nightlight on. This makes Marty frown just slightly, because she'd really like Zabrina to get over her fear of the dark.

"In the time between," Marty whispers to Avril, "you can think about all the different possibilities. You can let your imagination run wild."

Marty follows Avril into her room.

"I like Herth," Avril says as she climbs into bed.

"Me too."

Marty kisses her goodnight and turns the light off.

In the kitchen, she makes a pot of coffee and sits down to work on the VRTV presentation.

***

Saturday.

Marty is driving home. She's happy with her progress today. She's done the shopping and the laundry. She cleaned up the house a bit. She went for a light run.

She's bought a new suit to wear for the presentation on Monday. The sales assistant said the colour is "calming blue."

But she hasn't worked on the presentation. Avoiding, she thinks with a smile, the horsephant in the room.

There's still time. Tonight. Tomorrow night. And there's a good chance Greg will be late, again. Not because he loves spending time with the girls, but just to spite her. She finds it annoying that Greg uses the Saturdays to buy the love of Avril and Zabrina away from her.

She can sit down now and work. The problem is not with organising the slides, which is what Janice struggled with; she can't get a handle on how to frame the narrative of VRTV.

She pulls into her suburban street. It's a safe neighbourhood, but no kids are playing in the street. All the front yards are deserted. Some of the houses are for sale. Only her house has some action out the front: Greg, with a scruffy beard, leaning against his red SUV, and the girls playing with some woman who looks about Fiona's age.

The driveway taken, Marty stops on the street and gets out, leaving the suit she bought in the car, still in its big soft-plastic bag.

Avril and Zabrina run towards her. The three of them have a kind of group hug. Marty bends down and picks Zabrina up. She smells of popcorn.

"Hey, Marty," Greg says.

"You're early." Marty puts Zabrina down, checks her watch and adds, "Well, better said, you're not late."

"We got plans." Greg puts his arm around the woman. "This is Terri."

"Hi," Marty says.

Terri just smiles in reply, rather stupidly, as if she's a bit vacant. Marty thinks that fits. A girl with an IQ in the low two figures would be just about Greg's speed.

"And we gotta go," Greg says, opening the door to his midlife crisis. "Girls, say goodbye to Terri."

Avril and Zabrina wave. Their severe lack of enthusiasm fills Marty with vicious joy.

In the car, Greg lowers the window and says, "Hey, Marty. We're out of town next weekend. Going free-climbing. So, see you in two weeks, okay?"

Marty feels even more joy. "Free-climbing?"

"Yeah, should be a blast. It's Terri's idea. Never tried it before."

"Well, whatever. Have fun. Break a leg."

Greg laughs at this, but awkwardly. His limited sense of humour has him taking Marty's last comment literally. He backs out of the driveway and roars down the road.

"Terri the free-climber," Marty says. "With rocks in her head."

The girls head inside while Marty reverses her car into the drive. She takes the new suit with her, and the other odds and ends she picked up. As she does every Saturday, she's bought a present each for Avril and Zabrina.

Inside the house, the television's on.

"Av, turn it off," Marty says, dumping everything on the kitchen table.

When Avril ignores her, Marty goes to the set and switches it off.

"Hey," Avril shouts.

"You've had enough entertainment for one day. How many movies did your dad take you to anyway?"

"Two," Avril says, pouting and folding her arms.

"That's how he spends time with you? By taking you to the cinema?"

"Dad wasn't even there. He left us with her."

"With Terri?"

Avril nods. "And it was so boring."

Pleased, Marty says with sincerity, "I'm sorry, Av. But you know the rules. No TV tonight."

Avril whines some more, but Marty's not really listening. She's looking at the television, wondering how it would be if that TV could recognise Avril as a viewer, could interact with Avril and make all the content specific to Avril's tastes, and fill it with subtle, targeted advertising. How would she ever get Avril to stop watching?

"Wow," Zabrina shouts from the kitchen. "A colouring book."

Conditioned by several years of Saturday routines, she's found the bag with the presents inside and is clutching the book in her small hands.

"What did you get me?" Avril asks.

Marty smiles. "Something special. Take a look."

Avril runs for the kitchen, but Zabrina's already pulled the present out of the bag.

"That's mine," Avril says, snatching it.

She removes the crude wrapping and unfolds the shirt. It's green, her favourite colour. There's an image of the earth in the middle, shaped as a heart, and the line "Welcome to planet Herth."

"That is so cool," Avril says. She puts the shirt on. "I love it. Thanks, mum."

"I want one too," Zabrina says.

"Next time," Marty says. "I promise. Now, who's hungry?"

Both girls shake their heads.

"Good. At least your dad fed you. With junk?"

"Terri took us to a salad bar," Avril says.

"Oh, well, good. Hot chocolate?"

"Yes," Zabrina says.

Marty gets to work making it.

"Mum," Avril starts, "can you tell us the story again? The Herth story?"

"Yes," Zabrina says.

"Have you been thinking about it, Av?"

She nods.

"Me, too. Okay. Get yourselves comfy on the sofa and I'll bring the hot chocolate."

The girls do so, grabbing blankets and getting snug together. Marty hands them each a mug – Zabrina's has a straw in it – and sits down cross-legged on the floor, with the big TV behind her.

"Well, Herth part two," she says, wondering where to begin. She had a plethora of ideas today, discovered so many creative avenues. The whole Herth universe opened itself up. She imagined a series of books, movies and sequels, merchandise and fan clubs. The story inspiring girls all over the world. Changing the world.

"The special girls," Avril says. "They're gonna save Herth."

"That's right. But before we get to that, we need some context. We need to know more about Herth and its herstory. Because it was not always a peaceful place. You see, long, long ago, it was the men who dominated Herth. At that time, they were stronger and bigger than the women. But they were also selfish and rather stupid."

Avril sips her hot chocolate and asks, "They were?"

"Yeah, and they still are. Very selfish. Because that's how men are. Okay, not all men, but many of them. On Herth. It was like that on Herth. Anyway, a long time ago, the men were always fighting amongst themselves and destroying things. So, the women got together and decided to bring order to the chaos. There was a tremendous battle. Many people died, men and women. But because the women were better organised and smarter and braver, they won the battle. The men were captured and brought into line, and Herth has been peaceful ever since."

"Wow," Avril says.

"Yes. Wow. After that battle, Herth changed for the better. The women were very smart about it. Things were difficult at the beginning, because the men kept fighting back. But with each generation, the situation improved. With women in charge, the structure of society changed. The objectives changed. Instead of living from day-to-day, there was more future planning. And this included making the men weaker and more subordinate."

"How?"

"Good question, Av. What do you think? How do you keep someone from becoming strong?"

Avril considers this. She shrugs and says, "Food?"

Marty smiles. "You are brilliant. Zaby, look at your sister. She's so smart. And you'll be just as smart. You are both so special. Av, you are totally right. The women got control of the food. By feeding the boys less, they didn't grow as much or become as strong. They also controlled their education and trained them from an early age how to behave correctly. As the years passed, women became stronger, and they had the men fully under control. Herth was peaceful. It was a wonderful place to be. But ..."

"But what?"

"What about the princesses?" Zabrina asks.

"There are no princesses. But there are special girls. Like I told you last night, there are two very special girls."

"Sisters," Avril says to Zabrina. "With our names."

"Right. Avril and Zabrina of the planet Herth. And they're about to save the planet. Because even though the men have been controlled for centuries, very well-controlled, ensuring that everyone lives comfortably and in peace, they also haven't forgotten the herstory. They know that they once dominated, and they want to dominate again. It's only that they are too weak, stupid and disorganised." Marty lowers her voice. "But there are evil elements at work. Bad women, working together with rebellious men. These women want men to dominate them. They want to change the order. And there's one especially evil woman."

"What's her name?" Avril asks.

"Hmm. Why don't you give her a name."

Avril folds her arms and says, "Terri."

"Hah. That's great. Terri the Terrible."

The girls laugh. Marty gives Avril a high-five.

"That is just perfect. So, Terri was an awful girl, and she grew up to become a really awful woman. Worst of all, she was very stupid and she was desperate for attention. Okay? Now it gets interesting. Because even though she was totally dumb, she was actually very good at manipulating people. Especially the men. The men worshipped her. And she, er, she kissed all of them."

"Ew," Zabrina says.

"I know. That's why they called her Terri the Terrible. She was also very possessive, so they called her Terri the Territorial as well. And because she could be mean like a little dog, they called her Terri the Terrier." Marty leans forward and tickles both girls. "Grrr. She was a nasty, horrid woman. Grrr."

170

Avril and Zabrina laugh loudly, squirming on the sofa.

"Now, Terri started to get all these men together. And the dumb men just followed her blindly. She took them off into a dark, mysterious forest. It was there they made their camp and they started making plans for a rebellion."

"No," Avril says. "They can't do that."

"It was an awful time. Innocent women were kidnapped and taken to the secret camp. The men were like animals. They were all hairy and wild. They grew beards and they wore black suits with black ties. That was their uniform, you see. A black suit, white shirt and black tie. They called themselves the Black Ties. Because in Herth society, the men were classified by the colour of their ties."

"What does that mean?" Avril asks.

"Well, the tie, you know, it showed the man's status. Okay, say a red tie meant he was chosen by a woman and taken. A white tie showed he wasn't chosen yet. And other colours to signify their jobs and so on."

"What about black ties?"

"It was very bad to wear a black tie. It showed that the man had once been chosen by a woman, but then rejected, for whatever reason. It was the tie of the loser. The criminal. And this is why the rebels wore black ties. Because they were losers. They were society's rejects and cast-offs. And Terri the Terrible was their leader."

Having lost the feeling in her feet, Marty uncrosses her legs and shakes them a little. She does a few stretches.

"Now, this is where our story really begins," she says. "Because there's a brave woman, a truly amazing woman, who volunteers to let herself be captured by the Black Ties in order to find their secret camp. This woman is the mother of the two very special girls."

"That's you," Avril says.

Marty nods. "And because she knows her daughters are so special, she tells them about her plan. Follow the men to their camp and poison their water. She gives them a special magic potion and tells Avril to pour this into their spring. It will make them crazy." Marty pauses for effect. "The girls were scared, but their mother told them to be brave, that they come from a long line of strong, brave women. Herth is counting on them to stop the rebellion."

Zabrina is trying desperately to stay awake. Avril keeps shaking her whenever she nods off.

"The three of them go to the edge of the dark, mysterious forest,"

Marty continues. "Their mother tells them to climb a tree and hide, while she sits and waits for the men to come. It's not until after sunset that the men emerge from the forest and take her into the wooded darkness."

Avril lets out an audible gasp.

Zabrina is snoring softly.

"I think we better put you both to bed," Marty whispers.

"No," Avril shouts.

"Shh. Don't wake your sister." Marty gets to her feet and lifts Zabrina off the sofa. "Come on, Av. We can finish the story tomorrow night. Maybe you can think some more about what might happen."

Avril says, "We will stop the rebellion."

"Well, we shall see, won't we?"

Marty puts Zabrina to bed, reluctantly switching the nightlight on, then goes into Avril's room. Her new shirt is folded neatly on her desk.

"Are you gonna wear it tomorrow?" Marty asks.

Avril nods.

"Excited? The party should be fun."

"Does Zaby have to come?"

"Well, sure. We're a team. We'll all go together."

"Okay."

Marty kisses Avril goodnight and goes into the kitchen. She makes a pot of coffee and turns her laptop on. With the presentation open, she gets to work.

***

Sunday.

Marty is driving home. The traffic is heavy and ponderous. At one point, she sees Greg's SUV, with Terri in the passenger seat, but doesn't point the car out to her girls. It actually gets her thinking about contacting her lawyer, to see if it's possible to place some kind of restriction on Greg's Saturdays. Maybe one per month? Or maybe none at all.

Waiting at a traffic light, a few blocks from home, Marty looks through the back window of the car in front. There's a family inside, two kids in the back. There are screens lodged in the headrests of the front seats. One is showing some kind of cartoon; the other a game. The screens are occupying the attentions of both kids, and it's like there's a wall between the front and back seats. The parents fully disengaged, not even talking to each other. The driver is playing with his own screen, placed in the centre of the dash.

This makes her think about VRTV. Having been up most of the night working on the presentation, the best she could come up with was "the personalisation of television." That's how she's framing the narrative. Reach out and touch your viewer. Get personal with your consumer. Engage, entertain and influence.

It's a good story. She knows it is. One they'll probably be happy to hear. But perhaps not quite emotional enough. It still sounds too invasive. Yet, there's something about VRTV that she's really not liking: this vision of millions of people zombified in front of their screens. And all just to sell products.

A lot like what is happening in the car in front, she thinks. And maybe every other car.

But not this one.

"You girls have fun today?" she asks.

"Yeah," Avril says, though Marty had noted that she'd seemed bored most of the time. She'd even come over to where Marty and Zabrina were doodling and sketching pictures and joined in. That had gone all right until Avril told Zabrina to stop colouring outside the lines. Then Marty, lacking sleep and annoyed with all the divorcee dads hitting on her, had said that Zabrina can colour outside the lines if she wants. That there are no rules saying you can't, and that Avril should let her sister be creative. Avril had gone off in a huff, leaving Marty to wonder just how much standardised schooling was stifling, if not killing, her daughter's creativity. So, she'd run after Avril to talk things out and make it right.

The traffic creeps forward.

Marty yawns. "Sorry," she says. "I'm exhausted."

From the moment they got to the birthday party, Marty had wanted to leave. Zabrina, keen to be involved, had left her to play with the other kids. That's when the dads had swooped, one after the other, like they'd drawn lots. Or maybe they had some kind of twisted bet going on; pick up the single, independent career woman. Once rejected, they became rather nasty, avoiding her and talking about her amongst themselves. She noted that none of them got involved in the party. They were distant parents. She was thankful when Zabrina came back, crying a little because she'd been left out of the games. So, they sat down and did some colouring. Marty sketched possible logos for planet Herth. Then she drew the trees of that mysterious forest where the Black Ties were hidden. And so the hours passed.

Avril is now looking at those very pictures.

"These are so beautiful," she says. "You're really good at drawing, mum."

"Thanks, Av. So are you."

Avril looks closely at one elaborate tree Marty drew, which had a thick trunk and branches like arms, as if the tree would grab anyone who got too close.

"Not good like you," Avril says. "Can I have them?"

"Sure. But they're just scribbles."

Marty pulls the car into the driveway. They gather up all their stuff, including the small gift bags that Avril and Zabrina got, and head inside. Marty is expecting a fight with Avril over watching TV, but to her surprise, Avril joins Zabrina at the kitchen table and does some drawing. Marty watches. Avril sharpens a pencil, then meticulously starts copying the tree that Marty drew. After a few failed attempts, Avril puts Marty's picture underneath a piece of paper and starts tracing it.

Marty makes herself a cup of tea and sits down at the table with her girls. Satisfied that they're occupied, she turns her laptop on.

As she gets the presentation open, Avril says, "I'm ready to enter the forest."

Zabrina looks up. "Me too."

Marty sees that Avril has drawn two stick figures sitting in the tree.

"That's a good hiding place," Marty says.

"What happens next?" Avril asks.

"Hmm. Why don't you tell me?"

Avril writes her name in the bottom right hand corner of the picture and says, "The Black Ties kidnapped their mum."

"That's right."

"There were five of them," Avril continues. "They took her into the forest."

Marty recalls that there were five divorcee dads at the birthday party and wonders if this is a coincidence or not.

"Me and Zabrina waited in this tree." She holds up the picture and points at the two stick figures. "When they were gone, we followed them into the forest."

"And now you're in the forest," Marty says, closing her laptop. "It's very dark. Avril and Zabrina are both scared. They hold hands as they go deeper into the forest. Their mother is leaving a trail of white feathers for them to follow."

"That's clever," Avril says with a big smile.

Marty smiles back. "It takes over an hour to reach the camp. The reason the camp is so hard to find is because you have to walk through a long dark cave to get to it."

"I don't wanna go in there," Zabrina says.

"Don't worry. It's dark, but Avril and Zabrina are going in there together, and they are brave, strong girls. Inside the cave, there are giant bats inside, hanging from the roof, upside down and wrapped in their wings. There are bones on the floor. It smells awful. The girls have to walk through with hands over their mouths. It is the most disgusting place they have ever seen. And it's because the Black Ties have made it that way. In order to stop the women from finding their camp." Marty pauses, looking from one daughter to the other. "With every feather the girls find, they keep going forward. Because they want to find the next feather and because deep in their hearts, they are so very brave. It's inside this cave that they both start to realise how special they are and what kind of strength and power they have."

"Wow." Avril turns to Zabrina and says, "We're gonna get through this cave."

Zabrina nods feverishly.

There's a temptation for Marty to fill the cave with all sorts of obstacles and traps, like a computer game or children's book would, allowing each girl to showcase her special abilities. But she really needs to finish the presentation.

"And that's exactly what they do," Marty says. "They climb very slowly out of the cave and there in front of them is the camp."

"What does it look like?" Avril asks.

"Good question. How would an all-male camp look? A place where all the rejects and losers and evil men live."

"Awful."

Marty nods. "That's right. It was once a beautiful place, a wonderful natural place. But now it's disgusting. There's rubbish and mess everywhere. Some of the men are sleeping in it. From behind a rock, the girls can see it all. It's like something from your worst nightmare. The men have gone feral. There are dead animals and lots of bones."

175

"Ew," Zabrina says.

"Where's Terri?" Avril asks. "Terri the Terrible."

"She's not there. It's very strange. Where could she be?"

"She's a spy," Avril says. "She's spying somewhere."

"Hah. No way. She's not that smart. But maybe she's undercover, luring more rejected men to this place. There's her throne. It's placed on a small precipice, near the waterfall." Marty takes a piece of paper and starts sketching the scene, the precipice, throne and waterfall. "Behind the waterfall is another cave. This is where the captured women are kept. And I don't want to tell you what the men are doing to them."

"What? What?"

"Horrible things. Look. This is where those five men are taking the girls' mother, behind the waterfall and into their cave-prison."

"No."

"Yes. The girls will have to rescue her and all the other women trapped inside. If they can do that, and destroy the Black Ties, they will save Herth from this terrible rebellion."

"How?"

"Do you remember what the mother gave the girls?"

Avril thinks for a moment, then shouts, "Magic. She gave them a magic potion. To put in the water."

"You're brilliant, Av." Marty draws the bottle, shaping it like a deflated balloon. "The girls have to put the magic potion in the water. Because the waterfall is actually a crystal clear spring. All the men drink from it. In the pool below, you can see your reflection perfectly."

"So put the potion in it."

"They can't. There are too many men around. The girls need to wait until all the men are asleep. Only then can they poison the spring."

"They all sleep at once?" Avril asks. "Isn't that a bit stupid?"

"Do you mean that some of them should be keeping watch?"

Avril nods.

Marty is amazed by her daughter's thinking. "You are such a smart cookie, Av. You're right. They should have some men keeping watch, but they're just not that clever. They think their camp is so well-hidden, there's no need to keep watch. And because they're selfish men, they sleep whenever they want."

"Idiots," Avril says. "Boys are so dumb."

"I don't like boys," Zabrina says. "They hit me."

Marty makes a mental note to talk with Zabrina's teacher. If boys are hitting her, and the teacher's not doing anything about it, then she'll encourage Zabrina to fight back. But then she thinks of her busy schedule next week and decides to try to save herself the trip to the school.

"If they hit you," she says, "then hit them back, and hit them harder. Stand up to them."

Avril and Zabrina smile at each other.

"So, the girls hide behind a rock and wait. They're good at waiting. Patience is one of their very special skills. If they don't get the timing right, the men will capture them as well, and all will be lost. So, they wait, holding hands in the darkness." As Marty says this, Avril reaches across the table and Zabrina takes her hand. "They don't even look down at the camp, but they hear it. They hear the men shouting and fighting. It's very difficult not to look because they also hear some women screaming."

Marty sees her daughters' hands gripping each other's tightly.

"It's an awful night for the girls," she continues. "They think about running back through the cave, but they get strength from each other. They make it through this nightmare. The darkness doesn't scare them. Then, when it's very quiet and all they can hear is the waterfall, they look over the top of the rock and see that all the men are asleep. Very slowly, they creep around the rock and make their way to the waterfall. There are some men sleeping on the path and they have to step over and around them. They're repulsive up close, all hairy and smelly. Their suits are filthy and their ties are ragged."

"Yuk," Zabrina says.

"At the waterfall, the girls pour the magic potion into the stream. Nothing happens, and they look at each other, wondering if it worked."

"What do they do?" Avril asks.

"They decide to go back to their hiding place, to sleep and wait until morning. Just like you two."

"What?" Avril jumps in her chair a little. "No. Finish the story. Did the magic potion work?"

Marty puts both her hands on top of her girls' hands. "Tomorrow. I promise. Tomorrow night, I'll tell the final part of the story. But now, it's time for bed. You've got school tomorrow, and I've got a big presentation to give."

"Mu-um," Avril says.

"Hey, Av. Patience is one of your special skills. So, wash hands, brush teeth, don pyjamas and hop into bed."

Avril nods. "Tomorrow night," she says forcefully. "I want an ending."

"You got it."

Still holding hands, Avril leads Zabrina out of the kitchen. Marty is curious to see that neither of them seems remotely scared.

She makes a pot of coffee and turns her laptop back on.

***

Monday.

Marty is driving home. She left work early and is now stuck in traffic.

She's trying to decide if the day was a disaster or not. It had taken her all night, but the narrative she framed the presentation with was spot on; still working the personalisation of television angle, but the beauty was in changing the name to MYTV. That was gold, and it meant she could talk about details. Specific brands for specific consumers. Personalised messages and branded content. All that jargon that the big boys like to hear so much. Yet, those big boys, the brand managers, marketing directors and independent brand consultants, were all very young, and interchangeable. Slim-fitting black suits, three-day growths groomed to scruffy perfection, hair stylishly unkempt. Her brilliant presentation seemed to bore them. They asked questions the answers to which had been given a few slides previously. Many of them played with their phones throughout. A couple of guys stared at her with their arms folded and their mouths slightly open, like hyperactive children forced to sit still.

She yawns.

The traffic is bottlenecking around the entrance to the motorway. She thinks about taking a different route, down the back streets, but doesn't really know the way. This is Greg's hometown, not hers. She plays with the car's all-purpose interactive screen and gets a GPS route to her house. The female voice recommends taking the motorway, but Marty pushes her way off the entry ramp, forcing other drivers to let her in, until she's got some open road. The GPS adapts and tells her to turn around. She keeps driving forward.

Her phone rings. She presses the little receiver button on the steering wheel.

"Marty speaking."

"This is Janice."

Marty sighs. "What's up?"

"Please hold for Tyler."

Marty curses under her breath. Her boss hadn't spoken to her after the presentation; he'd been more concerned with making the necessary guy talk with the more important brand managers and marketing directors.

She has to wait a couple of minutes. Vaguely recognising the area, she makes a right, to cut through an industrial park and get to her suburban enclave the back way. Incredibly, the GPS is still telling her to turn around and go back to the motorway. She switches it off.

"Marty?"

"Hi, Tyler. What can I do for you?"

"Great presentation. Brilliant content. Really. I mean it. The guys loved it."

"But?"

"Yeah, hey, you're sharp. Yep, there's a but. Two actually."

Marty braces herself.

"We were talking about it after. My feelings are it's really important and you should add it to the pres before we send it to everyone."

"What?"

"Come on, Marty. You don't know?"

She knows, but decides to let Tyler say it.

He does a bad Pink Floyd impersonation: "Hey, Marty, we can't leave those kids alone."

"This technology's not for kids," Marty replies.

"Oh yeah it is. That was part of the brief you got. It was on page one in big, bold type. This is all about kids. MYTV – great name, by the way – MYTV was developed with kids in mind."

"I'm sorry, Tyler. I know it was in the brief, but the deeper I got into it, the more I realised that you can't have kids using it. Adults have a choice. They're old enough to make their own decisions, and they're old enough to know better. But kids. You can't put kids in front of this. They won't know where the borders are."

"What planet are you living on? That's the whole point. The differentiation between entertainment and advertising, it disappears. There's just content."

Too angry to drive, Marty pulls over to the side of the road.

"I know," she shouts. "That's why it's not for kids."

"Put it in the pres." Tyler's voice is steady, amused even. "Put it in tonight and send it to me. Tonight. This has gotta go out tomorrow morning."

"Tyler, I really don't think ..."

"It's in, Marty. No discussion."

Marty rubs her eyes and takes a few calming breaths.

"Okay, Tyler. You win."

"Hey, this wasn't a fight, Marty. It should've been in to start with. That's why the pres fell flat. That and the other problem."

"Which was? I thought the presentation went well."

"Yeah, it did. Sort of. Great content, minus the kids bit. But the problem was your presentation."

"What?"

Tyler clears his throat. "This isn't easy for me to say, so I'll just say it. Did you go out and party all night? Because you looked pretty wrecked."

Marty is speechless.

"You know that presenting has as much to do with the quality of the presenter as the content."

"Well, I was, Tyler, I'd been up all night working on it."

"You spent a whole night coming up with MYTV, and then you leave the kids out, which is the most important part? Better off getting some beauty sleep, Marty. Whack in the kids bit and go to bed. You would've looked a bit fresher then. And we would've got the content we needed."

Marty just keeps herself from screaming abuse at Tyler.

"Yeah, okay, Marty? We're all good, I know we are. Fix the pres and send it to me. Ciao."

Tyler hangs up.

A light rain starts to fall. The wipers come on automatically.

Marty pulls the car back onto the road.

She drives for about fifteen minutes, making turns down roads that look right. She gets lost and is forced to switch the GPS back on. The calming female voice directs her back to the motorway, where the traffic has cleared in the meantime.

The drive home is uneventful. She simply responds to the requests of the GPS woman.

She sees Avril and Zabrina standing at the living room window, waiting for her. The television is on behind them, with Fiona watching. When the girls see the car, they wave and come running outside. Avril opens the car door.

"Hi, mum. Hi, mum," she shouts, as does Zabrina.

"Hi, girls. My beautiful, special girls."

Marty hugs them both. They hug her back, and it makes her feel that things are right in the world. For the moment. But after the girls release her, she scoops the laptop off the passenger seat and follows them inside.

She's got work to do.

"Hi, Marty." Fiona says. "They've been at the window all afternoon waiting for you. What's going on?"

Marty turns to Avril, who's wearing her Herth shirt, and asks, "You didn't tell her?"

"No way. It's our story." Avril grins with pride. "Everyone at school asked about my shirt, but I didn't tell. It's our secret."

"You tough little girl." Marty looks at Fiona and adds, "I've been telling them a long story the last couple of days. I promised them the ending tonight."

Fiona puts her coat on. "Is it good?"

"It's awesome," Avril says.

"Me and Av are in it," Zabrina adds.

Avril grabs the hem of her shirt and stretches it. "We're gonna save planet Herth."

"Well, don't let me stop you," Fiona says, opening the door. "See you tomorrow."

When she's gone, Avril and Zabrina run for the sofa. Avril turns the TV off.

"Come on, mum," she says, as the two girls get settled. Avril puts her arm around Zabrina and they both get under the one blanket.

In the kitchen, Marty takes a swig of wine straight from the bottle, then pours some into a plastic cup. After a few steadying breaths, she switches the kitchen light off. In the living room, she lights some candles. As she does so, Avril turns the lamp off.

In the warm candlelight, Marty sits down on the sofa. She gets under the blanket and puts her left arm around Avril and Zabrina.

"I missed you," she says.

Avril and Zabrina nuzzle closer to her.

Marty takes a sip of wine.

"It was a long night," she says. "The girls took turns sleeping, just in case any of the men woke up. The forest made all sorts of noises. Groaning noises, like people in pain. Branches creaked and sometimes snapped. Wolves were howling in the distance."

Marty feels Zabrina shiver under the blanket.

"But the girls weren't afraid of the darkness or the noises. Just before dawn, when Avril was awake and keeping watch, an owl landed on the rock next to her. Barely two metres away. The owl had big eyes and was the colour of snow. It stayed on the rock for several minutes. Avril took this as a good sign, because when the owl flew away, it left a small pile of white feathers. The same kind of feathers the girls' mother had left as a trail."

"Wow," Avril says.

"And Avril knew then that the magic had worked, that they just had to wait for the men to drink from the water. They needed to be patient. To stay hidden behind the rock and wait." Marty takes another sip of wine. "When light finally came, they heard some of the men waking up. They looked over the top of the rock, just enough to see and not be seen. In the light, the girls saw that the waterfall landed in a very large pool. Already there were men sitting by the pool, staring at the water. Just sitting there, staring, not moving. The girls looked at each other, wondering what was going on. They watched one man walk to the spring, bend down and scoop up some water. He drank, then started to walk away. But he stopped. He sat down at the pool and started staring at the water."

"It works," Avril says to Zabrina. "The magic potion works. They're all dead."

"No, they're not," Marty says. "They're still very much alive. But they're not moving. It's like they're frozen in place, sitting by the pool. The two girls waited until all the men had drunk and sat down. It was a very strange scene, to see all those men sitting around the water. And it was then the girls realised that the Black Ties weren't such a big group after all. They were maybe a hundred all together, if that."

"They need to rescue the others," Avril says.

"That's right. With all the men by the pool, the girls walked slowly down the path and behind the waterfall. They were careful not to touch the water. They know it's the pool that's poisoned, but they're smart enough not to take any chances. When they were inside the cave, they found where the women were being held. They were in a crude cage made of wood and rocks. The girls got it open and their mother hugged them both so hard. All the women were happy. Some were very thin from lack of food, and they had cuts and bruises from different kinds of punishments. They were also tired and not looking very fresh, but their spirits were strong. They helped each other out of the cave. The girls led the way, followed by their mother. It was Avril who warned them not to drink the water. Seeing the men by the pool, some of the women wanted to go down and kill them. But the girls' mother stopped them. She explained that they will die slowly. 'They're hypnotised by their own reflection. That's what they're staring at,' she said. 'We'll leave them here to die and get eaten by animals.' And the women left the pool behind and entered the other cave."

"Yes," Avril says. "We did it."

Marty nods. "But it's not over yet. Because in the cave, the group encountered another group."

"Oh no."

"It was Terri the Terrible. She was bringing a group of men back to the camp. New recruits for the Black Ties, all of them with black suits and beards. And even though they were tired and hungry and battered, the women started to fight. All of their anger from being kidnapped and tortured came out. They fought so bravely. They worked together to kill the men. In the battle, Terri threw a rock that hit the girls' mother in the head. Then she tried to run away. She grabbed the two girls and tried to run, but the girls fought back. They kicked Terri repeatedly in the shins. Kicked her and kicked her until she fell. They were kids and she was a grown woman, but they were stronger and more fierce than her."

"Yeah," Zabrina shouts.

All three of them laugh.

"But she wasn't dead," Marty says. "The girls' mother said to leave her in the cave. Leave her where she is. They started walking out of the cave. Once outside, they stopped."

"Why?" Avril asks.

"Because Avril said they needed to close the cave somehow. The women discussed the possibilities. But it was little Zabrina who said the bats could do it."

Zabrina smiles brightly. "Really?"

"Yes, really. And the women knew what to do. If they could get the bats moving, get them really panicking, then they might destroy the cave. So, they gathered up some wood and went back into the cave. They put all the dead men together and covered them with wood. Terri was still unconscious. They threw her on top and set the whole thing on fire. It burned very quickly. And once it was burning, Terri woke up and started moving, but she was on fire. She tried to run, but the fire was too strong and it burned that wicked young witch. The fire woke the big bats as well, and they started flying around crazily, bumping into the walls and fighting with each other. Because these bats were the size of dogs, and there were hundreds of them. The walls of the cave started to shake and the group of women ran for it. But they were still so weak and tired. They had to help each other. Rocks started falling and there were crazy bats flying over their heads. They made it out of the cave just as the entrance was closed off."

Marty feels her two girls breathe out at once, and sneaks a look at the TV's digital clock. It really is time for the girls to go to sleep.

"They did it. They rescued the women and crushed the rebellion. Herth was saved. The two girls were awarded the highest honour for their bravery. And both girls would go on to become important leaders. More restrictions were put on the men, to prevent any further rebellions. Herth became an even more peaceful and happy place. And that's the end of the story."

Avril and Zabrina stare at her, taking it all in. Marty wonders if Zabrina got it.

"That was so good, mum," Avril says. "You should write books. And draw the pictures too. A picture book. All about Herth."

Marty yawns, and this makes the girls yawn as well.

"Worth the wait, wasn't it?" Marty asks.

"Definitely."

"Can you sleep?"

"Sure."

"Sure," Zabrina echoes.

"All right. Well, off to bed. I'll come in and say goodnight in a minute. Av, help your sister."

Avril does so, taking Zabrina by the hand and leading her out of the living room.

Marty blows out the candles and takes her wine into the kitchen, where she turns the light on and fires up her laptop. She fills her plastic cup and has a long sip. On the table are the pictures she drew yesterday. She looks at them, briefly, before heading for Zabrina's room. She's already in bed and asleep, without the nightlight on.

Avril is also in bed, and in darkness. Marty stands in the doorway.

"Mum?" Avril asks.

"Yes?"

"I don't think I wanna see dad anymore."

"Oh."

"Or Terri."

"Hmm. Let's talk about it in the morning. Goodnight, Av."

Back in the kitchen, Marty sits down and gets to work on the presentation.

Gregor

The recruitment agency is on the twelfth floor.

He's early and is told by the receptionist to wait. She points down the hallway, to two chairs placed next to the closed door of the interviewer's office. They look like they were put there this morning. They fill this narrow section of the hallway, seem out of place and temporary. To Gregor, they resemble the chairs outside a principal's office. But once seated, the chairs take Gregor back to all those drug tests, when he sat in a chair placed near a toilet and waited until it was his turn to go inside and piss into a special bottle in front of half a dozen people; when his legs were shaking, every joint hurt and he was exhausted, filthy and more often than not disappointed with his result, and all he wanted was to shower, eat and sleep. After fifty kilometres of race-walking, his urine always had a milky colour that caused the six observers to exchange glances and mumble in languages Gregor didn't understand. He'd once passed a small kidney stone during a test, screaming in agony, and this stone was put in a sealable plastic bag and taken away for examination.

Those days are over, the racing, the testing. Gregor's still not sure how he feels about it. His whole adult life devoted to walking, and never getting to the finish line first when it really mattered. Three hip operations, two knee arthroscopies, one herniated disc, constant cartilage problems in his left knee, bone spurs on his right ankle. Blisters upon blisters. His life rhythm dictated by base training, build up, race-readiness and recovery, and by a multitude of comebacks. Not to mention the crappy part-time jobs and the begging for a sponsorship or funding pittance.

He hopes the interviewer won't ask questions about it. Nobody gets race-walking, even after long explanations from an Olympian.

The door opens and a woman comes out. She's about Gregor's age, broad and heavy-set, muscular under her business clothes, which don't sit well on her. She doesn't smile at Gregor. If anything, she gives him a competitive stare. Then she walks down the hallway with a wide-legged, heel-toe stride, moving like an athlete. A power athlete, Gregor decides, a thrower perhaps. Or a lifter. An obscure event like weightlifting or shot-put, where funding is scarce and life is hard. Whatever it was, he thinks she's in the same boat; a retired athlete from a non-glamour event with no degree now trying to find a job.

She looks vaguely familiar. He wonders if he saw her at an airport, or at one of the ceremonies, or sat near her at an information session. Perhaps their younger selves had once swapped a bored glance at one of those tedious protocol meetings.

But then he thinks that a lot of power athletes look alike. The way swimmers do, and long-distance runners, and sprinters. How they always clustered together; different heads, but cloned physiques.

He assumes all the candidates for this position are in the same boat as he is, have all been recommended by contacts at the Ministry for Sport.

A head appears in the doorway, balding, smiling, the face slightly shiny.

"Gregor?" he asks.

Gregor stands and buttons his borrowed suit jacket, which is a bit baggy around his chest and waist.

"Come on in."

The office is small, with one narrow window which extends from the floor to the ceiling. The window is open, and there's a waste-paper basket placed on the floor to keep it open. The sounds of the city make it up the twelve floors and through the narrow gap. There's an orderly desk, with a closed laptop and several trays for papers and applications. In the corner behind the door, there's a circular coffee table with two chairs.

Gregor feels sorry for the recruiter. He can't imagine working here, day after day, reviewing applications and interviewing people. Arrive at the same time, regular lunch hour, go home again when the day is done. Eight hours sitting in a chair, at a desk, working.

The team-appointed therapist told him he would get used to an office job; that he would find the rhythm and adapt to life after sport.

Rather than sitting at the desk, the interviewer offers Gregor a seat at the coffee table. The chair is wedged into the corner and there's not a lot of leg space. Gregor, who's rather tall and gangly, which is unusual for a race-walker, sits and tries to get comfortable. The chair is warm. He reminds himself about the importance of positive body language, looking good, sitting with style and executing with form.

Contact, he tells himself. Keep contact and no negative thoughts.

The interviewer retrieves Gregor's CV from one of the desk's trays and takes the chair opposite. He crosses his legs and puts the CV in his lap.

"Thanks for coming. I hope you didn't wait long."

Gregor smiles and shakes his head.

"I got your details from Jarvis Haynes. He spoke highly of you."

"We went to school together," Gregor says. "We ran track. But we lost contact for a while, when Jarvis went off to university."

"Yeah, that happens. People's lives take them in different directions." The interviewer flips through the CV, frowns a little. "You didn't go to university."

"I decided to pursue an athletic career instead."

"Like the other sportspeople going for this job. All play and no work."

"I worked," Gregor says.

"Yes, I can see it here. Quite an ensemble of jobs. You delivered pizzas, stacked supermarket shelves, drove a van for a dry-cleaners. You were a bike courier for half a year. A porter in a hotel. All of them part-time jobs."

"Well, obviously I needed the flexibility. I had to earn money, but I also had to have a job that gave me time to train. And to travel. There's always a lot of travel involved, getting to races and meets." Gregor shifts in his chair, his right shin hitting the coffee table as he adds, "There was. I'm not travelling anymore."

"So, you're settled here. Retired from," he checks the CV, "race-walking?"

"Yes. I'm done with all that. I'm ready to work. Very motivated."

"Good, good. But you might be a bit too late. Because you're," checking the CV again, "thirty-six, and you don't have any tertiary qualifications or training."

"I'd be more than willing to do courses on the side, further training and night school, if necessary. I know I'm up against it, but I'm no stranger to overcoming adversity."

"Can you elaborate on that? Beyond the sporting analogies. I've heard enough of them for one day."

"I don't know if I can. Without making reference to sport? That's difficult. Sport's all I've ever known."

The interviewer looks disappointed. "Give it a try. Think back to all those part-time jobs. What were some of the things you learned?"

"I'll be honest. I only listed some of them on my application. I actually had a lot more." Gregor lets out a short laugh, but the interviewer doesn't respond. "What I learned is that everyone wants you to be reliable, no matter what the job. But if you're an athlete, you can't always be reliable, because you have to train and race. If you want to be the best, you have to sacrifice. Your sport takes priority over everything, and that requires discipline."

"Yeah, yeah. That's what they all said. But you made those choices, and now you sit here almost forty without much of a chance apart from taking some menial, unskilled job." The interviewer puts the CV on the coffee table, uncrosses his legs and leans forward. "Look, Gregor, I owe Jarvis a favour, but you need to give me more to work with. The position you're going for requires you to do research and to review grant applications."

"I know. I believe I can do that. I made such applications, every year, to get funding. And I was successful a few times. I know what to look for, and I'm now in the position to be reliable."

"Which is why we're sitting here. But do you think you're up for it? Working. The daily grind. You've never had a full-time job, Gregor. You'll be working for the government. They'll expect you to be reliable."

Gregor becomes defensive, and his competitive instinct kicks in. "I'm retired, all right? There's no sport to hold me back. I'm not racing. I don't have the travel commitments. I'm not even training anymore. Well, I'm tapering, but that will end in a few months. It's not a big deal."

"Tapering?"

"Training down. It's just as important as building up towards a big event. You also have to train down, otherwise your body goes haywire."

"I didn't know that. It's interesting."

"It's actually very boring."

"Why's that?"

"Because there's no goal to train towards. When you're building up, you're heading towards something. You're motivated. Training down is like the opposite. It's all over. There's no goal except your own health. That's important, but not quite the same as training to win an Olympic gold."

"You didn't win gold."

"No. I didn't."

"And you only went to one Olympic Games, which was earlier this year. At age 36."

"I qualified for other games," Gregor explains, "but I had injuries and wasn't able to compete."

"Sorry to hear that."

"But there's the adversity. Coming back from the injuries and disappointments. All that work to go from the bottom back to the top."

"And you finished," checking Gregor's CV, "eighth."

"Ninth, really. The American who won silver tested positive and the rest of us jumped up a place. That's why I got the diploma."

The interviewer flips the CV to the last page. "I was wondering about that. I had no idea they did this. The Olympic diploma. Does everyone get it?

"Only places fourth to eighth. I didn't know about it either, until it arrived in the post."

The interviewer holds up the diploma. "It's fancy."

"I know it's not the same as getting on the podium, but I'm proud of it. I went to the Olympics and finished in the top ten."

"You're right. Fancy as it is, it's not like winning a medal."

Gregor bristles. He's heard this too many times; whenever people find out he went to the Olympics, they all expect him to be a medal-winner.

"Can you imagine being in the top ten of something?" he asks, just keeping his anger in check. "Of all the people in the world, you're in the top ten. You, for example, are one recruiter in a world full of recruiters. There are thousands of you. Are you in the top ten? Imagine how hard you would have to work and how much you would have to sacrifice just to get into the top ten in this country. And then try to get in the top ten in the world. You'd have no social life. No relationships. Your whole life becomes about being the best recruiter in the world, and everything else is secondary."

The interviewer sits back and considers this. Gregor know it's a concept most people just don't get: actually being the best in the world at something. Many think they're one of the best at what they do, but are simply judging themselves against their own small, limited world. They can't fathom a whole world of people out there better than them.

"Hmm," the interviewer says. "Now that's an analogy I can understand."

"It's a sporting one," Gregor says, "but it can be applied to all facets of life. A person's level, no matter what we're talking about, is always relative. The best race-walker from this country may finish dead last in an international competition. Or they get disqualified for lifting, because they can't keep up the pace."

"Lifting?"

"When your feet lose contact with the ground. When you fly."

"Ah. You know, Gregor," the interviewer says, much friendlier now, more conversational, "I've watched walking at the Olympics. It's such a strange race. Why do you walk the way you do? The whole thing with the hips and the elbows. It looks bizarre."

Gregor shrugs. "Those are the rules. Your legs have to straighten from the point of contact, and stay straight. That's what makes the pelvis rotate. When you try to do that at speed, pumping your arms as well, I'll admit it looks weird. Especially when you get fifty guys all doing it at once, all of them trying to maintain good form at high speeds. Form is very important. That's why I could never train in public, because people stared and kids would run after me and make comments."

"I bet. So how did you train?"

"Running. I did walking drills on the track, with other race-walkers. We were behind closed doors, so we could look like idiots without being insulted."

The interviewer laughs.

"Believe me," Gregor adds with a smile, "it's not as easy as it looks."

"I don't think it looks easy. It doesn't look natural either. You all look like you're just keeping yourselves from breaking into a run."

Gregor nods. "That's about right. And that's why guys get the red paddle for lifting, because they fall behind and start running a little."

"So, the discipline is to walk and not run?"

"Yes. Something like that. But those days are over for me. My tapering is all about running."

The interviewer snaps his fingers. "That's good. You're willing to change. To move forward, hah, at a faster pace. That's something I can use. You've got passion too. And you're willing to do extra training, the hard stuff, like your taping."

"Tapering."

"Right. Also good. Gregor, you really should think about getting qualified, working towards a degree, part-time. Economics and analytics would fit the position. Throw in some sociology for good measure. Politicians and civil servants love that stuff. It might cost some money, but it'll be well worth it."

"All right," Gregor says, really not liking the sound of all that.

"Best to get signed up before your interview at the ministry, to show your commitment. Make it look like you're really serious about the position, long-term."

Gregor nods.

"That will give you something to say," the interviewer continues, "when they ask you the inevitable question of where you see yourself five years from now."

"Why five years?" Gregor asks.

The interviewer shrugs. "That's just the question. Is it a problem? Don't let it be a problem, Gregor. I owe Jarvis."

"It's not a problem. I just ... I always thought in terms of four years. From Olympics to Olympics. You'd start at the end of one and set up a plan to make the next, in four years time."

The interviewer stands up. "That's also good. More forward thinking. Find a way to apply that to the position. Put that together with your studies to come up with a four-year plan. They'll love that. Also talk about giving back to the ministry, because of the funding they gave you. Be extra grateful."

Gregor wonders why the interviewer is helping him, beyond the favour to Jarvis. He's not even sure he wants the help. As the interviewer extends his hand, Gregor stands and shakes it.

"Thanks," Gregor says. "What's next?"

"You'll be one of the two applicants I recommend." The interviewer moves around his desk, sits down and flips open his laptop. "You're actually the best of a pretty ordinary bunch. Why don't you athletes go to university when you're not training? Plan for the future? You can't play sport forever, and none of the sportspeople I interviewed even won a medal, including you. All that effort for nothing. Anyway, how it goes from there depends on you. It would be really smart to sign up for a part-time degree in the meantime. Get that four-year plan sorted."

"I will, I will."

"And buy a new suit. One that fits. You'll want to make a good impression. It's the Ministry for Sport, Gregor. Appearances count."

"Okay."

"Thanks for coming in." The interviewer starts typing and doesn't look up as he adds, "You should probably buy Jarvis a beer as well."

Gregor nods. "Have a good day."

He leaves the office and closes the door. The two chairs are gone.

He walks down the hallway. After a few steps, he almost gets into his race stride, straightening his legs and pumping his arms slightly. The balls of his feet are still strong, his pelvis limber. He feels that familiar twinge in his left knee; it's almost comforting. As he speeds down the hallway, past all the closed doors, he thinks that with a serious training regime, he could easily get back to top form, and qualify for the Olympics at age forty. It would give his life structure again, a rhythm he knows, goals he can aim towards, a four-year plan he wants.

He reaches the elevator, presses the button, circles around and stops.

"What's with the funny walk?"

Gregor turns to the receptionist. "Huh? Oh, just a bit of a celebratory stroll. You know, if you're gonna walk, you should walk in style."

"You call that style? You look ridiculous."

"Well, it, that kind of walk, it took me all the way to the Olympics."

The receptionist smiles, seems rather impressed. "Did you win a medal?"

Her phone rings, preventing Gregor from launching into a tirade. The receptionist answers it.

"Yes, Mr Haynes," she says, "I'll put you through."

As the elevator doors open, Gregor thinks he now owes Jarvis as well, and probably more than just a beer. How soon will Jarvis call in that favour? What will he want?

The sadness hits as the elevator descends: his retirement, his failed career, losing the one thing he'd defined his life by.

A man gets in on the eighth floor and his presence keeps Gregor from letting go of his emotions.

When the elevator reaches the ground floor, Gregor hesitates, pondering briefly if he should take it back up to the twelfth floor, squeeze through the interviewer's skinny window and jump.

But people are waiting to get in, forcing him to exit the elevator.

Outside, Gregor buys a bottle of water from a kiosk and starts walking home. It's not really home; he's been couch-surfing since coming back from the Olympics. He gave up his apartment, sold his car, sold everything he had in order to pay his way to the Games. And came home with nothing but a bunch of souvenirs and autographs. No one met him at the airport. He took the train to the city, then the bus to his father's house in the country. His dad was proud, yet clearly disappointed, to the point Gregor could stand it no longer and took the bus back to the city. He looked for work. He slept in youth hostels, sharing bunk beds with teenage backpackers. He tapered. He called in favours, looking for places to stay, for help. Jarvis was a long shot, but one that turned out to be useful.

Gregor knows this could be his last chance. He has to do everything the interviewer recommended, no matter what the cost. He doesn't want to end up as one of those athletes, retired, with no direction, unable to adapt to normal life, taking the elevator up to the twelfth floor and jumping. Or having to resort to drugs and alcohol, longing for days past. Or worse, coming out of retirement for one more shot at glory.

He walks slowly down the street. Ambling and drinking his water. Early-finishing workers are spilling out onto the pavement, walking fast. He could fly past them, if he wanted to.

And he thinks it's good he didn't win a medal. Didn't reach so high to have so far to come back down. The top ten isn't nothing. Disappearing into obscurity is okay, and made easier when you're obscure to start with.

Gregor stops in the middle of the pavement. There are more people now, walking from both directions, around him and passing him. He closes his eyes and enjoys this stationary moment. The contact of both feet planted firmly on the ground.

John

The man wakes up, naked and strapped to an operating table. He blinks slowly and tries to move.

Already in his scrubs, and with a surgical mask just below his chin, John stands over the man and holds up a battered photograph.

The man's eyes narrow, focusing. His arms struggle against the straps as he regains more of his strength.

"Have you seen this girl?" John asks.

The man looks away.

"Is that a yes? I guess you've looked at a lot of young girls. Can't even tell them apart anymore."

The man laughs, somewhat bitterly. He lifts his head to look around. "Where am I?"

"You're about to die," John says. "I'm going to give you another dose of ketamine, to knock you out. Then, I'm going to remove your organs and put them in those special cold-storage containers. I'll start with your kidneys, and then I'll take your liver, pancreas and lungs."

When this information sinks in, the man really starts to struggle against the straps. The operating table is bolted to the floor and doesn't move.

"Don't worry," John says calmly. "I'm not going to take out your heart. I couldn't live with someone walking around the world with your heart."

"Help! Help!"

"And what's left of you will be fed to the razorbacks. I've been starving them for a few days. They're ravenous."

The man screams some more, and struggles.

"Finally, I'll clean everything up so the practice is ready for work tomorrow. Then I'll have a shower, some dinner, deliver the organs and go to bed."

"Oh, God. Help!"

John holds up the photo again.

"Have you seen this girl?"

"Who the hell is she?"

"She's my daughter," John says, and he jams the needle into the man's arm.

~~~

It started with a list. John at age thirty-seven, listing all the reasons why he was unhappy:

Sexless marriage.

Can't connect with daughter.

Veterinary practice only mildly successful.

Spend most days dealing with sick dogs.

Don't sleep enough.

Married to someone who's become a stranger.

Pursued by demons.

Worse for John was the keeping up of pretences. Every day, he got up to be someone he wasn't and to live a life that wasn't his. And the days blended into a jumbled mass marked only by the steady growth of his increasingly distant daughter.

But then there was that other list, the intangibles, the what-ifs. All the things he could have done and had wanted to do: the wild dreams, secret desires, crazy wishes and missed opportunities.

It wasn't a long list, but it was telling, and he kept it very secret. It was the list of another John. The John who was kept locked away.

For years, John was on autopilot. He was acting too, pretending to love and pretending to cherish. Showing fatherly pride despite its absence. Feigning community interest and awareness when he had none. Maintaining friendships he didn't care for. Healing animals he considered more suited for burial.

His one solace was the farm. The chores and the animals. He especially enjoyed the time spent with his razorbacks. In the sty, John could almost be himself.

That was another list: all the reasons wild boars were better company than people.

His wife had affairs, but he didn't care. He looked the other way, kept up the pretences. He did his duties as father and husband. He paid the mortgage. He signed permission slips for his daughter's school excursions. He went to dinner parties and events, was witty and amicable when required. He wore the hideous pullovers his wife knitted for him. He smiled a lot, and tried to be genuine.

Around the town, John was very well liked. He was reliable and trustworthy. He was very good with animals.

But John was fully aware that he was almost dead inside.

~~~

John watches the boars devour what's left of the man. It takes about twelve minutes. Every now and then, a boar looks up at him, chewing, and he swears the animal is smiling. Thankful and appreciative, the previous days of starvation forgiven by this veritable feast.

"There'll be more," he says.

The boars leave nothing.

Back inside the house, he crosses the man's name off the list. Despite his endeavours, the list continues to get longer, as these guys always seem to know other guys like them and have no qualms about shouting out their names just before John jabs them one last time with ketamine. The hope being that the guilty party will be named, thus sparing the man strapped to the surgical table.

What started out as a handful of possible suspects in the county area had grown to include nearby counties and bordering states. John knows the further he expands his reach, the more names will be added to the list.

Because these guys are everywhere, living normal lives, sheltered by their pretences.

John doesn't know what's happened to all the organs. The Rep takes care of that. John simply delivers the cold storage containers to the specified drop-off point and takes the money that's been put in an envelope for him. No questions asked. His only contact with the Rep is by pay phone, when he has a fresh delivery.

He'd called the Rep this afternoon. John likes the sound of her voice. Over the years, they've talked a bit more, started to develop a relationship of sorts. John knows the Rep is getting rich from his work, as the black market for organs is lucrative.

Reminded of his next drop off, John goes into his practice to grab the organ containers. He places these in his van and drives to the town's small industrial area.

~~~

197

John at age thirty-seven, after making his misery list, tried to fix what he considered the most important part: connect with daughter.

Then, Rosemarie was twelve years old, pretty, but she bore little resemblance to him. She liked horses. John bought her one. Things slowly started to improve. John would ride his bicycle alongside while his daughter rode Comet. He was always scared she might fall off and made sure she never rode Comet on her own.

They started to connect, a little.

When out on rides, John and Rosemarie would stop by the lake so Comet could have a rest and a drink. John would try to make conversation, but Rosemarie stayed out of reach. Something was wrong with her, he thought, and he likened her to a damaged animal. She would not let him touch her, save giving her a leg-up onto Comet, but even after doing that, she almost kicked him away.

So John made a list:

Read her diary.

Follow her around.

Buy her love.

Bully the truth out of her?

In the end, reading her diary was enough. While it wasn't blatantly spelled out, John discerned that someone in the local community may have fooled with Rosemarie. The diary entries were vague, but John thought the description of the man resembled Dr Elster, a rival vet. This made him angry.

He tried to talk about Rosemarie's distant behaviour with his wife, but she said he was overreacting and ordered him to leave her alone. He broached the subject with Rosemarie herself, but the sheer mention of Dr Elster led her to shut him out completely. She stopped talking to him, and she stopped riding Comet.

John went to the police. They weren't terribly helpful, beyond showing John some headshots of known child sex offenders in the area, to see if he recognised anyone. He didn't. Dr Elster wasn't among them.

Despite John's best efforts, things changed for the worse. His wife got together with another man and moved out, taking Rosemarie with her. John was sad, but also quietly relieved. The divorce was swift. He saw Rosemarie every Sunday, then once a month, then less after his ex-wife took up with another man and they moved away.

But John was convinced that Rosemarie had been abused, and he decided to confront Dr Elster.

John was methodical about it:

Drug the man.

Search his house.

If no evidence, take him back to the practice for interrogation.

In the end, John found some suspect photos, and Dr Elster did confess, but not to having fooled around with Rosemarie. He mentioned a girl named Becky, who was several years younger than Rosemarie.

John knew he had already gone too far. He killed Elster and fed him to the boars. And he felt good about it.

Then, as the only vet in town, John's practice started to get a lot more business. Though busy, he didn't give up on finding Rosemarie's abuser. He got active online, signing up to special chatrooms and forums, and this brought him into contact with some potential candidates. He would meet up with them under the pretence of being a young girl. As bait, he used photographs of Rosemarie, taken when she was ten and very cute. John found it surprising how many of the guys fell for the ruse.

He killed four men in the first year.

The whole thing with removing the organs came later, when it occurred to John that he could profit from his charitable work and give something back to the world. His attempts to sell the first batch of organs online brought him into contact with the Rep.

~~~

When John gets home, Rosemarie is sitting on the doorstep, shivering from the cold. She's got her backpack, handbag and laptop bag with her, all of it leaning against the door.

He stops the van and takes a quick moment to put the envelope of money into the glove box. The envelope is still cold to touch.

"Well, this is a surprise," he says, getting out of the van. As always, he keeps his distance from her.

"Hi, dad."

"Hi yourself. No contact since Christmas and now you just show up?"

"Can I come in?"

"It's nearly midnight. How did you get out here?"

"Hitched a ride."

John crosses his arms, angry. "What are you doing that for? There are some sick people out there."

"Are you gonna let me in or not?" Rosemarie asks.

"I'm not sending you back onto the highway. Not at this hour."

She stands up and gives him room to unlock the door's three locks. John takes the backpack. Rosemarie carries the laptop bag and handbag.

John leads the way into the kitchen. He gets the old pot-belly stove going while Rosemarie opens a bottle of red wine.

"You can have half a glass," John says, "and only if you tell me what's going on."

"I got in."

"What? Got in where?"

"Princeton."

"You did?" John turns to his daughter, but doesn't quite know how to congratulate her. He positions himself so the kitchen counter is between them, preventing any physical contact. "That's great," he adds, knocking the counter with a fist. "Really great. I'm proud of you."

They toast their glasses and drink. Rosemarie downs her glass in one go.

"But no scholarship," she says. "And mum doesn't have the money."

"So that's why you're here."

Rosemarie nods, seeming just slightly ashamed.

"I'm good for funding," John says, "and that's about it. Well, it's all right. Because good old John has been working hard and putting money aside for your college fund, while your mother blows every alimony cheque I send her."

"Which is why you shouldn't be surprised to see me here, dad. I need your help."

Rosemarie sits down at the table. She picks up John's list and looks at it.

"Who are these guys?"

"Oh, just some people interested in, uh, yeah. They wanna buy Comet."

"What? You can't sell him."

"How do you think I've put together your college fund? I've been selling off some of the animals. The boars have been breeding like mad and are the healthiest in the county. I've been getting good money for them, from local restaurants going organic. That's right. Those ugly razorbacks you always hated, they're gonna put you through college."

"But not Comet, dad. You can't sell him." Rosemarie looks at the list again. "Why are most of these guys crossed out?"

"You don't want to know."

"Yes, I do."

"Well, yeah, some of them are glue guys," John says. "Most of them are butchers. That's why I crossed them off. I'm not sending Comet to his death."

"Hell no! You can sell all the pigs you want, but you are not allowed to sell Comet."

"They're boars, not pigs. Now, give me that list."

She hands it to him, then pulls it back. "So many guys were interested? There's like fifty on this list." She turns the paper over and sees more names. "Wow."

John grabs the piece of paper. "That's what happens when you advertise online," he says, folding the list and putting it in his pocket. "All these people come out of their closets. Relax. I'll take the ads down tomorrow. First thing. I'll delete the ads, then I'll make us breakfast and then we'll take Comet out for a ride."

Rosemarie smiles. It's a pretty smile, but John thinks she's not nearly as pretty as when she was a young child. The older she gets, the more she looks like him.

"I'm glad you're here," John says, standing up. "It's great to see you. And that's fantastic about Princeton. But I've had a really long day. Make yourself at home."

Rosemarie pours herself some more wine. "I'm only staying tonight."

"That figures." John lets out a sigh and adds, "Don't worry about the fire. It'll burn itself out."

"I'll send you all the Princeton stuff."

"All right."

"Goodnight, dad. And thanks."

On his way to bed, John passes the door to the practice and checks that it's locked.

~~~

To call the Rep, John always uses a different pay phone. He's got into the habit of using a phone in the city or town where he's collected his latest donor; the guy is out cold in the van while John makes friendly conversation with the Rep.

She has a high-pitched, girly voice, and when she laughs, the pitch goes up an octave. John always tries to make her laugh. She calls him the Organist, and this makes him feel like he's strangely special.

His work greatly satisfies and impresses the Rep. Their business relationship has been profitable. John would like it to go further, to meet the Rep in person, but she said this isn't possible.

In order to further impress her, John experimented with removing other organs and body parts, including eyes, intestines and stomachs, but his attempts were less than successful and the Rep said they should keep it simple. Liver, pancreas, kidneys and lungs. John once suggested they get together to talk about it, but the Rep said she wasn't in the country. She had her base in Hong Kong.

John wondered if this was where many of the organs ended up: in the bodies of rich Asians. Or in the bodies of rich people who travelled to Hong Kong to receive their transplant.

The Rep knows where John lives. From the start, the drop-off point was set up in John's town: a medium-sized freezer placed in a storage garage in the town's industrial area. John was given a key. He would make the delivery and remove the envelope full of cash that was waiting for him in the freezer. He never waited to see who picked up the organs. Over the years, the amount of cash increased, with the Rep becoming more generous as John continued to deliver.

John used some of the money to pay his child support, turning cash into cheques which he sent by post. On the rare occasions he saw Rosemarie, he gave her cash, as his ex-wife was terrible with money. He also sent Rosemarie cheques for her birthday and Christmas. The rest of the money he kept in several locked briefcases that were hidden behind a stack of medicine stored in his practice's cooler. The cash would be for Rosemarie, when she needed it.

John fell into a rhythm of killing one man per month. He kept an eye on news reports and police investigations, but as there was never a body found, the men were often dismissed as missing. Sometimes, an investigation would keep the story in the news, because once the man was missing, presumed dead, some people revealed that they had been abused by him, or somehow his disgusting secret came out. When this happened, and when the victims and the victims' families were interviewed on TV, John felt a very special kind of satisfaction. There were people out there very thankful for his work, and they weren't even aware that the bastard had actually helped others by being an organ donor.

Over the years, John had to travel more to find potential candidates. He invested in a small campervan for the journeys and enjoyed seeing more of the country. The campervan's bed made it easy for him to transport a man. He met some interesting people on the road, though some were suspicious of him, a single man travelling alone in a van. He always claimed he was en route to visiting his daughter.

The killings succeeded in keeping John's own demons at bay. He liked the work, as it was profitable, charitable and useful. It sated his unhealthy urges and allowed him to live something close to a regular life.

The Rep was thankful. And the cash piled up.

~~~

When John gets up in the morning, he finds Rosemarie gone. She's left a note, with "Thanks" written in big block letters. The wine glass is on the table, empty and stained slightly red.

In her room, John sees that her bed is untouched. He assumes she left not long after he went to bed.

He has some time before the first appointments start arriving. There are plenty of farm chores to do. He makes a mental list and starts in the sty.

The boars are already hungry again. He feeds them, though he doesn't get the looks of appreciation he got yesterday.

And he thinks appreciation is something that's missing in his life, beyond the Rep's money.

The chores done, he heads outside. There's a small girl, with a scruffy dog bundled in her arms, walking down the road towards his farm. She's struggling under the weight, and struggling to keep hold of the dog. The dog gets free and starts limping next to the girl.

John jogs over to them.

"Morning," he says, picking up the dog. "Now, what's wrong with you then?"

"Something's up with his leg," the girl says with a lisp caused by a missing front tooth. He finds her lisp very sweet and endearing.

"I think we can fix him. Let's go inside."

At the door, John hears the sound of a car and turns. The station wagon comes to a stop and a woman gets out.

"Sally, there you are," she says. "I was looking all over for you."

John steps forward. "I'm Dr Smith," he says, getting a hand free. They shake. "I'm the local vet," he adds.

"She must've followed the signs from town," the woman says.

"Yeah, a lot of people do." He turns to the girl. "You're pretty smart to find me all on your own."

This makes the girl smile broadly. "Can you fix him?"

"I think so. And now you know where the vet is, so you can bring him here again when something's up."

Another big smile.

John leads the way inside and unlocks the door to the practice. The girl heads straight for the big pile of toys in the corner.

Clare & Ellis

They met at a wedding. They'd both come with partners, to avoid being dumped at one of the dreaded singles' tables. Ellis took a frisky colleague from work, while Clare went with her brother under the guise of being a couple.

As the bride was something of a control freak, the tables were set up with even numbers and with name tags placed to ensure two men never sat side-by-side, nor two women. From the head table, the bride watched to guarantee there was no switching. Everyone did as they were told, and nearly all had adhered to the bride's strict dress code.

To view the reception from above was to witness an impressive display of uniformity, right down to the dark suits the men wore and the pale, understated colours of the women's dresses.

Clare and Ellis were sat next to each other. They exchanged smiles and pleasantries, swapped stories of their connections to bride and groom, and settled in for what would be a long, arduous evening. Clare knew it would be a marathon and paced herself, drinking-wise. Ellis, regretting that he'd brought the flirtatious Evelyn, wanted to go home. As they worked through the courses and sat through the speeches, Ellis tried to conjure a clever means of escape. Alas, he wasn't creative enough, and Evelyn's laughter punctuated his thoughts, preventing him from concentrating.

Conversation was strained. Speeches were long. Guests drank to relieve the boredom, and to look comfortable. Soon, tables were attempting to outdo the others by being the loudest and appearing to be having the most fun.

Clare's first impression of Ellis was that he was dull, if slightly good-looking, and perhaps a high-functioning alcoholic. He was putting the beer and wine away with ease. She thought there might be something there, something for her to work with, but it really looked like too much work.

Ellis found Clare rather attractive, except for the fact she was a little bug-eyed and had a bad haircut. These two off-putting features seemed to soften as the evening dragged on. But she seemed rather intent on ignoring him.

Events, however, transpired to bring Clare and Ellis together. Neither liked to dance. Evelyn was drunk and keen, and Clare's brother was good enough to give into her child-like pestering and hit the dance floor. Alone at the table, with the post-dinner reverie having brought an end to the circular and gender uniformity, Clare and Ellis scratched at conversation. The booze gave Ellis false confidence. They started simple, origins and occupations, feeling each other out for commonalities. There didn't appear to be many. Ellis was from the Midwest and worked in purchasing at a pencil company. Clare was from the East Coast and was a kindergarten teacher. They managed to talk for a little bit about colours; Clare took drawing and painting as her context while Ellis showed the full spectrum of his expertise. Seeing that she was bored, he changed the subject to weddings. Clare said she wasn't married. When asked, Ellis said he was divorced, and he explained that he'd married foolishly just out of college, because that was what everyone was doing at the time. It lasted two years. He joked that two years was about the average for those hasty marriages. Clare laughed, then confessed that Corey was actually her brother. This made them both turn to the dance floor where Evelyn and Corey were getting rather raunchy with their moves, with other dancers giving them room and craning their necks to watch. Ellis made a few sly comments about their dancing and Clare laughed some more. Conversation became easier. They drank, and moved on to hobbies and popular culture, finding more things in common as each glass was drained. Eventually, Clare revealed her age; it turned out they were both thirty-eight, born one week apart. They toasted this.

But they didn't go home together. Clare wanted to, had reached that delightful point of inebriety when anything single with legs and only one head would do. She laughed and lolled at Ellis's side, doing the shoulder squeeze and the forearm pat, all the signals she knew. They even got up and danced a few slow numbers together. But as Clare got friendlier, Ellis seemed to go the other way, becoming more morose the drunker he got.

Then Corey, appearing dishevelled from a cloakroom tryst with the ladies room-bound Evelyn, became protective of Clare and said he would take her home. Ellis felt a similar, if not necessarily pressing obligation to Evelyn. As the party dispersed into taxis, with various singles having paired up, Ellis managed to give Clare his card just before she passed out. Ellis helped Corey get Clare into the back of a cab, then split a taxi home with Evelyn.

Clare called a few days later. Ellis was glad she did.

They started dating. Things went quickly, then slowly, as life got in the way, then settled into a nice rhythm. They rotated sleepovers. They bought extra toothbrushes. It seemed a given that they would eventually move in together, which they did after five months. They both terminated the leases on their small, one-bedroom apartments and moved into a larger place walking distance from Clare's kindergarten. It was on the top floor of a new building in a part of the city that was once derelict but now being gentrified. Clare took responsibility for furnishing the apartment. Ellis was good with a drill and adept at assembling IKEA furniture.

They made the place comfortable and got settled.

Both were happy.

On Clare's insistence, Ellis started to drink less.

Every evening, they sat at the kitchen table, had a light dinner and talked about their days. They did this with the curtains open so all the neighbours in the buildings opposite could clearly see that they were a couple who talked over dinner rather than watching television or eating alone. The conversation wasn't exactly forced, but it didn't flow either. On his way home from work, Ellis sometimes made notes of things they could talk about. Clare's main topic was bad parenting.

They went running together every Sunday morning. Ellis wore tights, no matter what the weather, and these accentuated the skinniness of his legs. He also had a strange, ungainly running style, loping with deep knee bends. Clare had once done a course, to learn how to run properly, and she had good form.

Their sex life was standard and mildly satisfying. If they fell behind or went more than a fortnight without having sex, they both marked their calendars and made time for it. Clare wished Ellis would be more dominant in bed while Ellis hated that they had to plan for sex. But they never talked about it.

While they had their share of rough patches, there was the general consensus between them that they were right for each other and would see things through. For her part, Clare wanted to start a family, and she knew that this may be her last chance. Ellis was glad to be pushed around, most of the time, as this saved him from constantly having to make decisions for himself. Clare's dominance also turned him on. He felt protected and cared for, and her sometimes talking to him like a child was a small drawback in exchange for such security.

The relationship was useful for attending parties, weddings and work dos. Clare ensured that Ellis never drank too much. Ellis always wore the clothes Clare picked out for him.

They kept their hobbies and circles of friends, while expanding the circles to include new couples. As Ellis was funny and could play the piano quite well, they got invited to lots of social events. And while they didn't get one of those annoying combined-name monikers, within their circles, it was hard to mention one without the other. Clare and Ellis were a given.

Ellis played social tennis on Tuesday evenings and Saturday mornings. It was mixed, but he never told this to Clare and she never went down to watch. In the same manner, Clare didn't tell Ellis that she had her therapy sessions at the same time.

They didn't delve too deeply into their pasts. They focused on the present, occasionally talking about the future. Clare wanted to marry Ellis, but never mentioned this outright in fear she might scare him off. She secretly stopped taking the pill and dropped hints about marriage until her patience ran out. She decided she would propose to Ellis during their first holiday together; a romantic two weeks in France.

They'd done weekends away, and the obligatory extended visit to each others' parents, but they'd never really travelled together. When discussing the holiday, Ellis suggested a road trip, an extended drive to the more wild parts of the country, where they could camp and live it rough. His hope was that being in the wilderness might spark their sexual relationship, perhaps even bring out the animal in Clare. But Clare dismissed the road-trip idea and said they were going to France. She hoped being in Europe might bring out the romantic in Ellis and make him more passionate. Clare organised the whole thing, booking three nights in Paris and ten days at the French Riviera. Ellis agreed.

They flew in late September. Paris was enjoyable, but they both found it hectic and crowded, with lines extending in front of all the main sights and swarms of tourists buzzing from museum to museum. Clare was annoyed by having to wait all the time and Ellis was too stressed by the crowds to be passionate. It seemed there were far more visitors than locals, making it hard to enjoy the city, to relax into Paris and get the most of what it had to offer. This gave them something to talk about, to vent and complain, and they also talked about how nice it would be at the Riviera. Clare said she'd booked an apartment in Menton, close to the Italian border.

When she had some time on her own, Clare bought rings in Paris. She also bought Ellis a couple of nice shirts, as she didn't like his holiday clothes.

After three nights, and with the jet-lagged passed, they took the TGV to Nice. Both spent the five-hour journey reading or looking out the window at the scenery. The croissants and coffee sold on board were very good. They didn't have much to say to each other. Ellis claimed he was unwinding from work, getting into holiday mode. Clare agreed. She wanted the silence to be comfortable, and Paris had been disappointingly stressful.

In Nice, they switched trains and headed for Monaco, where they would spend one night. Unfortunately, the hotel was a dump. Ellis didn't complain. They spent most of their time outside, exploring Monte Carlo. As in Paris, Clare held the map and guided their walking tours. Ellis loped behind and took photographs.

They went to bed early and took the train to Menton the next morning.

It was a short trip. They sat on the right side of the train and watched the Mediterranean, when it came into view. The scenery was lovely, with the train winding around the coastline. Clare and Ellis held hands and smiled at each other.

The small apartment was in the old town, close to the Basilique Saint Michel. The old woman who handed them the keys couldn't speak English, and she didn't smile to make up for this either. She took their money and gave them a smudged print-out of instructions that was in poor English.

While small, the apartment had everything they needed, including a fully-equipped kitchen. Clare decided they should find a supermarket and prepare their own meals, as understanding the French menus was too difficult. Ellis agreed. He suggested they have dinner on the balcony, from where a slither of water could be seen through a gap between the buildings.

They went exploring. Clare wanted to get a view, so they hiked up to the cemetery, perched just above the old town. While Clare took in the view of the sea, Ellis looked at some of the headstones and was amazed to chance upon the grave of William Webb Ellis. When Clare asked him, Ellis explained that his father was a big rugby fan, and as William Webb Ellis was credited with inventing the sport, his father chose to name Ellis in honour of rugby's founder. Clare commented that it was highly unusual to use a surname when naming a child in honour of someone else, but she was quietly glad Ellis's father hadn't gone with Webb.

The sun was very bright, glaring off the water. Ellis suggested that Clare should swap her contacts for her prescription sunglasses, but she refused, and she didn't like that Ellis suggested it.

The afternoon was hot. They went through two big water bottles and were still thirsty. A swim in the Med helped. The beach was pebbly and littered with sun-chairs, which looked to be free. While Clare was swimming, Ellis sat down on one, but then some guy with a bum-bag came rushing over demanding money. Ellis stood up and walked to the water's edge. As Clare came out, he handed her a towel and said that she looked good. Shrugging off the compliment, Clare took the towel and wrapped it purposefully around her.

Dry and dressed, they walked around some more. Both were quiet. They kept a bit of distance from each other; Ellis under the pretext of taking photos and Clare consulting the map.

The town was small. They saw everything that afternoon.

Clare was nervous, as she'd planned that this would be the night she proposed. She wanted to buy a good bottle of wine, a variety of local delicacies and some candles, so they could have a romantic dinner on the balcony. While Ellis napped, she did all of that, finding a supermarket and stocking up.

Ellis was just coming out of the shower when she arrived back, toting several plastic bags. She told Ellis not to get dressed. She put everything away, then got undressed herself. Their sex was slow and passive, as it was rather hot in the apartment. The small oscillating fan didn't offer much relief. Ellis had another shower at the end. When he came back to dress, Clare, with the sheet up to her chin, suggested which shirt he should wear. Ellis complied. He looked through his bag and asked if Clare had thrown away his favourite holiday shirts. She explained it was because she'd bought him nicer shirts in Paris and their luggage was already pretty full. Ellis was annoyed, but tried not to let it show.

They prepared dinner together. It was more of a picnic, with everything placed on the balcony table and the food still in plastic containers. Clare had found a blue and white checked tablecloth and a couple of candle holders. Once set up, everything looked rather nice. The sun started to set; through the slim gap in the buildings, they could see the colours reflecting on the water.

Ellis popped the wine and explained that his company's R&D department had tried to make pencils with sunset colours, but couldn't get it quite right, and never as good as the real thing. The company didn't have enough money for more research and the project had been cancelled.

Clare yawned and mumbled that she'd heard that story before.

The dinner was good, as was the wine. The evening was warm and still.

When Ellis had finished eating, he turned his chair to get a better view and was quiet for a long time. Clare left him to his thoughts, allowing the silence between them to be positive.

Finally, he said, "It's nice here."

"Yes."

There followed another long silence, ended by a commotion on the street below. They both leaned over the balcony to look: two old women, animatedly engaged in conversation. One was their landlord. She saw them looking and waved.

Clare and Ellis waved back.

"I wonder what it's like to live here," Ellis said.

"Brenda told me it gets really busy in summer."

"I bet it does."

"She's the one who suggested Menton."

"I know."

"She was here with her son, little Finn, who's such a brat and I think Brenda's doing just an awful job with him. Finn is always well-behaved when I'm around. I got him figured out. You know I don't like saying it, Ellis, but Brenda is a terrible parent."

Ellis nodded. He'd heard Clare say that about pretty much all the mothers, and some of the fathers, of the kids at the kindergarten. He thought she was harsh in her judgement, but had to concede that her intentions were good; she cared about the children. There was just the problem that he considered her not very good with kids. He'd observed this the few times he'd picked Clare up from the kindergarten, detouring from the train station on the rare days he finished early so they could walk home together. He saw that the kids were well-behaved around Clare, as she always claimed, but Ellis thought it was more because they were scared of her, almost intimidated. She was loud, bossy and aggressive, and she always stood over the kids rather than getting down to their level.

"I'm glad we came," Ellis said. "You should thank Brenda for the recommendation."

"I will, I will. You don't need to remind me."

There was another long silence, this one rather uncomfortable. Clare broke it by asking, "Have you ever lived abroad, Ellis?"

Ellis shifted slightly, surprised at the question. They'd always skirted around the subject of their pasts, both seemingly content to not scratch too deeply.

"Abroad?" he asked. "Does Canada count?"

"Sure. Why not? It's another country."

"Well, I spent half a year in Windsor, Ontario," Ellis explained. "But I don't know if it counts, because it's just over the river from Detroit."

"Why were you there?"

Ellis took a sip of wine. "It was just after my divorce. We'd moved up to Detroit, from St Louis, because I got a job there, but things got messy pretty quick. We'd bought a house together. Shelley wanted to keep it and that meant I had to move out. But she didn't have the money to buy me out."

"What did you do?"

"I cut my losses and moved to Canada. I went over to Windsor because things were cheaper there. And I just had to get out of Detroit." Ellis looked across the table and smiled. "You know how it is, Clare. You make all these plans and jump through all these hoops and do it all with the person you're committed to, and it turns out you don't know that person at all."

"Oh, I know. I've been burned too. You men are terrible at keeping promises." Then Clare caught herself. "Not you, Ellis. You're a rock. You're my rock."

Clare reached her hand across the table and Ellis took it, stroking her fingers.

"Tell me about it," Ellis said.

"About what?"

Ellis was about to stop himself, but the wine had loosened his tongue. "Getting burned," he said, taking another sip. "Your old boyfriends."

"You don't wanna know about that."

"Sure I do. It's something we haven't talked about." It was then Ellis recalled an article he'd read in *Cosmopolitan*, while waiting for Clare at the doctor's a few weeks back: what women want is honesty and openness. That had resonated.

"Should we?" Clare asked.

"If we're serious about each other, we should also open up about our pasts," Ellis said, almost quoting the article verbatim. "It's what loving someone is all about. Loving who they are, and loving who they were."

Clare was on the verge of crying. In her pants pocket, she looped the rings around the fingers of her right hand, getting ready. "That's the most romantic thing you've ever said, Ellis."

"I think I can be more romantic than that. We're in France, after all. On the Riviera. It's so nice to be here. To be here with you."

"I know. It's wonderful. Look, Ellis ... "

But he interrupted her. "I'd really like to know who came before me. And what you were like in college. In high school. You've shown me some photos, but you never really said anything. Who was your first love? Did you ever do something just completely wild and crazy? Did you do drugs? There's so much about you I don't know."

Clare suddenly realised the same thing. She wanted to marry Ellis, but he was a stranger in so many ways. He'd already shocked her on this trip, with those hideous holiday shirts and trying to speak French when he didn't have a clue. And what about that sleeping on his back business, his hands at his sides, like he was dead? He never slept like that back home. Or did he?

Clare pressed the rings deeper into her pocket and said, "I think it's only fair that we both confess our sins. You haven't always been forthcoming with personal stuff, Ellis. I never knew about you living in Canada. You never said you owned a house either. With your ex. Is that why you wanted to rent?"

"No, not at all. The renting thing ... I just thought the apartment would be the first step for us."

"So, you're not serious."

"Clare, I am, really, otherwise we wouldn't be having this conversation. I mean the apartment is just a stepping stone to where we live next. Some place bigger. With a yard. That would be something we'd buy. But appreciate that I learned my lesson the first time. I don't want to rush into anything."

"Good. Okay. I can understand that." Clare folded her arms, satisfied that Ellis had such a vision for them. A yard would mean kids, maybe even a dog. She still wasn't sure if Ellis would be a good father, but she would more than make up for it by being a superb mother.

Ellis filled their glasses with the last of the wine, giving Clare just a tad more than himself, and placed the bottle on the table. Clare grabbed the bottle and laid it flat on the table. A few drops dribbled onto the tablecloth.

"Truth or dare, Ellis?"

"Are you serious?"

Clare spun the bottle. They both watched it turn, both smiling expectantly.

It stopped closer to Ellis.

"Again, Clare. Are you serious?"

Clare nodded. "Truth or dare?"

"I'm too tired for any dares. If that bottle lands on me, I'll take truth each time. So, truth."

After a brief, thoughtful pause, Clare said, "Tell me something about you that no one else knows."

"Like what?"

"A secret. Something you've carried your whole life. Something you're ashamed about. I wanna know it."

"Well, uh."

"Come on, Ellis. Share with me."

"Okay. I steal pencils from work."

"I know that. I want something a bit deeper. A bit more shocking."

"All right, all right. Keep your pants on. I got a secret, but I'm not really ashamed of it." Ellis took a deep breath, smiled, then confessed: "When I was at school, I had a lot of trouble learning. They said I was slightly autistic, then they said I had ADHD, but in my opinion, I was just distracted. They gave me Adderall, but I didn't take it. My parents went through like ten really messy years until they finally got divorced when I was sixteen. All that time I struggled at school."

"So did I," Clare interjected.

"I think everyone does, in some way. Yeah, so, the only chance I had to pass tests and exams was to cheat. I was on the school tennis team, training every day, and I was always having problems with blisters on my hand. I used to wrap the hand in bandages. When I had an exam, I would slide cheat notes under the bandages."

Clare's mouth was hanging slightly open. "God, I wish I'd thought of that."

"Everyone was cheating," Ellis continued. "One guy had a fake cast on his arm. Another guy wore shorts and wrote things on his inner thighs. He just had to lift the hem of his shorts to get the answers. And all the girls wore boots on exam days. They slid their cheat notes down inside their boots. I heard other people stashed cheat sheets in the bathrooms."

"So clever."

"Yeah, when really we should have just studied harder. All this effort that went into cheating."

"And you never told anyone?"

"You're the first. There's my truth, Clare. Now you." Ellis picked up the bottle and placed it to the side. "We don't need to spin this thing. Let's do it like tennis. Truth shots, back and forth. I served, now you can return."

"Cheating on exams is not really such a big confession. But I'll keep with the school vibe, and I am ashamed. Don't hate me, Ellis, but I had to repeat a couple of years."

"No way."

"It's true. Once in junior high, and again in high school. It's why I started college so late."

Ellis shrugged. "Not so bad. I got close too. The cheating got me through. What happened to you?"

"Well, there was this boy." Clare paused, enjoying the memory. "I beat the crap out of him. He was spreading rumours that we'd slept together, which we totally had not done. But he wouldn't shut up about it and everyone was calling me a slut. So I beat him up. Put him in hospital."

"You're kidding?"

"And I got suspended as a result. Missed a whole lot of school, had to go to counselling. That's why I fell behind and couldn't finish the year."

"Good on you for standing up, Clare," Ellis said. "I'm impressed. But what about the other time, in high school? Was that also you rupturing some poor guy's scrotum?"

"Ha, no. That time it really was sex. There was this massive scandal. I had to change schools."

"For sleeping with a boy?"

"With a teacher." Clare sighed, but she wasn't embarrassed. "My parents wanted to press charges, but I went on the record that it was consensual. Leo got fired and I never saw him again. We had to move in the end."

"Leo?"

"My physics teacher. He was like this total nerd, but he was really cool. He knew so much stuff."

"Leo the physics hero. Didn't see that coming."

Angered, Clare said, "You started it, Ellis. You're the one who wants to know everything about me."

"I do, I do. It's ... it's interesting."

"And now it's your turn."

"I can't top that. Was Leo your first sexual experience?"

Clare nodded. "What was yours?"

"No, no, no. We're not going there."

"Then we're not going anywhere, are we, Ellis? You're totally right. We need to be more open with each other. So, come on. Who popped little Ellis's cherry?"

"It certainly wasn't my physical education teacher."

"It was physics. And excuse me, but Leo was only nine years older than me. If we met now, no one would care about that difference."

"I think people care when the guy is twenty and the girl is eleven."

"I was sixteen, Ellis."

"All right. Don't shout. Don't ruin the mood."

"You're the one doing that, with your stupid comments. You don't know how it was."

"I'm sorry, Clare."

"You should be."

They lapsed into silence. The slight smile on Ellis's face really annoyed Clare. She wanted to push him, insult him, but decided instead to wait; because he always gave up in the end.

"We just never had stuff like that happen at my school," Ellis said at last.

"It happens a lot more than you think. You just never hear about it."

"I guess. Yeah. Maybe I was too busy coming up with cunning plans for cheating."

"So, you didn't lose your virginity in high school."

"No. In college. And that was pretty forgettable."

216

"You're lying. I hate it when you lie to me."

"What? It's the truth."

Clare let out a grunt. "Ellis, I spend all day with kids who lie. And then I talk with parents who lie as well. I think I can tell when someone's on the wrong side of the truth."

Clare and Ellis shared a look. Ellis didn't like Clare's blatant expression of arrogance, or the fact that she was right.

"We can't stay together if you're not honest with me," Clare said.

"Okay. Fine. Although, now that you told me about physical Leo, I don't think this is so bad. It was in high school. And she was an escort."

"A hooker?"

"An escort," Ellis said firmly. "She wasn't some runaway hustling on a street corner. She was working her way through college."

"Oh, that makes all the difference."

"Look, Clare, it's like this. Will you just listen for once? I had real problems with acne when I was in high school. All of us on the tennis team had it. I worked out later that it must've been the supplements the coach was giving us."

"He gave you drugs?"

"Yeah, steroids or something. I never played such great tennis as I did in high school. I nearly got a college scholarship."

"Too bad screwing escorts isn't an Olympic sport."

"Jesus, Clare, it was one time. And it was because I couldn't get a date for the prom. Because of the zits. No girls would go out with me. Some of the guys on the team took dates from the girls' team, but I was left out. I couldn't go alone. It was the prom."

"So you went with some hired help. And you had enough in your piggy bank to go all the way with her."

"I think we should stop this. I've had enough."

"No, go on. Tell me about your trip to the doctor to get checked for an STD."

"I used protection, Clare. I'm not an idiot."

"And the second time?"

"It was only one time. God, you're worse than Shelley."

"Excuse me?"

When Ellis didn't reply, Clare stood up.

"Don't overreact, Clare. That's not what I meant."

"What did you mean then?"

"Sit down."

"No. Explain yourself. Don't you ever compare me to your ex."

Exasperated, and regretful, Ellis ran a hand through his hair. "Look," he said, "one of the problems I had with Shelley was that she kept changing her opinions. She'd be all puritanical and conservative one week, and then she'd want to go to swingers' club the next. A Democrat in March and a Republican in April. She was all over the place. Imagine trying to live with someone like that."

"Did you ever go?"

"Go where?"

"To a swingers' club."

Ellis shifted in his seat. "A couple of times, yeah. But it wasn't my thing. And Shelley got all jealous when any women hit on me, which kind of defeats the purpose of it all."

Smiling, Clare sat back down. "I'd never pick you for a swinger."

"I'm not."

"Shame about that."

"What? Why?"

"No reason."

Ellis looked at Clare from the side of his eyes. "Is that a truth or a dare?" he asked.

"Could be a bit of both."

"Are you serious? Is this a recent development?"

"I've been true to you, Ellis."

"And before I came along? No, don't answer that. A devil's threesome with a couple of teachers or whatever. I don't want to hear it."

"But that's how all this started, with you wanting to know about my former boyfriends."

"Boyfriends sure, but not your sordid affairs with grey-haired teachers and professors."

"It wasn't like that. And you're one to talk, with your hookers and your swingers' club. That stuff's not for me. Okay. I confess. I did have a bit of fun in college, but it was all above board. Just some fun in a co-ed dorm."

"God, this is getting worse."

"You started it, Ellis. Besides, that was ages ago."

"And now? Don't tell me some kindergarten parents invite you in to spice up their sex lives."

Clare raised her voice. "Absolutely not." Then she calmed herself and added, off-hand, "There were a couple of affairs with some of the single dads, but I never got into bed with both parents. I'm not that depraved. And I was taking care of their kids during the day."

Clare kept talking some more, but Ellis wasn't listening. He was thinking of their own kids; being married to Clare and having a family together. How would that turn out? Clare bossy and aggressive, telling them all how to behave. Telling them what to wear. Bug-eyed Clare with her exaggerated sense of her own abilities and her smartest-person-in-the-room complex. A nightmare.

"Ellis? Say something."

Snapped from his thoughts, Ellis asked, "Why do you wear contacts?"

"Huh? What's that got to do with anything?"

"Why do you wear them? You look much better in glasses."

"I don't."

"You do."

"Don't try to change me, Ellis."

"But don't you get it, Clare? That's your problem. You think you know everything better. I'm telling you honestly. You look better in glasses. But you won't even listen to me. You tell me not to drink so much and I hear you. You tell me my shirts are ugly and I stop wearing them." He pulled the collar of his purple shirt for emphasis. "I'll wear what you buy for me, Clare. I'm open for it. I'm willing to meet you halfway. But you're not."

"Now wait just a minute. Why do you sleep on your back?"

"What? I always have. Did you only just notice? Maybe you need new contacts."

This really pissed Clare off. She launched into a verbal tirade, pointing out all the things that had annoyed her on this trip. The photography. The attempts at speaking French. She was abusive and nasty. Ellis returned this volley by saying Clare was dominating and stubborn, always wanting to hold the map and thinking she knows which way to go. She was needy as well, constantly seeking confirmation and affirmation. Clare complained that Ellis didn't earn enough money. Ellis said Clare was bad with kids.

They argued into the night, confessing things they'd never told anyone. They tried desperately to hurt each other.

Clare said Ellis was putting on too much weight. Ellis said Clare had a bad haircut.

At one point, Clare fished a bottle of wine out of her suitcase, the wine she'd planned to give to Brenda as a thank-you present. Ellis opened it with gusto and poured full glasses.

Clare said she still had the lease on her apartment and had simply sublet it to a colleague, just in case things didn't work out. Ellis said that social tennis was mixed, and that all the female players wanted to play mixed doubles with him.

On and on it went.

Much later, a man appeared on the balcony opposite and ordered them to shut up. Clare told the man to fuck off. With the wine finished and both of them pretty drunk, and with the night turning cool, Clare and Ellis took it inside.

Ellis said that Clare was bad at her job and should find another line of work. Clare said that Ellis should be more motivated at work, to get promoted and earn more money.

"You've got the biggest pencil, Ellis," Clare shouted, grabbing his crotch. She laughed as his pencil responded. "See? Put it to work."

"I will, if you put your glasses on, you dominating bitch," Ellis shouted back.

Clare did as she was told, even going so far as to ceremoniously smash her contacts with the heel of one of her shoes. She grabbed Ellis by the collar of his new shirt and ripped it to pieces.

Their sex bordered on violent. A lamp broke. The wrought-iron bed-head dented the wall. A vase of flowers fell to the floor, breaking and leaving a puddle of slimy water that the carpet absorbed. Clare's nails drew blood from Ellis's right shoulder. He hit her so hard with a pillow that it burst.

A neighbour called the police, who banged on the door.

"Don't you even dare, Ellis," Clare said.

"And don't you ever talk to me like I'm a child. Never again."

"And don't you stop."

When the landlord came to let the two officers into the apartment, they found Clare and Ellis tangled in a bed sheet in the floor. They'd stood the bed on its side and sprawled the mattress onto the floor. It looked like Clare was trying to suffocate Ellis with the last remaining pillow. Her glasses were askew and there were little feathers everywhere.

The two policemen put their hands on their guns.

Out of breath, Clare managed to say, "It's all right. We're engaged."

"That's right," Ellis said. "Now, get out." Then he turned to Clare. "What do you mean engaged?"

"Hey, you, officer," Clare said. "Can you get my pants?"

The pants had somehow landed on top of the refrigerator. The officer did as he was told, holding the pants out to Clare with his thumb and forefinger.

Clare dug in the pockets and pulled out the rings.

"Ellis, will ... "

"Yes," Ellis shouted.

They put the rings on, embraced and started wriggling under the sheet.

"These guys are French, Clare," Ellis said. "Show them some tit and then maybe they'll go away."

"We leave," one policeman said.

"Américains," said the other distastefully, and he seemed ready to spit on the carpet.

The landlord peered from behind them, pointed a finger and said, "You pay."

"Don't worry," Clare said. "We'll pay for the damage. Now please, go away."

With the door closed, Ellis said, "So she does speak English."

"Shut up, Ellis," Clare said, covering his face with the pillow.

Marie

They took separate cars. She was glad to go alone; he drove like a maniac, working the steering wheel like a child playing a video arcade game. She could see his silver car up ahead, weaving between the traffic, rounding imaginary red cones. She heard his voice clearly: "Making great time," said about when her motion sickness would set in.

So he got to places faster. Big deal. He never enjoyed the journey. He was always thinking toward another place and time and not living the moment they were in. Forever playing catch up, living in haste. No wonder he had no idea of what bothered her. Never did. She smiled, remembering the distinct pleasure it had given her to see that he hadn't seen divorce in their immediate future.

Now, she was going to have to spend the whole day with him, forced to watch him anticipate buyers and listen to his inane comments delivered so steadfast and sure. Oh, he always knew what was coming. Right.

She pulled into the empty space next to his car and sat momentarily, gathering her strength for the coming day. She decided to let him do all the selling. She would just observe. That was her role. Nonsense, she thinks. You can't build a relationship just watching; participation is required.

She got out of her rental car and carried her stuff towards the flea market.

"Marie. What took you so long?" he asked, smiling pleasurably, savouring this small victory.

She didn't reply, and perhaps in retaliation, he didn't offer to help her with the box she was carrying. He had already set up his side of the table, arranging his wares so they shared the space equally. He had used his collection of toy cars to mark the division, putting them bumper to bumper, perfectly straight, each with a little price tag on the roof.

As she started to empty her box, deliberately scattering the table without order or style, she saw the accumulated knickknacks of their life together. This is what six years had amounted to: a table at the local flea market, to be picked over and judged by all their friends and neighbours.

It was embarrassing, yet every item seemed to spark a kind of warm ache inside her: the miniature Gateway Arch from St Louis, the bottle of Lambrusco they had never opened, all the packets of matches she had gathered from hotels, restaurants and cafes. She picked up a few, opening the flaps and reading small notes she had written, often just one word. Each word sparked a memory.

Like this one: Black Swan Hotel, Perth, late moon.

They had walked along the river at night, on the south side. A power blackout had the city in darkness, but the moon was full and it shimmered on the water, a spotlight illuminating their small, intimate theatre. And in that pristine moment, before they had even kissed, he had said, "We better head back before they lock us out of the hotel."

Always planning ahead.

"How much for the matches?" someone asked.

She wants to give a price, but realises she doesn't care. "Ask him."

Musa

"You're playin with fire, I reckon," the truck driver says.

"I have no trouble so far."

He sneaks a look at the driver, what they call a truckie here, wondering if that trouble might start now. Although the truckie is certainly rough around the edges, sliced and dented like an old can kicked down the street, he seems pretty soft on the inside. No danger, Musa decides.

"What's ya story?"

"My story?"

"Yeah. Where ya been?"

"I started in Sydney. Then north to Cairns, across to Darwin. Now I'm heading for Perth."

The truckie whistles. "Hitchin all the way?

"Yes."

"Your folks know you're doing this?"

"They know some of it. My mother, she is not very happy."

"Too right. Bet she's wettin herself."

"Yes, my father tells me she cries a lot."

"No, I mean ... Ha-ha. Where'd you say you were from?"

"Istanbul," he says softly, but then adds, trying to make a small joke and perhaps put the truckie at ease, "not Constantinople."

"Eh?"

"Turkey. I'm from Turkey."

"Oh yeah? A Turk?"

"My name is Musa."

The truckie looks at him from the corners of his eyes. "You a Muslim?"

Musa shifts in his seat. "I was born in Germany," he explains, trying to speak lightly. "I'm a bit of both."

"What? A Nazi and a terrorist?" The truckie laughs.

"No, no, my father is Turkish. I have a German passport."

The truckie nods as he works the gear stick. "You know, I don't normally pick up hitchhikers. There aren't many of youse round no more, not since Milat and that other fella up in the Territory."

"What happened?

"Let's just say you're much more lucky to be ridin with me than with them."

Musa tries to smile. He wants to speak, but can think of nothing to say.

The truck approaches a small rise and begins to struggle, slowing down as the truckie runs back through the gears. Musa checks his watch. The sun is beginning to set. He won't make it to Broome until late in the evening. He doesn't like arriving in new towns at night and rues the time he lost standing at the roadhouse that morning, the hours spent chewing the dust of passing cars and seeing the prejudice in the eyes of passersby.

"It's probably better to be a Turk than a Nazi," the truckie says, pumping the gear stick. He bangs the big steering wheel with his hands, urging the truck forward.

Musa doesn't respond. He looks out the window at the desolate landscape.

"So," the truckie begins, sounding eager to talk, "what do you lot learn about Gallipoli?"

Musa grimaces. When they're not judging him for coming from a Muslim country, they're shoving Gallipoli down his throat. He knew it as Çanakkale Savaşları, and what should he say about it? A foreign army tried to invade his country and his people successfully defended it, had courageously fought off a superior force just as their great Ottoman Empire was crumbling to nothing. They drove back the invaders, put them to the sword, and this success led to independence and the foundation of the Republic of Turkey. Gallipoli was the making of their first President and greatest statesman, Mustafa Kemal Atatürk.

It was a glorious moment in Turkish history.

"Not very much," he says.

"I guess you lot feel bloody ashamed for slaughtering so many Anzacs on the beach in cold blood."

"It was a battle. Soldiers die in battle and they die with honour."

"Yeah, our diggers did, but your murderers didn't."

The truck crests the long rise and starts to gather speed again. The truckie continues changing gears, the muscles of his left forearm flexing each time, the skin rippling under all that dark hair.

Musa can't contain himself any longer. "What would you do if someone invaded Australia? Would you just stand back and let them invade, or would you pick up a gun and defend your country?"

"Defend it of course, but this is Australia and it's bloody worth defending."

"To the people who live there, every country is worth defending."

The truckie shakes his head. "Nuh. No chance. If I lived in Iraq, I wouldn't defend it, and if I was a Turk in World War One, I wouldn't have gunned down our diggers in cold blood."

Musa knows he should let it go, but he is so sick of this talk, sick of the contradictions and unfounded superiority. Sure, there had been others who were open-minded and didn't consider him a terrorist or held him responsible for Gallipoli, but those people were few and far between, and because they didn't offend him, they also didn't stay long in his memory; he only remembered the people who had insulted him, the ones who were slowly eroding his Australian dream.

"I'm sorry," he says, "but I do not agree with you. The Iraqis have the right to defend their country, and I'm sure that if you were an Iraqi you would do the same. You say it's not a country worth fighting for, but that's because you live here, in a place most people think is paradise."

"It's the greatest bloody country in the world," the truckie declares, but he has an almost defensive expression on his face, and the suggestion of violence lingers around the sunburned creases of his eyes.

Musa wants to agree, had grown up believing this was the case, but now that he had seen it and experienced it, he no longer thought so. He knows that was as much his fault as anyone else's; his expectations had been far too high. The land, the scenery and the coastlines had met his expectations, but getting to know the people had been a crushing disappointment. He had found them friendly, yes, but in a superficial, suspicious way that left him never knowing exactly where he stood. He had hitchhiked specifically to meet the locals, despite the warnings and the long waiting for rides. And true, he had met some interesting, genuinely friendly and open people, but even those few gave hints at underlying prejudices.

"Most people think their own country is the greatest," he says.

"Well, most people are wrong."

Musa looks out the window at the rugged, flat expanse of the north-west. This area of Australia reminds him of the coastline around Çanakkale, where his family had sometimes gone for holidays. It seemed both hospitable and surreal, and haunting, as if spirits rose out of the sand and slithered through the cracks in the rocks. It had been his father's idea to visit the site of the battle, but not in April when it gets overrun by "drunks and flag-wavers." He remembers the memorial with the words of Mustafa Kemal: "There is no difference between the Johnnies and the Mehmets where they lie side by side here in this country of ours." And he was right, Musa thinks, for all soldiers feel they are fighting the good and noble fight. The only difference is in the interpretation of history; whose side you're on.

"I don't reckon I like the way you talk," the truckie says at last. "The diggers gave this country our identity. They were heroes sent to the wrong place by the bloody Poms and were then mowed down in cold blood on the beach by your lot."

The truckie begins to slowly work back through the gears. The weight of the three trailers makes the rig jerk as the truck loses speed.

Musa feels that there is something wrong. It's nearly dark outside. He camped out once on the side of the road, but had not slept because of his fear of what lurked beyond. Then, in the early hours of the morning, a police car had stopped and told him it was illegal to camp next to the road. They waited for him to pack up his tent and could have given him a ride to the next town or roadhouse, but left him standing there.

As the truckie goes through the laboured process of slowing down the truck, he continues to talk about Gallipoli. He seems to like the subject and jumps easily to Muslims and how they are all terrorists and how the cold blooded killings of Gallipoli were similar to acts of terrorism.

"It was murder. Pure and simple. There's no honour in terrorism. You Muslims are gonna pay for what you did, and for what you do."

The truck comes to a stop on the side of the road.

"Come on, out ya get," the truckie says, sounding surprisingly jovial. "I'm not givin a lift to no terrorist who doesn't know the truth about Gallipoli."

"Are you going to leave me out here?"

"Yep. Get down in the dirt and pray for help. But I dunno which way Mecca is."

Musa gathers up his backpack and opens the door. He lowers himself down, but then stops.

"Do you even know what they were fighting for?" he asks.

The truckie's sneering, sour face drops a little. "Well, you Turks, you lot, you were in it with the Germans. That was reason enough."

"Right. Thank you for the ride and for leaving me out here."

The truckie laughs. "Pray to what-his-name, Allah, or Mohammad Ali. He'll look after you. There's still a few camels running round out here. Maybe God'll bring you one."

He puts the truck into gear and the rig lurches forward before Musa can close the door. The force of forward movement slams the door shut. Musa coughs in the churned up yellow dust of the highway.

With the truck's lights enveloped by the night, it's very quiet. There's still a slither of burnt orange in the sky to the west, but the highway is dark.

Musa sits down on his backpack. He picks up small rocks and angrily throws them across the road.

An hour slowly passes. Scared of snakes, he sits in the middle of the road.

When he finally sees a car's headlights coming from the north, he turns on his torch and holds it above his head like a streetlight. Curious, the driver slows down, gives Musa a long stare, but doesn't stop.

Then, it's silent again.

The sounds of animals moving in the bush scare him.

Another hour passes. Musa wishes he had kept his mouth shut, wishes he was still sitting in the air-conditioned truck and on the way to Broome. He thinks about walking off the highway and pitching his tent, but the thick darkness, and all those snakes, scare him.

He turns his head with every sound, every rustle of bush. He's sure he can hear the snakes slithering across the gravel next to the road. The batteries of his torch are running out and he knows he can't keep turning on the light every time he hears a noise.

It's very dark, yet the sky is full of stars. More stars than he has ever seen.

So, he battles his fear, singing to himself to keep the silence at bay, to prevent him from listening for sounds in the dark.

A car comes down the highway with one working headlight, and this is blindingly bright. He shines the torch above his head and the car slows down and stops. The passenger's window is lowered, as is the window from the rear door. The engine idles loudly and whines as if gasping for breath.

"G'day," the man says easily. "Waitin for the bus?"

The other men in the car laugh.

"I'm trying to get to Broome."

None of his rides had been with Aboriginal people and he feels apprehensive about getting into the station wagon.

"Broome?"

"I don't think there is a bus."

"Ha-ha. Nah, mate. No bus. We're goin to Derby."

Musa peers into the car and sees four middle-aged men, all looking a little ragged and rough.

"You gotta sit in back," the driver says. "Go on. It's open."

Musa moves around to the back of the car. He finds the latch and opens the back door. He puts his backpack on top of a pile of empty cans and is about to climb in when the car jumps forward. The men cackle with laughter.

"Just kiddin. Carn, in ya get."

Slowly, Musa gets into the back and pulls the door down. He moves a couple of cans and empty bottles to the side and tries to get comfortable. The car smells of sweat and spirits. The two men in the back seat turn around to look at him.

"Where ya from?" one asks.

Musa pauses. He thinks it's really good to be moving again, to be off the dark highway, and he decides to treat himself to a cheap hotel room in Derby. But until he gets there, he's not taking any more chances.

"Greece," he says.

Victor

Victor stares at the blank page.

Third person, that's stupid. Sounds stupid. They're probably doing that. Filling whole notebooks with third person stories, maybe even with second person stories. Letter to self and that kind of crap. You always write about yourself.

No. This is me. Me, Victor, myself. I am me. Write about me. I am going to write about me.

I stare at the blank page. Because there is nothing to say.

Make something up, Victor says.

Not the exercise. Anyway, what can I make up? Everything's already been made up. There are no original ideas left. Art is just a rehash. All the good art's been done. Our originality peaked with cave paintings. With fire and wheels. With coming down from the trees. Evolving. Now that's art.

So evolve, Victor says. And rehash.

Must I? I guess I could just add slight twists to all the stories already told. Isn't that what the pros do? Old stuff, new packaging. Old products, new branding. I stories into he stories. She stories into we stories. Cover versions outselling the originals. Every new generation unaware of all the stories that came before. Writers who only write about writers, because they think writers like themselves are the most interesting people on the planet.

I hate it when you talk like this.

I know, I know. The poison of pessimism. Larissa hates it. But come on, Victor. Draw life from suffering. Art from gloom.

The page is still blank.

It is. And the gloom is getting heavier. I'm killing the room.

Write about me.

I am you. And I'm not interesting. You see? Victor is not interesting. I'm in this room, amid the deafening sounds of pens scratching across pages, pens that can't keep up with the rehashed creativity, because I want to be interesting. A technical writer for software documentation is not an interesting person. Manuals and help menus and error messages? Please. Where is my help menu?

Where's the pop up box that can answer my questions? Where's my tech support?

Outsourced?

Maybe. An automated telephone answering service. The Victor hotline.

Don't get frustrated. Frustration isn't sexy.

This class was supposed to help, to give me an outlet, but I'm worse off than before. All it's done is made me see how few words I've got in me and how crap my life is.

It's not crap.

Fine. I'll agree to shut you up.

Okay.

Focus, Victor. Just pick up the pen and start writing. Like everyone else is doing: a sentence, a paragraph, half a page. It doesn't have to be great. Just start. Look, they have plenty to say. It's easy.

Victor, there's no one to impress. There's nothing to prove. No big prize. No multi-million dollar publishing contract. There's no book lottery to win. No fawning agents and publishers all wanting a piece of you. No author groupies. No tours. No need to grow a goatee and pack your closet with puce skivvies. No reason to fake an arty-farty accent or adopt a superior writerly air. This is just about you and the page. Victor, the page, the pen. Three elements.

Write what you know.

I'm aware that's the exercise, Victor. And do you know what that means? It means I have to write about a software documentation specialist who's about to lose his girlfriend because she doesn't find him interesting and she wants him to be a novelist so she can brag to her friends and become famous and maybe he gets lucky by rehashing and slightly twisting an already big selling story something with vampires or mythology or something that outlines a far better world than the one we inhabit and the book's a hit and Victor and Larissa travel the world going from lit fest to book fair to Hollywood where the books get made into films and everyone's beautiful and happy and can drink as much as they want without getting a hangover and they're photographed here and clutching statuettes there and launching merchandise everywhere and no matter how people behave everything can be excused away because Victor's a bestselling novelist and the whole world is lining up outside bookshops at midnight just to read collections of his shopping lists and school reports and Victor ceases to be Victor the person or Victor the writer and becomes Victor the brand and the words dry up because he really has nothing to say never did have anything to say and can't bring himself to rehash another book using mythology or magic or chase-chase clock-ticking espionage with the hero a brilliant something-or-other with brown hair greying handsomely at the sides but Victor the brand is owned by a big corporate conglomerate and now there are ghost-writers writing the books for him with Victor the brand splashed in giant type on the covers and the brilliant whatever hero has hair that does continue to grey handsomely at the sides through a series of bestsellers and women are playthings and objects and sometimes tattooed but always have to be rescued and those books get made into films and Victor and Larissa continue to go from lit fest to book fair to Hollywood and Larissa hates Victor now because she's living in his shadow and all she'd wanted was fame for herself and not even stints on reality TV shows get her that and she's voted off this and has no talent on that and looks awful in ballroom wear and is subject to perpetual mockery and she hates Victor the writer and Victor the brand and especially Victor the person and she misses the simple life they had when he was a nobody software documentation specialist who wrote help menus instead of rehashed fiction and she was in the position to break up with him and leave him heartbroken forever but then she made the mistake of encouraging him to take creative writing classes so he could sit in stuffy rooms and watch other people write like mad with their tongues hanging just slightly out of the corners of their mouths like they're pre-schoolers drawing with crayons and listening to them murmur with pleasure as if every sentence is gold and then they read their tripe to the class with Jane Austin-type accents and get stirring rounds of applause for sharing and all the while his page remains blank.

Yeah. Write about that.

Or start with Victor. A cover version of Victor. The cover is better than the original. I know Victor.

I pick up the pen.

Title: Victor.

Victor stares at the blank page. He's holding a pen, but he can't seem to get the pen to make contact with the page. He has nothing to write about, nothing to say. He's not interesting. He's not even a real writer, even if his job title includes the word writer. He prepares technical documentation for software; incredibly weighty documents which take ages to write and which no one reads. He makes a good living doing this work, as much as he hates it. Software companies have money and they need good documentation for legal reasons; when a user crashes his own software, the complex, labyrinthine documentation normally gets the company out of any liability. That's because users never read the fine print, and Victor is an expert at fine print, rambling sentences that never quite say anything clearly. He works freelance and has a desk in a collective office where other freelancers work. Graphic designers, ad copywriters, journalists, people far more interesting than himself. People who wear hoodies and eat sushi. The office is on Shorts Gardens in the centre of London and they all gather there under the semblance of community to avoid the loneliness and caged animal-ness of working at home. They all agree that there is something very pathetic about getting out of bed, walking two metres in your pyjamas and sitting down to work. You never leave the flat and stop showering or changing clothes. Victor's been there. He knows. The desk is expensive and he feels out of his league, but still he pays the monthly rent and commutes half an hour each way on his scooter.

He's twenty-nine years old and wants to be a novelist. After tiring of listening to him whine, his kind-of girlfriend Larissa forced him to sign up for creative writing classes; sign up or she's leaving. It's been a disaster. The class is run by Nigel, an author who has published three novels. Nigel's feedback for Victor's work so far has always consisted of variations of this one sentence: "Show, don't tell."

Victor doesn't really get what this means, and when he asked Nigel to explain it, Nigel replied by saying, "Show me, don't tell me."

The writing class is on Wednesday evenings and takes place in an expanded cleaner's closet at Hackney Community College. The room has no windows and gets stuffy very quickly. Victor goes through nearly a bag of eucalyptus drops to keep himself breathing through his nose and to avoid having a claustrophobic panic attack.

Every session they do a variation of the same exercise: write what you know. But one of the things Victor hates, that he really hates, is writers writing about writing and writers; as if this is the only thing worth writing about. He can't recall how many books he's thrown across the floor or how many movies he's walked out of when a character is introduced as a writer. Sentences like "Rayomi is a successful author of young adult novels" make Victor scream violently. A minor character he can handle, sometimes, especially when that character is an abject failure as a writer, but a main character, no way. He wants to start a movement: Writers Against Writers Who Write About Writers (WAWWWAW).

But all those writers are just doing Nigel's exercise, writing about what they know. And he has to do that too.

Victor picks up the pen.

Title: Victor.

~~Victor is a technical writer for software documentation.~~ Victor is a technical writer for household appliances, working from a desk in a community office on Shorts Gardens, London. He writes instruction manuals which get translated into many different languages. It's important that he writes clearly and without word play or idiomatic language in order to facilitate easier translations, because the translations are done not by people, but by a computer running translation software. The documentation for this translation software, including the 1,342 page manual and the help menus, etc, was written by a man called Victor. Victor, who is also responsible for the translation of his instruction manuals and works with the software, hates Victor. He thinks Victor could learn a lot by writing instruction manuals for household appliances, and those skills would help Victor turn that convoluted, user-unfriendly software tome into a more concise and usable guide. Sometimes, he imagines beating Victor to death with the software manual or strangling him with the cord of a mouse. One of Victor's first stories written for his Wednesday creative writing class was called Killing Victor. Victor was very proud of this story, and even thought it might be stretched into a novel, but the feedback from Nigel was: "Show me the killing, don't tell me about it."

Victor wondered then if Killing Nigel might be a better story. But Nigel had also asked, after skimming Killing Victor, that if you don't know what it means to kill Victor, how can you write about killing Victor?

"Because it's fiction," Victor said. "Fiction is about making things up."

"But the reader will know that you're not writing with conviction. You haven't done what you're writing about."

"So, I should first kill Victor?"

"I thought Victor was you."

"You want me to kill myself?"

"No. Of course not. You should write about what you know. For example, write about being a writer. Or in your case, write about wanting to be a writer. Show me your struggle."

"That's a bit selfish, isn't it?"

"Try it. Always write what you know."

Victor picks up the pen.

Title: Victor.

Victor sits in creative writing class staring at the blank page. Victor wants to be a writer. Victor really, really wants to be a writer. He wants to write the greatest novel ever written and sell millions of copies and make lots of money and people who ignored him in high school would write fan mail to him saying they always knew he was a great talent and maybe they could go out for a drink some time and he could sign the first edition hardcover they lined up for at midnight outside their local bookshop. People would then remember him for his books and not for being the guy responsible for ~~badly translated instruction manuals for household appliances~~ those annoying automated telephone answering services. That's what his job is. He's a script writer for automated answering. Something like: "Thank you for calling We're Too Cheap To Hire A Receptionist Enterprises. Your call is important to us. If you'd like to listen to the on-hold music, press one. If you'd like your call to be placed in a queue of never answered calls, press two. If you'd like to not spend the next six hours holding the receiver, hang up now. The charges for this call are nine pounds per minute."

Victor makes a good living writing these scripts. He hates it, and would much rather be a novelist, but there is a skill involved. The scripts need to be long, especially the list of menu options, in order to keep the caller on the phone, because the calls cost nine pounds per minute. And the scripts need to tell a story of sorts; that the company values the call, but is too cheap to hire any personnel to deal with it.

Because he makes good money, Victor has a desk in a freelancers' office on Shorts Gardens in the centre of London. The other freelancers are engaged in much more interesting pursuits than his own. He shares the office with another Victor, who is the only person more boring than himself. That Victor writes software documents, or something, and never says a word except to ask if anyone would like a cup of tea. He also types very loudly, sometimes tosses novels across the floor in disgust, and is generally an annoying presence in the office. He occasionally smells, as if he hasn't showered, and once he showed up wearing pyjama pants. There has been a secret meeting to have this other Victor evicted, but as he is the only person who buys supplies for the kitchenette, which everyone uses, he has yet to be kicked out. Noticing this, Victor, who wanted to secure his own place in the office, started buying kitchenette supplies as well. It seems that, in the office, only he and the other Victor make any money. Being a freelance graphic designer sounded good, and it kept one in sushi and hoodies, but it didn't quite provide the means to purchase milk, sugar, coffee and biscuits for the Shorts Gardens office.

Every evening, after commuting home half an hour by scooter, but not on Wednesdays because he has creative writing class at Hackney Community College, Victor sits down to work on his novel. The book's working title is Victor Writes a Book About Himself. He's making very little progress because there isn't much to say about himself apart from the fact that he wants to be a writer, that he really, really wants to be a writer, even though he hates books and films that have writers as main characters. He asked Nigel to read the first chapter, but Nigel didn't get further than the first page.

"Now, you see, Victor," Nigel said, pulling at the neck of his purple skivvy, "you're telling me. You're not showing me. You need to show me. I, the reader, I need to see it."

"What should I do?"

"Show, don't tell."

"How?"

"By showing and not telling. And by writing about what you know."

"But I know this. I'm writing about a man who wants to be a writer."

"That's good. Go with that. See where it takes you."

Victor wanted to take the small bundle of printouts, roll it up into a tight tube and beat Nigel to death with it.

"It's not taking me anywhere," Victor said.

Nigel stroked his goatee. "Keep at it. Writing's a bit like tennis. You need to get up every morning and hit a thousand forehands. Then you'll get better at it."

"Forehands?"

"Yes. Writing is a skill and you can train it, like any skill."

"Is that what you do?"

Nigel nods.

"You play tennis? Hit a thousand forehands every morning?"

"No, I do writing exercises, like the write-what-you-know exercise."

"Every morning?"

"Yes. That's why I've published three books. I write about what I know."

"That being you. Nigel."

"Right."

So, Victor gets up very early the next morning, walks two metres in his pyjamas and sits down at his desk. He picks up a pen.

Title: Nigel.

Nigel wakes up and pads across the carpeted floor of his bedsit. He's naked. That's how he sleeps, because he read somewhere that's what writers do. He sometimes works naked too, but that requires turning the heat up and he's a little short on funds for such a luxury.

He pulls on his robe and folds the bed away, not bothering to tidy up the bedding. He kicks the mattress down, forcing the sofa to take shape again despite the sheets and blankets now stuffed inside it. He sits on the angled sofa, gripping the carpet with his bare feet. There's a little fold-out dinner tray next to the sofa. He pulls this out and sets it up, placing his notebook on top. He edges the pen out of the spiral and opens the notebook. He starts halfway down the page, picking up from where he stopped yesterday.

Exercise: write what you know.

My name is Nigel. I'm a complete and utter failure. I'm in deep financial shit. My books don't sell. All I have is my creative writing class on Wednesday evening in that torture chamber at Hackney Community College. I'm single and depressed. That's it. That's what I know.

The pen stops.

"Same as yesterday," he says, putting the pen back into the notebook's spiral.

He sits back, wondering how to fill the day. He yawns and scratches himself under his robe.

A knock on the door makes him stop mid-scratch. He gets up and opens the door.

"Victor? What are you doing here?"

"Can I come in?"

"How did you get my address?"

"I contacted your publisher. Your ... um ... self-publisher."

"Now you know."

"Yeah. Sorry. You really paid to have your books published?"

"I think of it as investing in my own work."

"How did that turn out?"

"Come inside and you'll see."

Nigel lets Victor enter the bedsit and closes the door.

"Cosy," Victor says, standing in the middle of the room.

"Yes. Look, what can I do for you, Victor?"

Victor loops the strap of his scooter helmet over his wrist and pulls his shoulder bag around. He flips the front open. "I've written something. I'd like you to read it and tell me what you think."

"I don't have time for this."

"It'll just take a minute. I'm halfway in and I'm stuck. I really need your help."

"Why are you stuck?"

"It's my main character. He's just not coming off the page. It's like, he's there, but not really doing anything. I want him to do something special."

"Why does he have to do something special?"

"So the reader will want to go on a journey with him. Like you said in class a few weeks ago. Take the reader on a journey. Show the reader the journey."

"All the way to some crappy bedsit." Nigel sighs loudly and rubs his forehead. "Listen, leave it with me and I'll have a read."

Victor takes out the bundle of papers.

"God, is it a story or a novel?"

"I double-spaced it. Like a submission. I want to submit it to a publisher."

"An unfinished first draft?"

"Yep."

"I don't think you're at the submission stage yet."

There's another knock on the door.

Nigel looks at Victor. "Did someone follow you?"

"Not that I know of."

Nigel opens the door. "What the ... ?"

"Hey, Nigel," Victor says. "You got a minute?"

"I'm a little busy, talking to your twin."

"I don't have a twin."

"Then I must be dreaming."

Victor uses his scooter helmet to push past Nigel, but stops when he sees Victor, still standing in the centre of the room and holding a bundle of paper.

"Who are you?"

"Victor."

"No, I'm Victor."

Victor smiles. "I guess we're both Victor."

"All right," Nigel says, closing the door. "Stop this stupid twins game. I know you get a kick out of this, but I'm not in the mood. Which one of you is the writer?"

"I am."

"No, I am."

Nigel rubs his temples. "Who comes to Hackney on Wednesdays?"

"I do."

"So do I."

"That's ridiculous," Nigel says. "Then you'd both see each other. Wait. Do you hear that?"

Nigel goes to the door and opens it. Victor and Victor are shouting at each other.

"Hey. Hey! Shut up. What the hell is going on?"

"Hi, Nigel."

"Can I come in?"

"No, can I come in?"

"Both of you come in."

Nigel pushes them inside and closes the door.

The four Victors stare at each other. They're dressed slightly differently, but in the same style, as if they all pulled their clothes out of the same wardrobe.

"This is weird," Victor says.

"Very," Victor says.

"No, it isn't," Nigel says. "I'm dreaming. That's the only explanation. You're all figments of my imagination."

"That's wild."

"This isn't going to turn into some nasty sex dream, is it, Nigel?"

"I hope not."

"Me too."

"It won't," Nigel says.

"I don't know. That robe is pretty suspicious."

"Like you were waiting for us."

Nigel pulls it tighter around himself. "What do you all want?"

"If you're the one dreaming, then you've brought us here."

"Yeah."

"That's right."

"What do you want from me? I mean, from us?"

"I want you to leave me alone," Nigel says.

"I just want you to read my story."

"Me too."

"And me."

"I've also got a story."

Three of the Victors loop their scooter helmets over their wrists and reach into their shoulder bags. They pull out large bundles of paper.

"It appears we've been busy."

The Victors look at each others' pages.

"You reckon we've written the same stuff?"

"What did you write about?"

"Me. Victor. He writes scripts for automated telephone answering services."

"That's a mouthful."

"Oh yeah? What did you write about then?"

"Well, uh, I also wrote about me." Victor turns to Nigel, who's a little dumbstruck, like he's watching an extended rally at the tennis, one extraordinary shot after another. "You told me to write what I know. I know me."

"Is Victor a writer in your book?" Victor asks.

"Yes. A technical writer. He writes instruction manuals for household appliances."

"My Victor writes software documentation."

"Did he write the manual for a translation software?"

"I think so."

"Then my Victor hates your Victor."

"That's not very nice. My Victor's totally likeable. Although, if someone was trying to kill him, it would mean I'd have somewhere to take my story."

"That's my problem too. I'm stuck. Nothing's happening to Victor. He just gets up and goes to his office."

The other three Victors chorus: "At Shorts Gardens."

"Ha. Yeah. He goes to creative writing class on Wednesdays, but apart from that he's really boring."

The Victors nod at each other, then turn to Nigel.

"This is all your fault," Victor says.

"Me? Why?"

"You told me, us, to write what we know. That's what we did and now we're all stuck."

"Right. And no publisher's going to be interested in a dull guy who gets up every day and goes to work."

"Unless he kills people."

"Or he's Superman."

"Or he's a vampire."

Nigel calms himself and chuckles a little, bitterly. "That's exactly what a publisher said to me once. You take an ordinary guy and make him a hero. You send him on a quest. That's how it works. That's what people want to read. You get the average Joe, make him not so average anymore, and have him save the world."

"That's right," Victor says. "Being a technical writer, it's the perfect cover for some fantastic superhero. The mild-mannered software documentation specialist who fights crime and catches the bad guys."

"Yeah, but what should he be? We can't make Victor Superman."

"Just twist it," Nigel says. "Take something that's already been done and do it with something else."

"How?"

"I don't know. Maybe instead of an all powerful ring, you give the hero a watch, or shoes, or whatever. These are your stories, not mine. I don't agree with any of that. Popular fiction trash. Selling out. I don't want to write books like that."

"But that's what gets published. More than wannabe writers writing about writers."

"Yes."

Victor points a finger at Nigel. "I get it now. They wanted you to change your book, exactly the way we just talked about. But you didn't want to."

Nigel nods. "It was more complicated than that, but that's the essence of it, yes. I wasn't prepared to compromise."

"And look where that got you. All that write-what-you-know garbage. Forehands, Nigel? What a load of bollocks."

"And you're holding me back."

"He's holding all of us back."

"Stifling our creativity."

"Making us do what he wants."

"I want to write a bestseller, Nigel. I want to get published."

"And not self-published."

"You're stopping us from doing it."

"Shut up, shut up," Nigel shouts.

The Victors go quiet.

"Fine," Nigel says. "You want to publish a book? A big money contract? Here. You, um, Victor One, make your Victor some kind of beast that Victor turns into, maybe as a result of some botched science experiment. That Victor's caught between doing good and following his animal instincts. Someone in the government takes him in and turns him into a do-gooder. But even with that, Victor's always an outsider. Love interest, villain, calamity, another beast who's evil, such and such."

Victor One sits down on the sofa and starts writing on the back page of his manuscript.

"Okay, Victor Two. Your Victor finds a magical set of, uh, of contact lenses. When he puts them on, he sees all these things other people don't see. He can look into the future and see through walls. He uses the lenses to become some kind of superhero. Victor the Seer, or something. I don't know. There's a girl involved, maybe a high school sweetheart. The fate of the world. Armageddon. Blah blah."

Victor Two furiously scribbles notes.

"Victor Three. Your Victor is from another planet. He has whatever kind of powers you want him to have. Give him some kind of motivation, like having to do a certain amount of good deeds to get back home. Like he's a boy scout earning badges. Throw in a bad guy who wants to take over the world, and so on. Victor Four, uh, I guess you're getting the point now."

"My Victor is one of a select group of warriors," Victor says. "Their skills lay dormant until they're thirty years old. Then, close to his thirtieth birthday, Victor feels the urge to travel to Tibet. There he finds the ancient school where he gets trained."

Nigel snaps his fingers. "That's good. Go with that. See where it takes you. All of you, see where it takes you."

"Thanks, Nigel."

"Yeah, thanks."

"Glad I could help." Nigel moves towards the door. "I guess you all got what you came for."

"Maybe you should write a book like we're writing," Victor says. "With a Victor who's a tech writer but becomes a hero."

Nigel shakes his head. "We can't all do that. Anyway, it's not really my thing. I need to stick with what I know."

The Victors chorus: "Nigel."

"Right. The writer who's not quite making it as a writer."

"So go with that," Victor says. "Make it a tragic comedy. The story's so tragic, it's funny."

"So bad, it's good," Victor says.

"And then, in the book, the Nigel character writes a book about the pathetic failed writer Nigel and it becomes a hit."

"That's been done," Nigel says.

"So? Everything's been done."

"I guess I could just steal your ideas instead," Nigel says.

"What?"

"Actually, they're my ideas. I just gave them to you."

"You wouldn't."

The Victors exchange worried glances.

"I think I will," Nigel says. "That would get me out of this bedsit."

Victor gets the strap of his scooter helmet into his hand and swings the helmet so it connects with Nigel's head. The Victors descend on Nigel, raining vicious blows down on him with their helmets.

"Victor, are you done? Victor? Can you stop writing, please?"

"What? Oh, sorry, Nigel. Hang on."

Victor puts down the pen.

Victor puts down the pen.

Victor puts down the pen.

I put down the pen.

"That was a very constructive session," Nigel says. "I could feel the creative energy in the room. So, who would like to share what they've written? Hmm? What about you, Victor? You seemed pretty busy over there."

"Yeah, right. Sure. This is called Victor." I clear my throat. "Victor stares at the blank page."

Travel Page (cont.)

Lightning Source UK Ltd.
Milton Keynes UK
UKOW06f1614220315

248295UK00008B/68/P

9 783981 624922